A CROWN OF FATES

WOLVES OF LUNARA - BOOK TWO

HEATHER RENEE

CONTENTS

For more information on reproducing sections of this book or sales of this book, email heatherreneeauthor@yahoo.com.

ISBN: 979-8306153926

Editing: Danielle Fine

Cover: Covers by Juan

Cave
Alklo Falls
Selaris
Lunara
WOLVES OF
LUNARA

Portal Cave
Lunara Academy
...aris
Venaris
Altaris
The Bridge

CHAPTER ONE

ESTEE

Being a princess sucks. No amount of luxury can make up for the torment my dearest sister has inflicted on me. Damn Isla for dragging me into her mess, no matter how important it seems. She wanted me to set an example, but I didn't sign up for this, and no matter how much I adore her, I can't even muster a hint of a smile as I walk toward the ship like a sacrificial lamb.

The warm ocean breeze teases my dark hair as I approach the wooden plank leading up to the ship. If I could find a reason, outside of my stubbornness, to flee back to the castle, I would. But the eyes of the pack—the entire kingdom—are on me. Isla might be queen, but I'm still a princess in my own right, and I'm expected to represent the strength of Polaris.

Great. Just great.

The massive ship looms before me, its sails billowing against the pale blue sky, carrying the hopes and ambitions of far too many women—most of who are here for one reason: to parade themselves in front of the Alpha

King of Selaris, Theo Northcroft, hoping to be his fated mate, or possibly his chosen one if all else fails.

I scoff inwardly. If these women want to throw themselves at some king's feet, they can be my guest. But me? I'd rather jump into the frigid waters below than spend my life tied to a lazy, pompous ruler who couldn't be bothered to leave his kingdom and find his mate on his own. Instead, he's summoned us all to present ourselves like cattle at auction.

My black heels click sharply on the sturdy gangway as I make my way toward the guard standing at the top.

"Estee." Isla's sharp, firm tone sounds behind me. "You didn't even say goodbye."

I pause, turning slowly, as though this conversation is an inconvenience. Secretly, I'm glad she's here. I might've been wallowing a bit too much in my woe-is-me attitude by not going to see her this morning. A choice I would've regretted later this afternoon.

Just below me on the dock, Isla is magnificent in her royal attire, her pinkish-auburn hair glowing in the sunlight. Her blue eyes, always so piercing, narrow in disapproval.

Another wolf shifter named Drea stands between myself and my sister. I only met her briefly yesterday—there are plenty of pack members I haven't gotten to know since returning just a few weeks ago—and I address her before my sister. "Excuse our queen," I say with a wry grin. "It seems she left her manners back at the castle today."

Drea tucks a strand of brunette hair behind her ear and averts her hazel eyes as she bows deeply. "It's quite all right, Your Highness." She turns to Isla, curtseying. "Your Majesty."

Once the young woman passes, I offer my sister a saccharine smile. "Did you need something?"

Just as I step within reaching distance of her, she grabs my wrist, jerking me toward her with unnecessary force as she chooses to mind speak with me instead of airing our drama for all to hear.

"I asked you to set an example. The least you could do is show a little grace." The sharp look she gives me matches the terse tone echoing through my mind.

"Yeah, well, this is ridiculous," I reply honestly. *"I don't want to go. Plenty of these women want to be here. They don't need me to pretend I'm thrilled with the prospect of two full days at sea followed by an afternoon of primping to stand before a king I want nothing to do with."*

Her brow arches, that knowing expression creeping into her gaze. *"So you keep saying."*

"What's that *supposed to mean?"* I love my sister more than the moons and all the stars, but ever since we came back to Lunara and she officially took her place as queen of Polaris, she's become stronger and more intuitive. While I'm thrilled to see her finally find her footing, I don't like these new abilities being used on me.

"It means there's a chance King Theo is your mate, and after centuries of doing whatever you want, the idea of settling down terrifies you," she says, her voice filled with more compassion than I probably deserve after the way I've been acting these last few days. *"It's okay to admit that you're scared."*

My chest tightens. She's not wrong, and that's the

problem. The vulnerability of the truth claws at me, but I refuse to let it show. *"I'm not scared. I'm annoyed."*

That's a lie, and she knows it. Still, she wraps her arms around me, pulling me in for a hug that feels like home, and finally speaks out loud. "I love you, Estee. Whatever happens over there, you're going to be okay. I feel good about this, and once you get to Selaris, I think you will too."

I snort softly, muttering under my breath, "Slim chance." Once I pull out of the hug, I tell her, "I love you, too."

She lifts my chin with her fingers and grins at me. "Slushies and shifters on me when you're back?"

I bark out a laugh and shake my head. "I thought Asher destroyed all those human-made supernatural movies you had smuggled in?"

Isla winks. "He might be the king, but I'm also the queen. He can burn as many copies as he wants. I'll keep getting more. It's good entertainment."

Again, she's not wrong.

I wrap my arms around her, and any irritation I felt before is gone. "I'll be home soon, we'll have a night of gossiping about my travels, and then things can go back to normal."

She holds me tightly, her joy a palpable warmth. "In the meantime, I'll enjoy watching Declan mope around the castle because you're not there for him to chase after."

Oh, that man.

He's exactly what one would think I'd want. A sweet guy on the inside, mischievous on the outside, and more than three hundred years ago, he was rather talented between the sheets, but he's held no interest for me since I returned.

In fact, nobody has. I've wanted nothing more than to spend time with Isla and our parents. The three of them are all I need in my life now that I have them back. Not a mate, not a *good time*, and certainly not a lazy king.

With a soft sigh, I pull away from Isla and offer a smile that doesn't feel quite right. "I'll be back in less than a week."

If I keep saying it, the words will be true. The universe and gods will bring me back home to my family. I won't somehow get stuck in Selaris. King Theo won't be my mate.

I control my own destiny and my thoughts are powerful, filled with their own kind of magic.

These are all things I've been telling myself more often as of late, and one of the few things I'm thankful for discovering while I was on Earth. Manifestation and tapping into the power of my subconscious isn't something I'd ever have learned in Lunara, but now that I know how impactful my thoughts can be, I wield them wisely.

Well, most of the time.

Sometimes a girl needs to conjure a chocolate cake to make the world right again.

With one final glance at my sister, I step away from her and make my way onto the ship. The plank's drawn up behind me, and the engines come to life beneath the wooden deck. A sense of finality washes over me as I lean on the sleek railing, watching the horizon slip further from my grasp.

Isla blows me a kiss then folds her hands regally in front of her, her bright blue eyes seeming to glow under the morning sun as she gives me one last piece of advice. *"Just remember what you used to tell yourself every morning while getting ready for the day: Everything is always working out for me, and I'm on the path that benefits my highest good."*

Damn her. My chest grows heavy as I repeat the words to myself. For the first time in years, I don't believe them. Still, that's something to sort out later. I've committed to being on this ship, and there's no going back now.

The deck behind me is already abuzz with activity. Dozens of women bustle about, most wearing expressions of excitement or nervous anticipation—though some cling to the side, pale-faced and ready to hurl into the sea. I'm not sure which group I fit into yet. Probably neither. I've never been good at masking my emotions, and it's going to be a struggle to do so in the coming days.

My sister might think this is some grand adventure, but it's an unnecessary, ridiculous tradition. Still, the people of Polaris are watching, and there are those who'd love nothing more than to see Isla fail as queen. I refuse to give them any excuse to question her leadership.

Geena, one of the handmaidens, comes rushing toward me. Her cheeks are flushed, and her rich brown eyes are hidden beneath her onyx hair as she bows her head, the strands falling forward. "Your Highness, I apologize, but it seems there's been a mix up with the rooms."

"If there's no room for me, I'm happy to swim back to shore," I tease with a soft smile, leaning casually against the exterior wall of the ship, but she doesn't seem to appreciate the joke.

Her gaze widens. "I don't think that would be wise, Princess Estee," she stutters. "The waters are frigid, and people would—"

"I was only kidding, Geena," I tell her before she can spiral much further. "Whatever the mix up is, I'm sure we can work something out."

Her shoulders slump in relief. "Currently, you're sharing a room with one of the other ladies, Your Highness. Drea has offered to sleep on the deck so you can have your privacy, but Captain Peters is refusing to allow that, and—"

I place a hand on her shaking shoulder and give her a reassuring smile. "I don't mind sharing. I promise. If you'll show me where the room is, I'll tell Drea myself."

I might be a princess, but that doesn't mean I don't have a heart.

"Yes, Your Highness." Geena bows before turning sharply to lead the way.

The hundred-foot vessel is already cutting swiftly through the waters now that we're away from the dock. As we hit a wave, I shove my arm out to catch myself on the wall before we get to the door leading to the rooms.

Please, be a smooth trip.

The handmaiden turns the wheel on the steel door to disengage the lock, opening it for me and gesturing for me to enter first.

The hallway has whitewashed wooden slats on the wall and dark floors. Between the windows to the closed-off areas, there are framed photos of past captains and the crew on different excursions. All the doors down this hallway are shut, but through the glass openings, I see we're passing the laundry and food storage before going by the kitchen, where I can smell fresh baked goods that have my mouth watering.

We go down a narrow set of stairs, with Geena in the lead this time, and we get to the next level of the ship, where most of the sleeping quarters are located. Halfway down another hallway, Geena stops at a door that's ajar and moves aside. I enter to find Drea picking up her suitcase.

"I hope you don't mind top bunk," I tell her cheekily. "Heights of any kind aren't really my thing."

She gapes but still bows. "Your Highness, I was just leaving so that you could have your privacy."

"Not necessary," I promise with a warm smile. "Plus, being alone on a ship for the next couple of days doesn't sound very fun to me."

Drea swallows thickly, not seeming thrilled about getting to know one of the royal members of her pack. "Of course not, Princess."

I wave a hand. "Quit with the formalities. I'm not in line to be queen of anything at the moment. Consider me just one of the women forced to be on this boat with you."

She clutches the handle of her suitcase, shuffling her feet until she's further back in the modest room that contains one bunk bed, a small dresser, and an overhead light that flickers above us. "As you wish."

Well, this should be interesting.

I turn to Geena. "Will you find out if the sugary smell coming from the kitchen is brownies or cake? If so, bring some for me and my new roommate, please."

Geena curtsies. "Yes, Princess Estee."

She closes the door behind us, and I address Drea again. "Please, don't feel weird around me. I'm not as royal as some think. Sure, I was in line for the throne in one of my past lives—and my sister is the queen—but right now I'm perfectly content to be a wolf shifter within the Polaris pack."

Her breath comes out in a shudder. "I'm just glad I'm not the only one who doesn't want to be here. I wouldn't be if my mother hadn't threatened to burn all my clothes."

A bubble of laughter builds within me as I feign horror. "That's sacrilege. How could she?"

Drea finally giggles, dimples forming in her round cheeks as her shoulders relax. "I don't know, but I couldn't let it happen, so here I am."

I walk toward her and throw an arm over her shoulder. "No, here *we* are. I actually really am glad I'm not going to be alone. Or with someone who's salivating at the thought of being the next queen."

Drea's face twists. "No, thank you."

And just like that, this voyage is a little better. I'll gain a new friend, one who might even help me to blend in easier with the other women, and make it out of this week without too much excitement or drama.

Before I know it, I'll be back in Polaris, and everything will go back to normal.

Do you hear that, Universe?

Everything will go back to normal.

CHAPTER TWO

ESTEE

I stumble off the boat with an uneasy groan, my legs still swaying from the motion of the sea. The ground feels like it's rocking beneath me, and if it weren't for Drea's firm grip on my arm, I'd be face-first in the dirt by now. While I appreciate her quick reflexes, the sudden jerk upward only worsens my already spinning head.

"Who the hell invented seasickness?" I grumble, rubbing my temples. My hands do little to steady the world still swirling around me.

The two days of our voyage were nothing but misery. Spending the entirety of the trip confined to my cabin, hunched over a bucket, was not how I'd envisioned this *grand* journey. I'd imagined at least a bit of ocean air, maybe some time spent on the deck under the sun, but instead, it was me, my trusty bucket, and whatever crackers Drea could convince me to consume. None of which stayed down for long.

Drea chuckles beside me, her amusement only adding

to my irritation. She's been a saint—helping me by braiding my hair back, wiping the vomit from my chin, and ensuring I didn't starve or become dehydrated.

"Oh, Estee," she teases, her tone light, "you don't have to pretend anymore. We're here. There's no going back."

A growl rumbles low in my chest, and it's enough to make her flinch, just a little. "What kind of psychopath would fake this misery?"

She shrugs, a playful glint in her eyes. "One who really doesn't want to risk being mated to a king."

Touché.

Before I can retort, a voice cuts through the air—a familiar, and not entirely welcome, one. "It's a good thing you're not fated for a sea dragon."

I lift my head up. Elyn, the pack's elder healer, is standing a few feet away. She's grinning, her wrinkled face folding into a look that's part amusement, part mischief. The last time I saw her, she'd performed magic that had—technically—killed me. And Isla. Sure, it was to break a curse, but I'm still convinced she enjoyed draining the life out of us a little too much.

Before I can respond, Elyn blows a handful of silvery dust directly into my face. I double over, retching and coughing, certain my lungs are about to flee my body.

"What the hell, Elyn?" I manage to snarl once I can breathe again, my throat burning from the assault.

Elyn raises a greying brow, her weathered face showing no remorse. "Unless you *wanted* to spend the next few hours being poked and prodded by handmaidens while attempting to keep the projectile vomiting to a minimum, I suggest you be grateful."

I blink, my irritation dimming. The nausea that had gripped me for days has vanished. Damn her for being helpful in the most infuriating way possible.

"Thank you," I mumble begrudgingly, brushing off the last remnants of sparkly powder from my travel-worn dress—a simple blue cotton thing, wrinkled beyond repair after spending most of the journey hunched over a bucket and too tired to change.

Elyn cackles, a sound that somehow echoes in the stillness around us as she begins to walk away, but not before leaving us with what I assume is supposed to be an ominous warning. "You'd best hurry along, girls. You never know what might find you out here. Head for the side gate. I'm sure someone is waiting for you."

Drea grips my arm tighter, her unease clear as she whispers, "We're going to be the last ones to arrive. I can't see the others anymore."

I sigh, glancing up the path toward the looming castle ahead. Its stone walls are weathered, the large tan bricks fitting together like pieces of an ancient puzzle. It's a far cry from the pristine castle of Polaris, where every stone gleams as though freshly laid. Here, the windows are dark, and the turrets stand empty, no sentries visible. Even the arched wooden doors, set with dark metal studs, look worn, as if the weight of the world has pressed down on this place for far too long.

"Yeah, well, I'm a princess of Polaris," I remind her, my tone laced with exhaustion. "We'll get there when we get there."

I may no longer feel like hurling my guts out, but I'm still bone tired. It's not just the seasickness or the sleepless nights on that ill-fated ship. It's life. Sure, the past few weeks spent with Isla and our parents have been a blessing, along with reigniting my love for our pack, but it's been a whirlwind of responsibility and uncertainty. A part of me craves a break, knows I need something just for me —time to myself, away from the demands of bloodlines, curses, and summons from kings I have no desire to meet.

Maybe after this.

An uneasy pressure settles deep in my chest, one that no amount of rest will shake. It tells me that this journey, this whole ordeal, is only the beginning of something more sinister than I can imagine. A fact that terrifies me considering I've been cursed to Earth for three hundred years and forced to forget my own identity and family, lifetime after lifetime. How much worse can things get?

Elyn disappears into the shadows, scurrying off in the opposite direction as we make our way along the fanned cobblestone path. Drea leads, her pace faster than mine, but I don't force myself to rush. Not with the castle closer, its aura thick with age and mystery.

As we approach, there's a man in his thirties that steps out from a small door near the gate we've been heading toward. He moves forward, impeccably dressed in a charcoal suit, complete with a maroon tie and pristine white shirt. His green eyes flick over Drea before settling on me. He bows deeply. "Princess Estee. My name is Cecil. We're so pleased you could make the trip on behalf of Polaris. Please, allow me to escort you to the private chambers we've arranged for you."

Before I can respond, another figure exits from wherever Cecil came from, but this guy goes straight for Drea as if he means to take her elsewhere. Instinctively, I grab her wrist, pulling her toward me. "She stays with me." My voice is firm, leaving no room for argument.

I've only just met Drea, but something about this place, about the way the shadows cling to the corners, makes me feel like I need to keep her close. The hairs on the back of my neck bristle. There's something off here, more than just its wear and tear.

Cecil gives a curt nod, and the second figure retreats back where he came from without a word.

"Where's everyone else?" I ask, noticing the distinct lack of women. The ship was full of them, all giddy with excitement, and yet the castle grounds are eerily quiet. I may not be queen, but I know enough about protocol to realize something's off. I should've been one of the first to be greeted, not the last to arrive, regardless of how slow I was.

"They've been taken to a separate building to be prepared for the king's audience, Your Highness," Cecil replies smoothly. "I'll be taking you to a room within the castle itself." His eyes flick to Drea. "Both of you."

His lips curl slightly at the end of his sentence, as if he has to force himself to seem friendly, or maybe he hates this situation as much as I do. Either way, I nod before pulling Drea a little closer as we start to walk again.

Her face is pale and eyes wide, confirming she's as uneasy about all this as I am. But I squeeze her hand in silent reassurance. She'll be fine. We both will.

We follow Cecil at a distance, my feet dragging slightly as we walk on the smooth cobblestone pathway leading to the main doors. On either side of us are patches of sparse green grass, statues half-hidden in the gloom, and twin fountains, each with three tiers of stagnant water. Even the air feels heavy, like it's hiding something that I hope not to be here long enough to understand.

Cecil pushes open the main door with little effort, and I hesitate for a moment before stepping inside. My wolf stirs within me, and I briefly close my eyes, calling her heightened senses forward to scan our surroundings.

The castle is quiet. Too quiet. The faint scent of cooking meat and bread baking wafts from somewhere deeper within, but it lacks the tantalizing richness I've come to expect from the grand kitchens of Polaris. A staleness overwhelms me as I inhale; yet, no matter how hard I try, I can't pick up on anything exact to confirm the unease within me.

Annoyance gnaws at me. Maybe this place is just old, and my nerves are getting the better of me. After all, I've survived worse.

Cecil, ever patient, says nothing as I inch further into the castle. The large wooden doors close behind us with a dull thud, and we're left standing on a maroon rug that stretches toward a grand staircase. The interior walls are the same tan stone as the outside, adorned with oil paintings, old armor, and ancient weapons—no sign of dust or decay.

Okay, so I might've preemptively judged. Just because they haven't given this place a complete overhaul doesn't mean there's anything wrong.

Maroon and gold banners hang from the walls, bearing the sigil of Selaris: a crescent moon with a howling wolf in front of it. A reminder that this is a kingdom of shifters, one I hope to leave behind sooner rather than later.

Though, we still haven't seen anyone else. Again, I try not to make assumptions. Maybe the staff is elsewhere, tending to the main group of women who arrived with us. A perfectly logical explanation.

Thinking this kingdom is in disarray and this sudden need for King Theo to find his mate is nothing more than a plot to ferret money out of whatever pack his mate might be from would just be crazy.

Right?

Cecil stops at a double set of doors, the same dark wood as the main entrance, but with smaller studs placed in rows of six. He grips the rose-shaped silver handle and twists before stepping back.

"Your Highness." He gestures for me to proceed. "Since you've brought your own handmaiden, would you like me to cancel the one King Theo has reserved for you?"

I hold my chin high and narrow my eyes on Drea's behalf. "Drea isn't here as a handmaiden. As an unmated adult female of Polaris, she's here at your king's request, and we will both require assistance to prepare for this evening's festivities."

Cecil's face flushes slightly at my rebuke, but he maintains his composure, bowing gracefully. "As you wish, Princess." He keeps his voice smooth, but I sense shock beneath his formalities. Something that's not my problem.

As soon as the door closes behind him, Drea lets out a soft gasp, her eyes wide with disbelief. "This is insane." She places a hand to her chest, exhaling deeply.

I grin, satisfied with her reaction. "Which part?"

"All of it, but most importantly, I can't thank you enough for taking me in," she says with relief. "I wasn't looking forward to being carted off to wherever the others are, but I would've gone without a fuss. Though, watching you make your demands with such authority, as if you're the queen here, not a visiting shifter… The strength you hold, it's inspiring."

I lean in closer, giving her a conspiratorial smirk. "That's the secret to life—believing in your worth. We're all queens in our own way. And when someone disrespects you or those you care about, you don't back down. Make sure they know who they're dealing with."

Drea's face brightens, her wide smile lighting up the dim room. "I'm really glad to know you, Estee."

I squeeze her wrist gently, and a genuine warmth blooms between us. "Same here. Now, let's see what we're dealing with."

Together, we turn to take in our surroundings. The room is large but simple—stateliness stripped down to the basics. A grand bed dominates the space, its maroon and gold bedding matching the castle's colors. Heavy curtains hang over the windows, and Drea moves instinctively to open them, allowing the pale light of the late afternoon to filter in, casting long shadows across the stone walls.

Despite the austerity of the space, there are small touches of care—fresh bouquets of vibrant flowers sit on either side of the bed, their colors a welcome contrast to the otherwise muted room. A wardrobe stands against the wall, next to a tall dressing screen, and a small tea cart is tucked into the corner, steam still rising from the kettle.

"A drink while we wait?" I ask, crossing to the cart and

pouring a cup of tea for Drea. I hand it to her with a grin. "As I told Cecil, you're not here to be a handmaiden. We're in this together, whether we like it or not."

Drea takes the cup, her eyes filled with gratitude. "I appreciate the sentiment, Estee. But I don't think there's any universe where I could be your equal."

I raise a brow, giving her a playful wink. "You never know. Maybe you'll be King Theo's fated mate and outrank me by the end of the night."

That has her choking on her tea, sputtering as she laughs. "Gods, don't ever say something like that again!"

I laugh along with her, but a dark weight still hangs at the back of my mind. As much as I joke about the situation, the reality is sobering. We've both been thrust into something neither of us can control, and I can't shake the feeling that this whole event, this mate-selection nonsense, is meant to distract us from something far more dangerous.

Drea wipes her eyes, still chuckling. "I'm serious, Estee. I don't want anything to do with being queen, let alone being mated to a king. Can you imagine the pressure?"

I nod, feeling the gravity of her words as I tug on one of the purple highlights in my dark hair. "Trust me, I know exactly what that's like." My thoughts flash to Isla. I've seen the level of expectation on her, and I wouldn't wish it on anyone who didn't truly want it, least of all myself.

Drea leans back against the wardrobe, her laughter finally subsiding as she gazes at me, her expression softening. "Still, I'm glad we're in this together. It's nice to know I'm not as alone as I thought I'd be."

I couldn't agree more. Even though I'm trying not to think negatively about all of this, I hope, for both our sakes, that these days away from home will have been nothing more than a waste of time.

Well, outside of the two of us meeting.

CHAPTER THREE

THEO

Pacing my room does little to quell the storm inside me. My wolf, restless and growling, claws at my mind as Jerome approaches. I already know what he's about to say.

"The women of Polaris have arrived, Your Majesty." His light blue eyes seem hopeful, but the tense wrinkles around them tell me he's just as unsure as I am.

I don't tell him that I've already sensed them. That my wolf's been on edge since the moment their ship docked. Jerome may be my most faithful advisor, but after nearly a year of ruling, I've learned not to trust anyone completely. Not even myself.

Hell, I'm not even sure if my wolf sensing that our mate is near is real or completely fabricated at this point, but knowing this could all be a lie doesn't lessen the panic growing within my chest.

"Very well," I say, my gaze drifting to the window. Beyond it, the castle grounds stretch toward the horizon, where dozens of women now gather. One of them could be *her*. The answer to the mess I've found myself in.

"Dinner will be held promptly after you've met with the eligible females, Sire," Jerome continues, his voice neutral, as if we haven't already played this charade twice before. "Princess Estee and her guest Drea are secured in her private chambers. They'll be prepared separately before joining the others."

Princess Estee.

Gods, please don't let her be my mate.

As if this situation weren't complicated enough, having my wolf claim the princess of Polaris would be a disaster. The last thing I need is to pull their family into the web of lies and destruction I've found myself tangled in.

I turn from the window and head toward my closet, opening the door to reveal a row of formal tunics adorned with medals I haven't earned. The polished silver shines proudly, yet only serves as a reminder that I'm a king who doesn't deserve his kingdom.

How did I let it come to this?

"Sire, would you like me to draw a bath?" Jerome asks, ever the attentive advisor, though his eyes don't meet mine. If he managed to face me, I know what he'd see.

Dark circles shadowing my charcoal eyes, evidence of too many sleepless nights and stubble on my cheeks that should've been shaved days ago, but I haven't had the energy to care. My brunet hair, once neatly cropped, now falls in unruly waves above my ears. I run my fingers through the strands in a half-hearted attempt to tame them, but it's a lost cause. It all feels pointless after all I've endured.

"No." My voice is harsher than I intended, and Jerome stiffens slightly.

He adjusts the lapels of his maroon suitcoat, nodding. "Very well, Your Majesty. I'll return within the hour to escort you to the gathering."

My wolf is practically panting to claim the soul created specifically for us, but I wonder just how much things are going to change. And, most importantly, if the one I hope to call mine will ever be able to forgive me for what I've done.

I slip my arms into the sleeves of my formal tunic, the dark wool sliding over my white dress shirt. The maroon piping around the edges matches the kingdom's colors, and the golden buttons gleam. Securing them one at a time, I force myself to straighten to my full six-foot-four-inch height and call on my wolf healing to take away the bruises under my eyes. I may not be worthy of the crown I wear, but I'll at least try to look like it. For *her,* my mate.

With a heavy sigh, my gaze shifts toward the mirror near my closet. There's still a bleakness within my stare, hollow and tired. The weight of the crown atop my head feels heavier with each passing day, pressing down on me, suffocating me to the brink of death, but never offering the sweet relief.

I shake my head, a useless attempt to clear the darkness from my mind as I move to the drink cart. My hands tremble as I pour a whiskey. It's not the answer, but for a moment, it dulls the edge of uncertainty clawing at me. I toss it back, the liquid burning down my throat.

I've lived four lifetimes—nearly one thousand years in total—and in all that time, I've never felt as lost as I do now. Sometimes, I want to blame my mother, but the choices I've made are mine alone. Even when forced to do things I'd never thought I was capable of... The truth is, there was always another way. A way I never took.

Death could have stopped this years ago.

But I was too selfish. Too determined to keep fighting.

And now, with my wolf pacing inside me, impatient and agitated, I wonder if I'll be able to make the right choice when it matters most.

Whoever my mate is, she deserves better than this. Better than me.

I wish I could believe that today will be the beginning of something good. That finding her will be a turning point. But I know better. After all I've been through the last few years, this feels more like the beginning of the end because no matter how much I'll want to cherish her...

She'll hate me for what I've done, and I won't blame her.

A strange sense of relief washes over me as I imagine the near future. Maybe this is how it's meant to end. Maybe my mate is meant to be the queen Selaris needs, and my death is the price I'll pay to give her that chance.

Maybe, just maybe, there's still a way to fix this.

CHAPTER FOUR

ESTEE

The threads of my embroidered bodice burn against my heated skin as I stand with Drea in the crowded ballroom, awaiting King Theo's arrival. The more time passes, the stronger the fire building in my stomach grows—a sensation so severe I keep glancing at my arms to make sure they aren't actually smoldering.

A sheer cape hangs over my shoulders, and the added material makes me want to tear it from the carefully sewn seams. A center opening in the fabric exposes the top of my chest, but that does nothing to keep me from feeling suffocated.

The maroon material of the skirt sways around my ankles as I fidget until Drea grabs both my hands and growls at me. "Stop."

I raise an eyebrow, smirking. "Someone's found her confidence."

She blushes, dropping her gaze. "Sorry, but you're driving me nuts."

I chuckle, though it's brief. Drea looks stunning—her simple silk gown drapes effortlessly over her curves, the light grey fabric soft and fluid, unlike the overly embellished nightmare I'm trapped in. She looks comfortable, while I'm about two seconds away from ripping this dress to shreds.

But before I can voice my envy, Drea stiffens beside me. A low growl vibrates from her chest, and when she looks up at me, her doe-like eyes are wide with shock but also a certainty that I don't understand.

"Mate," she whispers, her voice breathless.

I blink. "What? I'm not your mate."

"Not you," she hisses, her gaze darting around. "He's here. I can smell his scent… Gods, it's so sweet, like chocolate."

Oh no.

I'd hoped—really hoped—that Drea would be returning to Polaris with me, but now? If she's found her mate, who am I to stand in her way?

Before I can say anything, a large figure barrels through the crowd—a warrior clad in black, medals gleaming across his chest. His eyes, dark brown and glowing with intensity, are locked on Drea.

Well, I didn't see this coming.

Neither of them speak. Drea turns toward him, and in an instant, he scoops her into his arms, kissing her with the kind of passion that makes it clear they're no longer aware of the hundred people in the room with them.

Her hands move over his dark, shaved hair, and when he gropes her backside, I decide I should intervene.

I step forward, grabbing his arm firmly. He snarls but

doesn't turn toward me. That's fine—my nails extend into claws, and I dig them into his skin, piercing through his sleeve.

He pulls Drea to his side, and this time, he spares me a glance, his hand twitching as though ready to reach for my throat.

I shake a finger at him. "I wouldn't recommend that."

Drea steps between us, panting. "Estee, I'm so sorry."

I don't look at her. My gaze is still fixed on her mate, whose burly form practically radiates with possessiveness. "Mauling this incredible woman in public doesn't equate to cherishing her. I expect you to respect Drea—mind and body. Whatever the two of you do in private is your business, but here?" I glance around the room briefly. "This isn't the place."

The warrior bows his head, grumbling. "Yes, Your Highness. My apologies. It was unintentional."

I flatten my lips even though I've seen the way Isla and Asher are with each other. Desire between mates is typically the furthest thing from rational in the beginning. Still, I want better for Drea if I'm already going to lose her as my companion and friend. "See that it doesn't happen again."

His face flushes with shame as Drea giggles softly, her cheeks red but eyes sparkling. "I'm sorry," she says again, unable to suppress her smile. "This is…unexpected."

That's an understatement.

"Why don't the two of you excuse yourselves?" I suggest, my tone gentle. There's no reason for her to stay here, not when she's found her mate. I'm not selfish enough to ask her to stick around for my sake, not when her future's standing right beside her, practically drooling.

Without hesitation, Drea nods, and they rush off, disappearing into the crowd. Women from Polaris watch with interest, but I ignore them as a trumpet sounds. Great. Now I just have to survive this ridiculous display, feign a headache, and retreat to my room until it's time to sail back home tomorrow.

I'll take seasickness over this any day.

"His Majesty, Alpha King Theo Northcroft," the announcer bellows between the trumpets.

I shouldn't care. I shouldn't even be curious, but I find myself staring at the vaulted doorway, waiting. This man didn't exist to me when I last lived in Lunara three hundred years ago, and I told myself I wanted nothing to do with him, yet here I am, wondering what kind of king he is.

King Theo steps through the doorway, a gold crown resting atop brunet hair that's disheveled, as if he couldn't be bothered to properly clean-up for the occasion. His dark eyes scan the room before landing on me, and I swear a flicker of disappointment crosses his face.

Well, screw you too, buddy.

I keep my head high, my back straight, refusing to let his reaction affect me. There's a faint flutter in my chest, a sensation I can't quite place, but it vanishes as quickly as it appears. Relief washes over me. My future isn't set in stone. Whatever fleeting connection passed between us isn't enough to bind me to him.

But then, King Theo nods to the man beside him—the one who introduced him—and steps back into the shadows beneath the archway.

What the hell is going on?

"The king has found his mate," the man, whom I assume is an advisor, announces. "Everyone may make their way to the dining hall except Princess Estee Blackwood."

The words hit me like a punch to the gut.

There's no way. There was no connection. I felt nothing. Well, I mean, there was a twinge, but as I just witnessed with Drea and whoever that guard was, I should've felt a hell of a lot more than *that* if he was truly my mate.

Murmurs and whispers swarm the room as women side-eye me while they walk toward the exit. Hell, some even glare, and I almost offer to switch places with them, but something tells me that won't help my situation.

The room empties, and I'm left standing there, with no clue what I'm supposed to do.

Maybe he asked me to stay behind because he thinks I'm some sort of royal liaison, and he wants to find out more about the one he's identified as his mate. Yes, that would make more sense.

That has to be the reason.

The advisor comes forward and bows before me. "Princess Estee, I'm Jerome Graves, First Advisor to King Theo. If you'll follow me, I'll take you to his office so the two of you can have a private conversation."

"He doesn't need to ask for my permission to claim his mate," I state without moving, even though he's gesturing for me to proceed toward the archway. "Any of these women are free to stay here with him. King Asher won't stop that from happening."

Jerome pales, and his throat bobs. "Princess Estee, it's *you* that King Theo believes to be his mate. Can you not feel the connection as he does? Are you unwell?"

Motherf— I was right the first time.

I guess I'm about to have an awkward conversation with the King of Selaris.

"Show me to his office," I demand, leaving no room for further conversation. This has just become a royal matter, and even if Jerome is the top advisor, I'm not discussing this with anyone other than Theo. Well, maybe Asher and Isla if I need to bring them into whatever's happening here.

He nods and turns on his heel before leading the way. We move through the now empty space and into the arched hallway. My jaw is locked tight with frustration and my eyes fail to focus on anything other than the back of Jerome's head.

My intuition knew coming here was a bad idea before I even boarded the ship. I should've listened, but… Damn my sister for making me love her so much that I didn't want to disappoint her.

One foot in front of the other. I curl my fingers into my palm and take a deep breath before slowly letting it back out.

Okay, Estee. Think. What's really happening here?

Why would King Theo think I'm his mate when I hardly felt anything after seeing him? Or why did I hardly feel anything if he truly is my mate? Is he trying to attach himself to me as a way to gain something from Polaris? Gods, I might actually kill him myself if that's true.

I bite the inside of my cheek to keep my thoughts from getting out of control. Thinking clearly is a must, and I need to rein in my emotions. As of right now, King Theo isn't my mate. He's just a desperate man who's up to something, and I need to figure that something out.

Yes, that's it. Another mystery to solve. While this isn't as dire as figuring out who killed Isla, and then me, that doesn't mean this won't escalate depending on what's really going on here.

If my sister can figure out who murdered us, surely I can learn why Theo thinks he can get away with calling me his mate. I mean, he's never met me, but I'm sure he's *heard* of me. I chuckle to myself. Maybe this will be fun, after all. A princess bringing a king to his knees.

That thought finally has my grin returning.

With my little pep talk taken care of, I pay more attention to my surroundings. Jerome is leading us up a set of stairs. Though, I have no clue if we're heading to the first or second or even third level by now. Oh well. It doesn't matter. I've got this.

After two left turns on the next floor, Jerome knocks on a large arched door before grabbing the metal knob, this one diamond-shaped with intricate carvings that are too worn to make sense of. The advisor waits a couple of seconds then opens the door and steps aside.

"Your Highness." Jerome nods, gesturing for me to enter.

I hesitate before squaring my shoulders. This doesn't change anything. I know what's in my heart, and I'm not going to let some desperate king rewrite my future. Whatever King Theo thinks this is, he's about to learn a hard lesson in being wrong.

Because if he believes tying himself to Polaris through me is going to get him anywhere, he's in for a rude awakening.

CHAPTER FIVE

THEO

This is exactly what I *didn't* want to happen. How can my mate be Princess Estee? More importantly, why? Is this some sick joke or another twisted scheme orchestrated by...

No. I can't even think his name right now.

Regardless, I've had all the time I'm going to get to prepare for this moment. Estee is here, standing in my office like a magnificent force of nature, and I can only hope that whatever I'm about to say will be enough to placate her. Though, based on the raised brow and smirk on her perfect face, I can already tell this isn't going to go as smoothly as I'd like.

She walks through the threshold, radiating a confidence that pulls me in despite the danger. Her maroon dress flows around her with an air of regality that doesn't require the diamond tiara upon her long wavy strands for me to know that she is every bit the queen I could have ever dreamed of.

My wolf stirs as I gaze at her. Every instinct begs my

feet to move closer, my canines extending so we can taste what's ours. My heart pounds as I lose myself in her golden eyes. There's a promise in them, a glimmer of something that could be joy—a future that seems so out of reach for someone like me.

But then her lips twist, and she clears her throat, yanking me back to reality. "Are you just going to stand there or are you going to start explaining what the hell I'm doing here?"

Her words hit like a punch, and my pulse stumbles. "What do you mean? You're my mate."

She laughs, but there's no warmth in it. "You're kidding, right? You might be able to lie to your advisor back there, but that's not going to work on me. I'm not your mate."

"You don't... But I... I don't understand." An unease fills me. I was told I had to find my mate, that Selaris needed its queen so a proper heir could be born—one the previous king was unable to provide—before I would be released from this nightmare. If this pounding in my heart is nothing more than a fabrication, I don't know what I'll do.

Estee steps closer, her presence like a heatwave crashing over me. The cape draped over her shoulders floats behind her, ghostly and delicate, but there's nothing fragile about her as she closes the distance between us.

I inhale deeply, unable to help myself. The scent of pomegranates and orange blossoms fills my senses, and a low growl escapes me.

She pokes a finger into my chest, sharp and insistent. "Don't you growl at me." Her touch sends a shock of need coursing through me, but I grit my teeth against the powerful need. "I want answers, Theo. Why. Am. I. Here?"

Gods, why can't she feel it? How is she resisting what's so clear to my wolf?

And then the voice I hate most slithers into my mind, dripping with amusement. *"Because you have to work for your mate, Theodore. Did you really think I was going to make it* that *easy for you? I gave you a crown, a purpose, and now, you'll entertain me. Unless, of course, you'd rather your mother take that role instead."*

Bile rises in my throat. *"You—"*

He clicks his tongue. *"Careful. Choose your next words wisely. You now have a mother* and *a mate to protect."* There's a pause then a slight moan. *"Estee is quite lovely, isn't she?"*

I clench my fists, jaw tight with the effort of holding back. I've never won with this monster, and that isn't going to change today. He's enjoyed watching me suffer every moment since meeting him, a trickster with his own agenda that I haven't quite figured out. But at least now I know what he's doing—blocking the bond between Estee and me, twisting reality to make me fight for what's mine.

And I will. I have no choice. Losing Estee isn't an option. Not now that I've felt the intensity of the bond pulsing through every inch of my body.

Her chest heaves as she waits for me to speak, her eyes full of fire, and gods help me, I want her more than should be possible.

I don't want to lie to her. Yet, seeing her now, feeling her wrath, I need to speak carefully if I'm to convince her to stay long enough to show her that maybe... Well, I don't know what I hope for besides keeping her. Though, a future where everything works out feels nearly possible. I have to at least try now that she's this close.

"I don't know why you can't feel the bond as I do, but I assure you, my wolf isn't wrong," I say confidently, drawing on the power of the alpha king that flows through my veins. "You are my mate, Estee Blackwood. Don't tell me you didn't feel *something* the moment you saw me."

Her expression hardens, but there's a glimmer of doubt behind her eyes. Good. If I can pull on that sliver of uncertainty, I may have a chance to break through whatever barrier *he's* created. It's a long shot, but she hasn't left yet. That has to mean something.

She shakes her head, and as the long strands move, I catch a hint of purple highlights woven through her dark hair. They're beautiful—just like the rest of her—and I want nothing more than to reach out and touch her, to prove that what I sense is real.

But before I can, she takes a step back, hands on her hips. "Something is happening here," she says, her voice low but fierce. "I knew it before I came here, and I know it even more now that I'm standing within the castle walls. I may not understand what kind of game you're playing, Theo Northcroft, but I'm not going to be a pawn. I'll figure out what you're up to, and then, I'll destroy you for dragging me into this mess."

Her fire should scare me. Instead, it only makes me want her more. "I know this isn't conventional—"

She snorts. "Conventional? This is insane."

"But," I continue, determined to press on, "if you'll just

let me try something, maybe I can make you understand." I take a step toward her, and she moves back two paces for every one of mine. "Estee, please."

I'm not above begging, especially when the stakes are this high. I can't lose her. I thought I could, that keeping her at a distance would be better, but being in her presence, everything I thought before has changed.

"Don't come any closer," she warns, eyes flashing.

It's a threat I know I should heed, but I can't seem to force myself to retreat. "You said you wanted answers," I counter. "I'm trying to give you something that will lead to them."

She mutters briefly under her breath, a word that sounds a lot like "Bullshit," but I ignore her and continue across my office, intent on getting my hands on her if she'll allow it. If she can't sense our bond just by looking at me or being in my proximity, maybe she'll be able to feel it by touch.

Estee stops backing away. Though she's near the door, close enough to grab the handle and run, she remains still. There's a slight shake to her shoulders, accented by the embroidered fabric of her dress, and while most of her is covered, I can still see the rise and fall of her chest peeking out between the small opening above her breasts.

As much as I want to wrap my arms around her and hold her close, I know better. Instead, I settle for gently pushing the cape back and trailing my fingers down her forearm until I'm able to capture her hand.

Her creamy skin pebbles, and I expect her to shudder in response, but she stays frozen. I stare at her oval face, transfixed by her beauty.

Estee's eyes are firmly on the wall behind me, but I don't let that stop me. I hold her small, warm hand between my palms, keeping my gaze on her face. Drawing my wolf closer to the surface, I focus only on the connection to this woman that thrums like lightning through my veins.

She is mine whether she knows it or not, and the longer I stand here, holding her as much as I'm allowed, the more I know that nothing will stop me from getting her to realize this truth.

Though, I'm not a fool. I know this won't be easy, and she'll likely hate me before I get close to righting my wrongs, but I won't give up. Not now that I can see the slightest shift in her movements, telling me I've done just as I hoped.

Her breath catches, and her eyes flutter closed for the briefest moment. When she reopens them, it's as if the night sky has exploded within their depths.

That's right, my Starlight. I'm right here.

At least until she jerks her hand out of my grasp and growls from deep within, her golden eyes narrowing. "I don't know what I hoped to get out of that, but we're done here."

Gods, I hope she's wrong about that.

CHAPTER SIX

ESTEE

This is *not* happening. It doesn't matter that I'm not even sure what *this* is. I'm not doing it. I'm not getting mixed up in whatever mess Theo's found himself in. It doesn't matter that the moment he grabbed my hand, peering into my eyes as if they might be a window to my soul, my wolf surged forward, her interest in him almost too much to keep at bay.

None of that matters because I'm getting the hell out of here.

I spin around and clutch the door handle. "I'm taking the women from my kingdom, and we're leaving. Right now."

The metal knob feels icy under my palm, grounding me for the briefest moment as Theo reaches for me again, this time wrapping his hand gently around my bicep. "Estee, please. Just give me time."

I whip my head around, a snarl already on my lips. "Remove your hand before I remove that arm from your body."

My wolf howls within me, a low, mournful sound. She doesn't like the hostility, but what does she expect? How can I trust this man? Whatever fleeting and almost hollow…gods, I can't even call it a connection. Whatever that was, it wasn't real. It can't be. Especially because now all I feel is anger.

She whimpers, clawing at my mind—pleading, but not forcefully. She wants to see him for herself, in her true form, but I can't let that happen. I can't allow myself to be vulnerable when there's so much uncertainty.

Theo lets go of me and holds his hands up innocently. "I won't force you to stay, but I will beg you to reconsider. I know this isn't how it's supposed to be, and you have no idea how sorry I am about that. I wanted more for my mate, for you. I didn't…" He grips the back of his neck, his eyes pleading with me to believe him as he lowers himself to the ground. "Just know that this *is* real. I'm not lying and, if you'll let me, I'll do whatever it takes to prove the truth to you. Give me one week." He drops to his knees, desperation etched across his face. "Please, Estee. Don't leave me yet."

Gods. He's literally groveling at my feet, staring up at me with those dark, tortured eyes. His hand twitches, like he wants to reach for me again, but he stops himself.

"I'll do whatever you ask," he pleads, his voice trembling. "Please, just give me more time to sort this out."

"What is 'this,' Theo?" I demand, looking down at him, trying to ignore the pulse of sympathy that grows within me.

Damn it. Bringing a king to his knees isn't as fun as I imagined it would be.

Still, I can't falter. Not when I know something is wrong.

He drops his gaze, shoulders slumping. "I know this will sound like a lie, but I swear on my life, two things are true." Slowly, he looks back up, his eyes locking onto mine with a fervor that makes my skin tremble. "One: you are my mate, Estee Blackwood. Two: I don't know *exactly* what's blocking you from openly feeling what I do, from knowing what I know without a shadow of a doubt, but I will figure this out, and when I do, I'll explain everything to you. I promise."

His words pierce my chest, each one like an arrow. His desperation is tangible—so much so that I can almost taste it, heavy and bitter on my tongue. Yet, I still don't know what I'm going to do until the words leave my mouth.

"I'll give you twenty-four hours," I say curtly. "Tomorrow, you'd better have something more to tell me, or I will leave, and you'll never see me again. That's a promise."

He nods, swallowing hard. "I understand."

I slip out the door, closing it behind me. Leaning against the wooden surface, I press my palm to my chest, trying to steady my breathing, but the emotions inside me are too wild to contain. That wasn't a strong enough connection to be a mate bond, but even I can't deny that there's something there when he touched me. A curiosity that might be better left alone.

"I'm so sorry," Theo's words are a hushed whisper that barely make their way through the door. "More than I can possibly explain."

I don't know if he meant for me to hear him, but the

anguish in his voice wraps around my heart, squeezing until I almost want to cry. Gods, why is this happening? Why can I sense these emotions so deeply, yet not feel the bond? How can he claim I'm his mate when my own heart is this conflicted?

It isn't supposed to be this way.

Shoving myself away from the door, I force my legs to carry me down the hallway. I can't afford to be distracted by Theo's sorrow. There are questions to answer, and I'm not going to find them standing outside his office, wondering why I care. Heading back toward the room I was given, I try to focus on a plan for the next twenty-four hours. First, I need to call Isla, let her know what's going on. Then, I'll find Drea and convince her that she and her mate should transfer to Polaris. I've only known her a short time, but I won't let her stay in Selaris with all this uncertainty.

And then I have to decide what to do about Theo.

I know I told him he had a day to bring me proof, but really, that time is for me. To clear my head, to figure out if there's any truth to this intermittent and weak connection. I can be stubborn—brash, even—but it's not without reason. I spent a childhood on Earth feeling like an inconvenience, not knowing who I was, searching for a sense of belonging that came decades later than it should have.

Three hundred years of living as a human, cursed to be reborn over and over again, without my memories... I can't just shove all that hurt aside. Not as easily as Isla did.

She had Asher before she left, and she has him now that we've found our way back to Lunara. I've only ever had her, and a lot of the lifetimes I lived on Earth, I didn't even get that. I floundered for so long, always searching and never finding. Though I didn't know it was Isla I was searching for, I knew something was missing.

Once again, I find myself alone and searching, but this time, it's not for my sister or the world we belong to, it's for answers that, depending on which way this goes, have the power to destroy me.

Years have passed since I've allowed myself to be vulnerable. I worked hard to strengthen my mind, to protect myself from those who sought to hurt me instead of lifting me up.

Now, I'm faced with Theo, who's claiming me as his mate and seems to want me to accept all of this on his word alone. No. I can't allow that. Not when there's only a flicker of a connection. One that not even my wolf is absolutely certain of.

Gods, this is a mess.

Beneath the frustrated growl that builds within me, there's a whisper that won't let me run from this place—a question plaguing my thoughts: what if my centuries of pain, of loneliness, have been leading me to this moment? What if Theo's not lying? What if, somehow, this is my fate?

For the last ten years, I've strongly believed that everything happens for a reason, that things will always work out for me eventually. Just because I don't want to accept the reason right now doesn't mean the sentiment is no longer true. I just have to find my center again.

With that in mind, I know what I need to do.

Still heading back to the room, I make a mental list of

all the things I need and have every intention of locking myself away tonight, but then I hear Drea's worried voice.

"Gods, Estee, when I heard…"

She doesn't need to finish her sentence. I understand her shock more than she knows.

"Are you okay?" she asks, reaching for my hand. "You look pale. Did you get sick again? Why aren't you with Theo still? Is he really as bad as we assumed? I know this isn't what you wanted, but at least we'll be here together."

I offer her a kind smile and shake my head. "One question at a time, but inside the bedroom, okay?"

"Right." She nods, pulling at the ends of her hair. The action reveals her neck, showing light scratches over her skin.

As soon as we're inside, it's my turn to pepper her with questions. "Why aren't *you* with your mate? Did he hurt you? He didn't abandon you already, did he? I'll kill him."

Drea giggles and shakes her head before starting to twirl about the room in childlike fashion, a smile growing on her face as she holds her arms out. "Orion is perfect in every way." She stops to face me, her cheeks flushed and eyes bright. "His only fault is that he didn't want me to leave, but his roommates came home, going on about the princess of Polaris being King Theo's mate, and I knew I had to come find you."

"Oh." Great, everyone knows. I shouldn't be surprised, but that means Asher will soon hear and so will Isla and, ugh, that phone call is going to be…interesting.

"So, why aren't you with *your* mate?" Drea presses, eyeing me carefully as I cross the room to get some water from the drink cart.

I hesitate to tell her the truth, not because I don't trust her, but because saying the words out loud makes them all that much more real. Or potentially so.

"It's okay," she says, nonchalantly. "I know I'm not royal. You don't have to tell me."

My head turns so quickly toward her that I hear a pop in my neck. "This has nothing to do with you or your stature, Drea. I promise. The situation is complicated, and I'm not sure how I feel about the whole thing."

"I know you didn't want a mate, but doesn't the euphoria of the bond override the reservations you had? Or are you really that badass that you can fight the connection with pure will?"

My entire body goes cold. Good gods, am *I* doing this? I know I believe in the power of thought, but I never considered...

Have I sabotaged myself because the fear of becoming someone's mate after centuries of loneliness was easier to hold onto than possibly having my heart shattered by the one person everyone always said would complete me?

My mate.

Drea's suddenly in front of me, helping me sit down before I collapse under the burden of my thoughts. "Hey, what's going on? Do I need to call a healer?"

I shake my head, trying to find my voice. "I don't feel the bond with Theo. But he does, and even my wolf thinks something is there. Yet, I just ripped him apart, blaming him for everything when maybe...it's my fault."

My wolf rises within me, her presence steady and calm, trying to soothe my racing heart. I wish I could hear her voice—any reassurances that I'm not going insane.

Drea clasps my hands in hers, her grip warm. "It's not you. At least, not *all* you. Even Orion says there's something off with King Theo. He only makes appearances when he must. He doesn't have any real friends and keeps his advisors at arm's length. Supposedly, the gods chose him as the next king since the previous one got sick and had no heirs, but the pack talks, and everyone believes something's being hidden."

I want to smack my head against the wall just to stop the emotional whiplash, but at least Drea's words are grounding. Something *is* off here. I wasn't wrong to be cautious. And while I might be at fault for not feeling the bond, there's more to this kingdom than meets the eye.

"You and Orion should go back on the boat with the others to Polaris," I state firmly. "If things are as bad here as they sound, you'll be safest back home. I'll make sure Asher knows that I sent Orion with you, and he'll get his transfer approved."

Drea's head is shaking before I've even finished speaking. "I'm not leaving you here on your own. You're going to need me."

"No offense, but what can you do that I can't?" I ask, genuinely.

She slowly smirks. "I can get the staff to talk. You're royal, I'm not. With the situation being that you forced me to stay behind, ignoring my desire to return home to Polaris with my newfound mate... Once they believe I'm one of them, I might be able to find answers for you. The help always knows."

While she makes a good point, just the fact that she's

willing to put herself in that position makes me reconsider.

"You can stay, but you won't be talking to anyone on my behalf," I tell her with authority. "I don't want you putting yourself in a situation where you might find more trouble than we're already dealing with. Do I make myself clear?"

She chuckles and reaches to hug me, tears shimmering in her eyes. "Thank you, Estee. Thank you for seeing me as a person."

"You're stuck with me now," I promise her, and I mean it.

It doesn't matter that she's never lived as a royal. Drea's quickly become a dear friend, and I intend to make sure she's taken care of.

Just as soon as I figure out what the hell is going on in this kingdom.

CHAPTER SEVEN

ESTEE

Later that evening, I finally convince Drea to go back to Orion, leaving me to have dinner alone—a moment of solitude I desperately need. The grilled chicken, fresh vegetables, and buttery rolls are a comfort, each bite easing the tension in my shoulders, leaving me with only the gentle hum of my thoughts.

After eating all of my dinner, I keep the candles that came with the food burning so that I can begin my healing-and-letting-go ceremony.

Nothing is physically wrong with me, but my mind and heart aren't seeing things the same, and before I do anything else, I need clarity.

Staying at the small dining table with a piece of paper and pen in front of me, I take a moment to center myself, breathing in and out slowly until I can feel my mind and heart start to open. Only then do I list the beliefs that have plagued me since arriving here. Each statement, raw and unfiltered, spills onto the page like inked wounds.

> *1.King Theo is a lazy alpha*
> *2.Something is wrong with Selaris*
> *3.Theo can't possibly be my mate, making him a liar*
> *4.I don't want a mate*

This last one is the hardest to write, but I force the words out because if I don't let go of this belief, I'm never going to know the truth, and that will be worse than any other possible outcome.

> *5.I'm better off alone*

My hand trembles as I finish. There it is. My thoughts laid bare, confessions that feel both damning and liberating. I fold the paper in half, hold it close to my chest, and whisper, "I willingly let these beliefs go, with the intention of returning to an open mind about my future and the king of Selaris."

I lift the paper to the flame above the pillar candle. The edge turns black before catching fire. Gently, I set it down on my empty plate, letting the flames devour my words. The parchment curls and dances before disintegrating entirely. Breathing deeply, I will the tension to release from my body.

The truth is, whatever secrets Theo holds don't matter. Not really. I can't control him or whatever forces are pulling the strings here. All I can control is myself. I need to let go of the outcome I've already decided on, trusting not only in my wolf's intuition, but the Universe to guide me. And as much as I don't want to trust Theo, I'll have to extend him an olive branch if I'm going to get answers.

Seconds after the paper is gone, I feel lighter than I have since Isla first asked me to make this journey. This won't solve all my problems, but it's a step in the right direction, at least.

I don't want to be spiteful or think I don't belong here just because I'm afraid. I want to understand what's happening and I want to feel good about whatever choice I make once I do.

Now, it's time for me to do what I should've done hours ago—call my sister.

There's a phone on the bedside table. I pick up the black receiver, and assuming it works like the one back home, I press zero for the switchboard, something we only need to use when calling outside our own territories.

"How may I assist you this evening, Princess Estee?" asks a sweet, elderly voice.

"Please connect me with the Polaris castle."

"Of course, Your Highness."

The line hums, and I wait patiently. After a few clicking noises, my sister's voice shrieks through the receiver.

"I freaking told you so!" Isla's breathless with excitement. "Tell me everything—unless you don't have time, and if you don't, that's fine—but gods, Estee, I'm just so freaking happy for you."

Well, this is going to be awkward.

"So, I take it you heard that King Theo announced me as his mate." I try to keep my tone light and teasing.

I can practically hear her eyeroll by the huff she makes. "Everyone knows. It's all anyone can talk about. Selaris hasn't had a king *and* queen in centuries. Now, *you're* going to be that queen."

Her joy is almost infectious. For a moment, I wish this was a different conversation, one where I shared her excitement. But I need to tell her the truth. At least the pieces I do know right now.

"Listen—"

"What did you do?" Isla's voice switches from excitement to sternness so quickly it almost makes me laugh.

Oh, she knows me so well.

"I might've played a part, but this isn't all me," I say earnestly. "I'm doing my best to keep an open mind now, but there's something going on here."

"Like what?" she presses, her voice lowering with concern.

I twist the cord attached to the phone between my fingers. "I don't know, but let me start from the beginning, and you tell me what you think."

I recount everything: arriving and seeing Elyn unexpectedly, being led to my own room with Drea, the brief and confusing flutter when I saw Theo for the first time, the confrontation in his office, and finally, the letting-go ceremony. I pour everything out, keeping nothing back.

"Holy hell, sis." Isla exhales like she's been holding her breath the entire time. "I don't even know what to say except that I'm sorry I'm not there with you. I'll get on the next ship and—"

I stop her right there. "I've got this. You're a newly crowned queen, and you've only just gotten Asher back. Enjoy this time. Stay with the pack. I promise to let you know if I feel like things are getting out of hand."

"I don't like that you're by yourself, though," she says with a huff. "Maybe I'll send Declan. I'd ask Noen, but we still haven't heard from him and—"

"I have Drea," I say before she can spiral over our childhood best friend who took off after wrongly being blamed for our murders. "If she's not enough, you'll be my first call, but let me figure out if my resistance is the biggest problem here or if the staff is right and there's something off with Theo."

She tries to apologize, but I don't want to hear anything of the sort. "I love you, Isla. That's all that matters. I'll be fine."

Silence stretches between us then she speaks softly, earnestly. "You *will* be fine. You always have been. I'm so proud of you, Estee. You're strong—mind and body. You're brave, and you're kind, and you have so much love to give."

A chuckle escapes me, though it's tinged with something raw. "I don't know about the 'kind' part."

"I do," Isla insists. "Look at how you befriended Drea. You could have sent her to be with the others, but you kept her close and are still trying to protect her. You have the biggest heart even if you're afraid to share it with people who might hurt you if you allow them fully in."

And that's the crux of it, isn't it? Letting someone in. Opening myself up to be left scarred. Regardless of whatever Theo's secrets are, if I let him in, if I accept that he could be my mate, and then everything falls apart... That's a kind of pain I don't want to face.

"Thank you," I murmur, leaning back against the

bedframe and closing my eyes. "Everything is going to be okay."

"That's right," she replies softly. "No matter what, you're an incredible person with so much to offer. Nothing and no one can take that away from you. Just remember, I'm only a phone call and ship ride away. And if Theo hurts you, well, Asher will tear him to pieces, because anything that hurts you hurts me. You're not alone, Estee."

Tears burn in my eyes and my throat aches with the pressure of my emotions, but I manage to get off the phone without my sister knowing how out of sorts I really am.

I take a few extra moments to let myself feel the importance of this situation before I rein in my pain. The need to escape nearly overwhelms me. The walls feel like they're closing in, whispering thoughts I don't want to hear. I need air, and I need to be anywhere but inside. I push myself to my feet, then go to the wardrobe, hastily putting a long jacket over the silk pajamas I'd changed into before dinner. Black flats slip easily onto my feet, and I head to the exit.

The door swings shut behind me with a faint click, and the silence of the castle wraps around me once I'm in the hallway. There's a stillness in the air, heavy and old, as if this place is holding its breath, waiting for some long-forgotten secret to surface. My shoes tap lightly on the stone floors as I walk down the corridor, each sound echoing like a question I'm trying to ignore. The halls are dark except for the occasional flickering torch, and the castle feels like a maze of shadows, hiding passageways and doors I have no interest in uncovering right now.

I pass ornate paintings of past kings, their eyes following me as I move, judging. There's no life in these faces, only history and expectation. Heavy curtains line the walls, their fabric rippling as I rush past. In a different mood, I might have paused to study the intricate designs woven into their depths—the ancient stories of Selaris hidden in thread—but tonight I have no patience for anything that reminds me of Theo's kingdom.

I quicken my pace, the air growing colder as I descend a stone staircase. I have no clear path in mind, only a desperate need to be outside to rid myself of the ache in my skin and bones. Around me, the castle shifts from grand hallways to more utilitarian spaces. Rougher walls, older beams. Everything feels less polished, more real and raw. There's a freedom in it that I crave—a place that hasn't been forced into being something it's not.

At last, I find a door that leads outdoors. As I push it open, the night air hits me like a rush of icy water. It's bracing and cleansing, filling my lungs with the smell of damp earth and pine, a scent so different from the castle's stifling stone walls. The twin moons, both bright and silver, hang heavy in the sky, bathing the castle grounds in an ethereal light. The grass beneath my feet is soft, and for a moment, I just stand there, allowing the earth to ground me as the breeze whispers through my hair, over my heated skin.

I let out a long breath, and as I do, my wolf stirs within me, her presence urgent and strong. It's not like I can ignore her—not now. I pull my focus inward, and without a second thought, I release her, encouraging the shift to come.

In mere seconds, my bones crack, muscles contort, and my vision sharpens as I fall onto my hands and knees. My senses expand as my body reshapes itself, and then I'm there—my wolf, my truest self. The world comes alive in ways my human form could never perceive: the flutter of a bird's wing miles away, the scurrying of small creatures in the underbrush, the gentle rustle of the trees as they sway in the wind. Every sound is louder, every smell more potent. And then there's the castle itself—an unwelcome presence behind me, looming like a weight pressing down on my furred back.

But here, outside, under the warmth of the moons, I'm free.

I run, paws digging into the earth as I dart across the grounds, heading for the tree line just beyond the castle. The cool night air rushes against my thick coat, and with every stride, my mind clears a little more. My wolf lets out a triumphant howl, a sound that slices through the night and makes the castle seem small and insignificant. This is what I need to let go of all the expectations and fears clouding my thoughts.

My wolf senses my confusion, my doubt, and I feel her response—protective and certain. She doesn't understand why I'm fighting this so hard. To her, even the glimmer of a connection to Theo is enough. It doesn't matter if the bond isn't perfect. She sensed the *something*, and that was that.

But for me, for my mind, this is all terrifying. And I

can't help but wonder if she's wrong—if whatever temporary draw we felt is merely a trick.

I run faster, pushing myself through the tall grass until the castle is far behind me, nothing more than a shadow on the horizon. The forest opens for me like a welcoming embrace. The scents of pine and earth nearly overwhelm my nose as I weave through the trees, dodging branches, leaping over fallen logs. My wolf's joy is infectious, her exhilaration at being free spreads through me like wildfire. There's no room for thoughts here, no space for doubt—only the run, the feeling of being alive, of every muscle burning with exertion, every heartbeat pounding in time with the rhythm of the forest around me.

The world blurs into streaks of green, black, and silver, the light of the moons filtering through the shadows and leaves above. For this moment, at least, there's no Theo, no confusion, no mate bond that feels broken. There's just the outdoors and the wild abandon of the run.

I finally slow to a stop, breathless, chest heaving. I stand in a small clearing, the moons bright overhead, their glow cascading down and bathing everything in a shimmering light. My wolf's energy hums around us, her joy mingling with my own exhaustion. For a heartbeat, I let myself bask in the beauty of the evening, in the cool breeze moving through my fur.

Her low rumble reminds me that I don't have to be afraid, that I can take the euphoria of this freedom she's just shown me and bring that back to the castle with me. I don't have to fight the unknown. At least not yet.

I can be free no matter what answers I find.

Giving the moons and stars another longing gaze, my wolf howls into the air, her cry filling me with strength until there's no more room for fear.

Tomorrow, I'll speak with Theo.

Tomorrow, I'll do my best to trust the fates and the spirit inside me.

Tomorrow will be better.

It has to be.

CHAPTER EIGHT

THEO

The sun rises slowly, spreading a golden glow over the forest, but the sight that used to bring me solace now only reminds me of the burden I carry. There was a time when all I needed was my mother and the close-knit pack members who were more like family than friends. We didn't live near the castle. Instead, we formed our own pack far from prying eyes. It was a life lived in seclusion and simplicity—a pack carved out of strength and loyalty, where bonds ran deep. I grew up being called an alpha without realizing what it meant, without understanding what I could lose.

Then, they came for us. For me.

The memories haunt me even now. Darkness fell around me then, but it wasn't just the absence of the sun that night. A storm of death swept through our lands, cloaked in shadow and silence. I awoke not to screams, but to an eerie, suffocating quiet. And when I stepped outside, blood rained down on me—every person I'd loved was slaughtered, each felled by their own hunter.

My mother, the last soul still alive, crawled toward me, begging me with her dying breath to stay hidden.

But the intruders were gone. They'd come for me, but not with the intention of taking my life. They sought to destroy me in the worst way possible, leaving me to live with the guilt of surviving and the weight of the lives that had been so cruelly stolen.

That was the end of everything I once knew about our world.

It's been three years, but the silence of that evening never truly ended. It lingers, darkening my mind, never allowing me peace. And now, I've found myself further ensnared in a web of choices I can't untangle, some of my own making and others thrust on me by one who wields his power like a weapon, unstoppable and uncontrollable.

Hope was fickle, death was welcome, and then...Estee arrived.

I'd spent months searching for my mate, a task given to me by way of threats and demands that I had no power to refuse. I thought of *her* as a means to an end, someone to fulfill a role. I didn't expect her to be so enthralling, to have a presence that would unsettle me in ways I still don't understand.

Though, none of that matters if I can't fix what I've done, if I can't find a way to my freedom without sacrificing anyone else.

I spent the night locked in my office, the walls closing in as I mulled over my options. Estee gave me twenty-four hours to prove to her that she shouldn't walk away. Twenty-four hours to find a way to keep her here and safe. And as much as I wish that just being me could be enough for her, I know that isn't the case. Nor should it be. Not when our bond is being used by another to create his own entertainment through my misery.

My wolf snarls within me, his growl echoing through my chest and making the silence in my office feel heavier. He's not pleased with my thoughts of inadequacy, but that's nothing new. He hasn't agreed with anything I've done since the day I traded our future for my mother's peace. A decision that's shaped the fractured life we now live.

But that's the past, and I can't change it. The only path forward is to face what's coming head-on, starting with the mess I've found myself in with Estee. It's the only way I know to protect her, even if that means putting myself in more danger.

For hours, I've sat there, my hands in my hair, tugging until pain pulls me back into focus. I keep circling to the idea of telling Estee everything—laying bare the truth of my past, the bargain I made, the way my life's been damned. But even now, there's a voice in my head warning me away from that path, whispering threats and consequences I don't fully understand. Though, I don't know if it's my own fear or *his* voice, creeping into my thoughts.

Jerome, my advisor, nudges at the edge of my consciousness, and after ignoring his presence for the last several hours, I let him in.

"Good morning, Your Majesty," he states respectfully, even though I know I've frustrated him on too many days to count over the last year. *"Princess Estee is still resting, but I thought it would be wise for you to take a walk through the*

town before she wakes, maybe address the people about your new mate."

He's not wrong; the pack deserves to see their king. But I've avoided them for a reason. How am I supposed to face them, knowing the truth of how I got here? That I was chosen not because of any honor I might possess or my strength, but because of a deal that's bound me in unparalleled ways. When the truth comes out—as it almost always does—they'll despise me. And that's a future I'm not prepared for. Not now that Estee's come into my life.

"The pack is eager to hear about their new queen, Sire." Jerome's urgent tone tells me I shouldn't decline his suggestion as I usually do.

I give myself a once-over. My clothes are wrinkled from having spent half the night sitting on the ground beneath the window with my back against the wall. Hell, I don't even smell the best. Yet, I yearn to have my mate's acceptance. With a shake of my head, I realize it's time I began treating myself better. I said yesterday that I would fight for her and no matter how twisted my thoughts have become over the years thanks to the mind games I've been trapped in, I can't forget there's more at stake now than ever before.

By overcoming the self-doubts and no longer hiding behind these walls, maybe I can show Estee that I'm worthy of the bond we share and not the coward of an alpha I've considered myself these past months.

I open my office door and greet Jerome, who stands on the opposite side of the door, patient as ever. "I'll shower and change first then we'll head out."

His eyes widen. "Yes, Sire. I'll organize a group of guards to join us."

My head shakes. "It's not necessary. The two of us will be plenty."

"Your Majesty, if I may insist—"

"You can, but just the same, I can decline." My voice is stern. "Be ready within the hour."

As I stride past him, guilt nips at the edges of my thoughts. Jerome's been nothing but loyal to me, and I've repaid that allegiance with stubbornness and silence. Though, that doesn't change my mind about the guards.

I make my way to my private quarters, pushing open the doors and entering my bedroom with a renewed sense of purpose. Everything I do now has to be in pursuit of Estee, of her acceptance. The motions of showering, shaving, and changing into fresh clothes are routine, but with my new motivation, the small acts feel significant. As if I'm shedding more than just the grime of the night and previous day. I'm also freeing myself from the layers of doubt and fear that have held me captive for years.

It's no longer about what I've lost, but what I have to gain. At least that's what I need to keep reminding myself of.

Dressed in a crisp charcoal shirt and fitted black slacks, I stand in front of the mirror. The dark circles under my eyes are gone, the stubble on my cheeks has been shaved clean, and my eyes have regained some of their old spark.

My wolf paces within me, his pride and strength bolstering my resolve. I can't change what's happened, but I can change how I move forward. Estee deserves a mate who fights for her, not a king who cowers to his demons.

When I enter the formal sitting area of my private quarters, Jerome is standing near the fireplace, his hands clasped behind his back, patiently waiting for me.

Fine lines stand out around his eyes and sparse strands of grey are woven through his short hair. Gods, I've really been mentally absent if I didn't notice my closest advisor is much older than I believed.

Moving to stand in front of him, I meet his gaze respectfully. "I'm sorry, Jerome."

"Your Majesty." He bows his head. "As king, you should never have to apologize."

"Yet, I have plenty of reason to. But maybe what you and the rest of the pack need isn't an apology. You need me to show you that I haven't forsaken our home, that I can be the leader Selaris deserves."

His curiosity is tangible as he looks up at me. "I think the people would appreciate that, Sire."

"Then, let's start with showing them I'm still here and available to them." I move toward the door, but Jerome clears his throat, stopping me.

"I must prepare you, Sire." His tone is uncertain. "Going out into the public, you might find that there are those who wish to see you gone, that believe you unworthy of the throne."

My smile is genuine as I try to ease his concern. "That's nothing I didn't already assume. I'm prepared for them to question my authority. I know I have a lot to make up for, but I can't do it from inside this castle."

"No, Your Majesty, you can't." He turns toward the door and opens it for me before bowing.

As I pass him, I stop to clasp his shoulder. "Thank you for never faltering in your duty, Jerome. Your support hasn't gone unnoticed."

He nods. "Thank you, Sire."

I walk past him, and together, we make our way down the castle's winding staircases. I've kept the staff within this palace sparse as there hasn't been a need with so few guests staying within these walls, but maybe that's something else I need to change.

Bringing life back into this kingdom is second to fortifying the bond I share with Estee, but that doesn't mean I can't strive for both.

I make mental notes as we walk and share my thoughts with Jerome. Things like adding color into the castle by updating some of the portraits and tapestries on the walls.

Once we exit through the main doors, the path leading to the outer gates of the castle goes right into the heart of our market. The morning light touches everything—cobblestone streets, the wooden stalls of the merchants, the quaint, weathered homes—and as I walk deeper into the area, I feel the eyes of my people fall on me like a physical touch. Shocked stares turn to worry, distrust, and even anger as the murmurs begin.

"How dare he show his face now?"

"*Now* he comes to walk among us?"

"Someone should take his head off."

The hostility rolls over me in waves, but I knew this was coming. Nothing close to a warm welcome, yet still more than I deserve. I let my wolf rise within me, his presence steadying me, grounding me in the strength of our bond.

At the center of the market square, I stop, tapping into the mental connection I share with my pack. They may not respect me as their alpha, but today they're going to hear me.

"I know you have no reason to trust me." There's no point pretending otherwise. *"But I'm here to ask for your forgiveness anyway. I've been an absent leader, and I sincerely apologize for that. I also know that my words won't be enough to earn your pardon, but I come to you today, vowing to do better as your king, to be better for our pack."*

The emotions swirling through the shared bond are chaotic—fury, disbelief, suspicion—but there's a sliver of hope as well, hidden beneath the bitterness.

"As you've heard, I found my mate," I continue. *"While the details of that are being worked out, I'm also going to be opening my doors to speak with anyone who wishes to voice the issues that have gone unresolved for far too long, and I promise to begin making changes to better all your lives, one day at a time."*

"Lies!" a man yells from a shadowed alleyway. "How about *we* start making our own changes, beginning with ending your reign?"

The voice doesn't belong to anyone I can find a connection to. My wolf pushes forward, enhancing my senses, but the presence is gone before I can pinpoint him. Yet, the damage is already done.

"Yeah, maybe we should," one shifter agrees then another.

"Who's to say you're even fit to lead?"

But before the muttering can turn into a full-blown uprising, a clear, steady voice cuts through the noise. "Or perhaps," a woman says, "our time for struggle is over. Perhaps King Theo, alongside the soon-to-be Queen Estee, will unite Selaris in ways we haven't seen in centuries."

Elyn Holton.

One of the oldest members residing in our kingdom and a healer. I've never spoken directly to her, but that seems about to change.

She approaches me and places a hand over my chest before speaking into my mind. *"The debt you bear is strong, but you must find a way to see the truth."*

"What truth?" More importantly, how the hell does she know about my *debt*?

She doesn't answer me. Instead, she walks away as if her show of support didn't just shock every pack member crowding in around me.

"Might I suggest we go back to the castle, my King?" Jerome's concerned voice sounds through my mind next. *"I think this was enough for today."*

He may be right, and I'll go, but our business isn't done just yet.

Tapping back into the connection with my pack, I leave them with one final statement. *"If you'd like to meet with me, I'll set aside several hours a day, four days a week, beginning within the next few days. Changes will be happening as quickly as I'm capable of implementing them, beginning with a celebratory ball for all that's to come. Expect an invitation within the coming weeks."*

Jerome's displeasure is clear, but the castle isn't only mine. It's an extension of our pack, and I want them to feel welcome. Not only that, but I also want Estee to know how much her presence is going to mean to our people if she chooses to stay.

She wouldn't only be my mate; she'd also become the queen of Selaris.

Something that I hope to see happen because there has to be a way that I can still protect my mother *and* have Estee in my life.

No matter what it takes, I'm going to fight for that future.

CHAPTER NINE

ESTEE

After returning from my run, the focused energy I'd clung to out in the forest stayed with me. But between the day's emotional upheaval and the physical exertion, I've managed to sleep most of the morning away.

Getting up slowly, I stretch my arms above my head as I let out a deep yawn. A tiny smile breaks across my lips—one that feels almost foreign.

Secrets and unease aside, today I feel ready to deal with whatever I've stumbled on here in Selaris. I want to know the truth, and I'm going to have an open mind. There's a reason I'm here. I may not know what it is yet, but I will soon.

I swing my legs over the edge of the bed, and the cool hardwood floor sends a shiver through me as my feet touch the ground. When I enter the ensuite bathroom to get ready for the day, my toes sink into the plush maroon rug covering the tile floor, but the smell of food hits me, and I go back into the room.

I somehow missed a tray of fresh food on the table by the window. A small envelope sits beside the towering plates, my name scrawled across the front in delicate, looping script.

Curiosity gets the better of me, and I grab the note. *Did Theo leave this for me?* I tear open the seal with a startling urgency, but when I read the words inside, my chest tightens with unexpected disappointment.

Dearest Princess Estee,

My name is Keera, your royal handmaiden. I came to prepare you for the day, but you were resting so peacefully that I didn't wish to disturb you after your travels yesterday. Please ring for me when you've awoken, and I will return to assist you as needed. I've left your breakfast—a variety of local breads and fruits, along with some boiled eggs.

I look forward to serving you.

Signed,

Keera Brindle

The note is kind, formal, and carries no hard edges, but I can't ignore the fact that a part of me was hoping to see Theo's handwriting, to see his thoughts laid out before me. Why that absence bothers me, I don't know, but my stomach twists with an odd sensation I can't quite place.

I shake my head and force myself to focus, so that I can at least brush my teeth before my thoughts run wild. As I pass the tray of fresh berries and breads, I grab a ripe strawberry and pop it into my mouth. The sweet taste floods my senses, but I decide to clean up before sitting to eat. Leaving the food for now, I step back into the bathroom.

My shower is brief, but the heat of the water is soothing. Once I'm dried off, I dress in a pair of loose cream pants and a navy-blue sweater—a comfort outfit pulled from the depths of my steamer trunk.

As I brush my teeth, I realize the note mentioned that Keera was meant to help me prepare for the day, which would normally include assisting with my clothes. While that's part of the role for handmaidens, it's not something I've ever taken advantage of—except when it comes to ballgowns. I've yet to meet a woman who can cinch herself into one of those torturous corsets.

Once I'm done, I go back to the table, piling a few things on a plate then butter some toast. As I lift the bread to my mouth, a soft knock sounds at my door.

"Come in," I call before I take my first bite.

A young woman enters, wide green eyes, a sprinkle of freckles across her round cheeks, and a nervous smile on her face. "Good morning, Princess Estee. I'm Keera."

She brushes a loose strand of deep red hair back behind her ear and keeps her gaze on my feet. Her light grey dress is clean but thin and almost stiff as it hangs from her lean frame, accented by a white waistband.

I offer her a warm grin and motion for her to step forward. "Please join me."

She does, quietly closing the door behind her, but doesn't come much closer. "What may I do for you this morning, Your Highness?"

"You can come help me eat this food," I tell her, doing

my best to keep my tone light. She reminds me of a frightened animal, one that might run at any moment.

"Oh." Her cheeks somehow pale even further. "That's not… I can't—"

"Keera," I say a little more firmly, "come and make yourself a plate and tell me about yourself. Anything less will make me very displeased."

So much for taking it easy on her, but she looks as if she hasn't eaten in a week. I'm trying not to be furious about that fact since I don't know how this kingdom is run, but I certainly intend to find out. No member of the pack should look as frail as this one. Not for any reason.

Hell, she barely looks old enough to be working in the castle.

Keera shuffles closer to the table, her fingers twisting together and her head down as we both take our seats. With a shaking hand, she grabs a croissant and puts it on a plate.

"How old are you, Keera?" I ask, no longer interested in my food.

"Sixteen, Your Highness."

My teeth grind together. This girl should be in school, not coming to tend to a princess.

"And what of your mother and father? Are they proud that their daughter works in the king's castle?" I do my best to make her job sound like an accomplishment, even though this is the last place she should be right now.

She chews her next bite slowly before answering. "They, um, well, I never knew them."

An orphaned wolf? Outrage storms through me like an uncontrollable wildfire. This is unacceptable on so many levels, yet I know this growing rage has nothing to do with Keera and everything to do with how this kingdom has been run, even before Theo took the crown.

"I'm very sorry to hear that," I tell her gently. "Do you live here in the castle? Is that why you've been asked to work at such a young age?"

"No, Your Highness. I applied for the position myself and they've only just offered me a room." Her fingers twist the fabric of her dress, and her voice shakes. "Today is my first day."

I pull a harsh breath in through my nostrils, the air tearing through me like jagged blades. "And it's going to be your last day."

She gasps and begins to cry. "Please, Princess. Whatever I've done, please let me fix it. I need this job."

I kneel before her, grabbing her hands and holding them tightly as I look up into her fearful eyes. "You haven't done anything wrong, Keera. It's your king and the pack who've failed you. You will live here in the castle, but you won't work unless that's what you choose for yourself later in life. I'll make sure you have clothes, food, and a warm bed to sleep in. Anything less is unacceptable to me, and it should be to you as well."

Keera's tears begin to ease and she's silent for too many beats. I'm nearly certain she's going to reject my offer based upon the paleness of her cheeks, but then she tries to speak and only deep, wrenching sobs escape her.

I try to ask what's wrong, but before I get the words out, she throws her arms around me, clinging to my neck. Her cries are muffled against my shoulder, but I think she's whispering "thank you" over and over, her voice breaking. I hold her tight, trying to pour every bit of warmth and compassion into the hug she so clearly needs.

How has this been allowed to happen? What has become of Selaris?

In that moment, I make a silent vow: Even if Theo isn't my mate, I won't leave this place until I know the people are safe and cared for. I won't walk away until I'm sure that children like Keera have the support they need, the lives they deserve.

When she finally pulls back, her face is streaked with tears, but a small, fragile smile plays on her lips. "Thank you, Princess Estee," she whispers. "You're everything we've been wishing for."

Gods, I hope she's right, because my need to help these people isn't something I can ignore.

"Until we find a place for you to call your own, why don't you stay right here in my room?" She should at least be safe in here for a while.

She nibbles at her lower lip. "That's more than I should accept."

I offer her a friendly wink. "But you're going to, with grace."

I don't want to force her to stay—it's important that she starts making good choices for herself—and luckily it seems she doesn't need much persuading.

Keera adds more food to her plate and nods. "Yes, Your Highness."

"I'm going to go speak with King Theo." I stand then point toward the bathroom and my wardrobe. "I'm not sure anything I have will fit you, but what's mine is yours until we have you settled. Make yourself at home, and I'll be back to check on you soon, okay?"

She looks up at me sweetly and sniffles. "You're going to be the best queen to ever reign, Princess Estee."

I rest my hand on her shoulder and smile. "We'll see."

There are several things I need to do this morning, and the first is finding Theo or, at minimum, his advisor Jerome. They're about to learn what I'm not willing to put up with.

Orphaned children being uncared for is at the top of that list.

I stride down the hallway, my mind a whirlwind of thoughts and feelings. Unlike yesterday, though, I'm capable of sorting through them without losing control. My rage isn't governing my actions, just fueling my motivation.

Bounding up the stairs two at a time to the next floor where I hope to find Theo, I do my best to keep my mind open. While he's to blame for hiding away in this castle while his people suffer, Keera not having a family to call her own didn't happen within the last year. She said she didn't know her parents, which means she's been alone since she was only a babe. *That* tells me I also have the previous alpha—King Airik—to blame.

Still, Theo's finally going to open his eyes and make strides to fix the broken pieces of his land, whether he wants to or not.

For his sake, I hope it's the former.

The office I ran from last night comes into view, the carved mahogany doors looming in the dimly lit hallway. I reach out to knock, my knuckles grazing the cool wood.

The door swings open, and I've suddenly forgotten why I've come here.

Theo towers over me, stealing the air from my lungs. He's different today. Stronger. Confident. A far cry from the disheveled man I met yesterday. He's wearing a charcoal shirt that hugs his broad shoulders and tapers toward black slacks that cling just right to his powerful legs, making my mouth go dry. He's freshly shaven, his jawline sharp and clean, and the unruly hair from before now lies in soft waves around his forehead.

Those dark, grey eyes lock onto mine. They appear alive today, glittering with a hidden light that wasn't there before, and his stare wraps around me, pulling me in as if I have no choice in the matter. As if we're the only two people in this castle. In the world. The air around us is heavy with something electric, making it so that I can barely move.

The space between us crackles with tension, hot and tense, and I don't know if it's my wolf awakening or just me, but I'm hyper-aware of every inch of room that separates us. My skin feels as if it's buzzing, my chest is tight with emotion that's almost akin to excitement, like my wolf knows something that I don't. She prowls within my mind, close to the surface, pacing back and forth, encouraging me to step closer.

Yet, despite all that, I stand my ground, my hands curling into fists at my side to steady myself. And still, he just stares. Like he's drinking me in, trying to memorize every detail of my face, my eyes, my soul. His chest rises and falls, the movement almost imperceptible.

Finally, after what feels like an eternity, he swallows,

the sound almost too loud in the charged silence. "Estee."
My name falls from his lips like a desperate prayer.

Gods, is *this* the bond? Is Theo really *mine?*

Or maybe this is merely lust because while I'm finding
this version of him suddenly irresistible, the uncontrollable need to touch him still isn't present. His essence isn't
the air I need to fill my lungs.

And as those thoughts become a truth in my mind, the
attraction begins to crumble. My chest shudders, and I
close my eyes, fighting off the growing disappointment
within me, a feeling I don't understand nor want. Yet, one
that is as real as the beat of my heart.

I don't know what that was, and I'm not sure I want to,
considering how overwhelming it was... But I came here
for a reason, and I'm not leaving.

I clear my throat, trying to steady my voice, but it still
comes out softer than I intend. "Are you going to let
me in?"

For a moment, he just stands there, and I can see the
struggle on his face—he looks like he wants to say something but can't find the words. Then, with a slow, almost
reluctant nod, he steps back, opening the door wider.
"Please, join me."

As I cross the threshold, my arm brushing his for the
briefest second, I swear a bolt of lightning passes between
us, scorching my heart.

Gods, what is happening to me?

CHAPTER TEN

THEO

The thundering in my chest makes my legs shake as I struggle to make it back to my desk. Estee's presence does something to me I've never experienced in all my lives. Her scent, rich and sweet, brings my wolf prowling to the forefront of my mind. And those eyes—the way they softened when she looked at me for those few moments, completely unguarded—it was like the sun breaking through darkened clouds.

For the briefest second, the bond between us flared, and I saw a glimpse of what could be: a world with no shadows, no underhanded deals, no secrets. Just the two of us—bound, whole. My wolf felt it too, and for that sliver of time, everything was right. And then…it shattered. Estee's gaze hardened, her walls went back up, and I was left scrambling for words that suddenly felt too small.

I manage to sit behind my desk, steadying my breathing. I'm desperate to ask if she felt the same, but I already know what she'll say. Her defenses are like steel, impenetrable and unforgiving.

"I didn't expect to see you so soon," I offer lamely, every word tasting like ash.

It's a poor attempt at beginning a conversation but also the truth. I thought she would avoid me, not seek me out first thing this morning. Unless she's changed her mind, and she's not giving me the day to convince her to stay.

Panic claws at my chest, and I grip my thighs beneath my desk. I have to keep control of myself before I lose her completely. I know this, but it doesn't make my mind stop racing.

"And I didn't expect to be greeted by a sixteen-year-old handmaiden," she fires back. "What's going on here, Theo? Why are children working in your castle?" Her voice is cold, sharp as broken glass, and I can't meet her eyes.

I look away, shame creeping up my neck like a noose. As Alpha King, I should know the answer to that question, but I don't. Something that's unacceptable on more levels than I can analyze right now. "I'm sorry, Es—"

"Don't you dare tell *me* that you're sorry. What about Keera? The child who woke up today thankful to have a job she shouldn't need if this pack was being run as it should be?" Tears glisten in Estee's golden eyes, but they never fall. "How many more are out there just like her?"

"I don't know," I admit ashamedly. "I've been an absent ruler. I know more than anyone else that I don't deserve the crown I wear, but you've woken a part of me that I thought lost long ago. I'm going to be better. For you and for the kingdom. I promise."

Rage simmers beneath the surface of her vibrant presence, but I can't tell if that anger is at me or because of what Selaris has become. Worse, I'm too cowardly to ask.

Estee stares down at me, and my wolf rises to the surface, no longer allowing me to wallow in disgrace. He pushes my alpha power through the room, and I see the moment that she feels my strength. She blinks several times and her shoulders tremble ever so slightly.

"I want to make it clear that while I still expect explanations, I'm not staying here for you, Theo. Instead, I'll be remaining in your kingdom for the people. I have no choice after all I've seen. These shifters need help, and if you can't do it, someone else has to."

Her words rush over me, but all I can focus on is the fact that she's not leaving. The relief is profound, yet I know I can't show it. Not when she's just admitted she's not truly staying for me. At least not yet. I have a fighting chance to change that, though.

"Thank you for giving me a chance," I tell her, but that must not be the right thing to say because she scoffs and turns her back on me.

"You clearly haven't been listening to anything I've said. I don't know why I expected anything more after being summoned here."

My wolf breaks through the fragile hold I've kept on him, and his snarl echoes through the room. I move toward Estee's retreating form without a second thought. My inner beast is in full control, and there's little I can do to stop him now. Not when our mate has basically been rejecting us since our first interaction.

"Stop."

I'm not sure if the word comes from me or my wolf, but either way, urgency claws at me as she reaches for the doorknob.

Before I can fully process what I'm doing, I wrap my hand around her wrist, pulling her back toward me. Her mouth twists in shock and fury, and I know I've gone too far, but I can't seem to let go.

Her chest collides with mine as I pull her further from the door. The heat of her body, the pounding of her heart sear into my memory as I keep her close, momentarily forgetting that I'm not supposed to be touching her like this.

A warning rumble echoes from her chest, clearing my head. I take control of my movements, start to back away, but she reaches up to grip my throat. "Touch me without my permission again, and it might be the last thing you do. Are we clear?"

Her threat is real and I should heed it, but I don't flinch. Instead, I lean in, our faces inches apart, my voice a steady thrum. "You might think you know me, but you have no idea what I've been through or why this kingdom is the way it is."

Her laughter is cold and dark. "The why of this whole mess becomes less important to me each time we speak. The only thing I care about now is making sure the people are taken care of."

"That's what I've been trying to do!" I don't mean to

yell directly in her face, but I'm so damn frustrated that I can't hold back any longer.

The weight of hiding from everyone, of being threatened and tricked, has become too much to bear on my own. Estee is supposed to be my mate, my partner, the one person in all the worlds I can trust and depend on. Even if she doesn't see that in me, I'm desperate to have that from her.

"I've sacrificed in ways that would make most crumble," I continue, every inch of me rigid with anguish. "I've lost everything, even things I didn't know I had to lose. But you're right, Estee. The pack deserves better, and I haven't been that for them since taking over, but that doesn't mean I don't care. Everything I have and haven't done is because I care too damn much."

She releases the hold on my neck but surprisingly doesn't step back even though I've also let go of her wrist. "Then why is your kingdom failing its people? Why are there children with no families, without enough food to keep them strong?"

"Because I haven't been enough." The words sound as pathetic leaving my mouth as they feel reeling through my mind. "I thought I could have a second chance. I thought I could keep everyone safe, but I've always been ten steps behind, and now is no different, but I'm going to change that. I'm going to find a way to make all this better."

Estee watches my face closely, her arms crossed as her foot taps softly on the floor. She says nothing for too many heated seconds and when she finally looks away, it takes every ounce of my strength to not grab her face and make her see the truth in my eyes that I can't find the will to share with words.

"What do you mean by 'a second chance'?" she asks, this time without as much malice. "Were you a king in a previous life as well?"

Even though it was only a few years ago that I was called alpha, it certainly feels like another lifetime. Not because I've been able to forget that time, but because so much has happened since. Watching my mother take her final breath, seeing our homes burn to the ground, thinking I found an ally, only to realize I'd been tricked into a future that was nothing I could've imagined.

"I was something," I tell Estee. "I had a small pack, people to care for, and they all died on my watch. I tried to avenge them, but..."

I can't tell her more. I've already said too much. If Estee finds out the truth before she feels the mate bond, I fear she'll never accept me. There has to be a way to keep her close and end this nightmare before I truly do lose everything.

"But what?" Estee presses, putting her focus back on my face. "How did you get to this point, Theo? If you expect me to believe you're worth my time and not better off meeting the end of a sword, you need to give me something."

"I'm your mate," I say, hating the way she shakes her head.

"It's not enough. Not like this."

I know what she means and she's right, but that

doesn't mean that I'm not going to fight to change her mind.

"This morning, I went with Jerome to the town center," I tell her. "I promised them that things would be better, and I meant every word. I'm going to make changes, and I'm going to find a way to make all this mean something. You don't have to believe me. In fact, I hope you don't, because then maybe you'll stay long enough to make sure I follow through on my promises and long enough to see that there's more between us than you've yet to feel."

She looks away from me, out toward the window that oversees the royal courtyard. "I'm going to stay and make sure the shifters here are taken care of, but I promise you nothing more than that. You're still not telling me everything. Mate bond or not, if I can't trust you, what's the point?"

My wolf howls inside my mind, the sound ricocheting through me.

"You're right," I tell her then take a risk I probably shouldn't after her earlier threat. I cup her face. "I'm going to be better. For the people of Selaris, for the future I still hope to have, and for you. But most importantly, so I can one day find myself worthy of the strength you've shown me."

When she doesn't immediately pull away, I decide to step back first. I want her to know that I respect her need for space, that I understand none of this is normal, but most of all, I want her to know that I won't give up.

I might've been ready to do so before finding her, but death no longer seems like the only way out of this mess.

Not when I still have hope that there's a chance for me to have Estee in all the ways I've yet to discover.

Estee is mine. This kingdom, even if it never should've been, is mine. My future is mine.

All the twisted threats be damned.

"We shall see about that..."

CHAPTER ELEVEN

ESTEE

I leave Theo's office, nearly stumbling over my own feet as I hurry down the hallway, away from the chaos swirling around us both. The corridor seems to stretch out longer with every step I take, my breath coming in shallow gasps as if the very air has turned into a heavy mist trying to keep me down. Once I've rounded the corner, I press my back against the cool stone wall, trying to steady myself.

My emotions twist like a storm-tossed sea, each wave carrying a different feeling—anger, attraction, doubt, and something I can't quite name. I close my eyes, leaning my head back until it thumps against the wall behind me, wishing for a calm I fear will never come.

Gods, why is this all so confusing? I thought admitting earlier that I might've been blocking the bond would open my mind up to letting Theo in, but after speaking with Keera and being back in his presence, all I can think about is how infuriated this entire situation makes me.

No matter what problems he's been faced with, how

could he let things get this bad? I don't understand, and I know that's why I'm reacting the way I am. Well, that and the sudden flare of attraction that nearly consumed me back there. I can almost believe that the draw to Theo is due to a bond, but having my desire to be with him disappear nearly as quickly as I'm able to sense it is going to drive me mad. Hell, it already has.

How am I supposed to let him in or show him sympathy when he's withholding information and I'm more confused than I've ever been?

The answer should be simple. I know I'm capable of offering him compassion without the whole story; I've done that a million times over with strangers throughout my many lives. Except Theo isn't supposed to be a stranger—*if* my wolf's intuitions are true, *if* he's right when he calls me mate. He's supposed to be more. At least in my mind. As much as I've feared having a mate, I've envisioned what it might be like to finally find my other half. Someone that I don't expect to complete me, but who will complement my strengths and weaknesses, empower me to do all I aspire to do, love me beyond reason, and feel like coming home every time I look into his eyes.

It's what my sister has with Asher, and I don't want to settle for anything less, which is likely half the reason I'm so damn frustrated right now.

I tug at my hair as my chest vibrates. I'm exhausted from this situation, from the whiplash of emotions I've been spun around in since stepping onto that ship. I just want it all to stop.

"Estee?" Theo's voice cuts through my thoughts like a

blade. "I'm sorry. I didn't like the way we left things and..."

I push away from the wall, straightening my shoulders as I face him. My chest strains as I take him in. I'm again forced to see that he's more presentable today. I also can't forget that he said something about going out and seeing his people this morning, facing them and acknowledging the problems within Selaris.

Taking all that into consideration, I have to admit that it wouldn't kill me to start focusing on the positives a little more. No matter how muddled my heart is.

"It's fine, Theo," I tell him, keeping my voice even. "Our conversation wasn't going anywhere productive, and I think some space will do us both good." And because I feel guilty about how harsh I was before, I add, "Thank you for sharing what you did with me and for promising to do better. I know I didn't make it seem like it, but your efforts do mean something."

He blinks several times. "I appreciate that, but I didn't come after you for an ego boost. I was more concerned with making sure you were okay. I don't want to push you for more than I deserve at this point, but I'm not going to give up either. I'll figure out this mess with our bond and find a way to make this right. All of it. With me, you, and Selaris."

The sincerity in his words reaches deep inside me, and for a moment, I let myself see him as more than a broken king. I can't ignore his strength and determination. Or his agony.

"What happened to you, Theo?" I ask him earnestly, because while I thought him lazy and incompetent before,

I can't deny that I'm sensing true sincerity from him now. Hell, if I'm being honest, I could tell he was frightened yesterday, but I chose to ignore that because it was easier to be angry with him than anything else.

Theo glances around the hallway as if the shadows might be listening, his eyes clouding with something like shame. "I've made mistakes, Estee. Choices that haunt me, but I promise I'm going to do whatever it takes to fix as much as I can. I know it shouldn't have taken finding you to admit that things have gone too far, but I can't change that now."

There it is again—hope. A fragile, desperate kind of hope that tugs at the edges of my resolve. I want to believe him, but every stubborn instinct I have tells me not to. Still, I can't shake the feeling that there's more beneath the surface than I understand. And that maybe, just maybe, he's trying to do right by this kingdom, however flawed his efforts have been. Yet, I don't see my walls coming down anytime soon. Not until he explains how things got to this point.

"The moment I saw you, your essence was as bright as the stars for me," he adds, his voice barely above a whisper. "You are the light I needed to remind me that things don't have to be as dire as I've allowed them to be. My Starlight."

"Theo…" I'm not sure how I'm supposed to respond to that. As sweet as his words are, I don't have that same connection to him.

His smile relieves me of having to say anything else. "It's okay, Estee. I'm just sharing to help you understand. I don't expect anything from you, but I do hope for time.

While you're here, you can make as many changes of your own as you'd like. I've let Jerome know that anything you want done is authorized by me without asking. You might not officially be the queen of Selaris, but I've made it clear you're to be treated that way until you decide what you're doing."

This is the conversation we should've had in his office —a rational one that focuses on solutions instead of problems. I almost offer to return to his private quarters so we can try again, but then Theo reaches for my hand, and when our skin meets, there's a spark—an electric tingle that makes my breath hitch. He bends low, his lips brushing my knuckles, and my heart clenches at the sensation. I don't pull away, and neither does he. An unspoken understanding forms in these brief moments of silence: this is a truce, a restart, nothing more.

"Thank you for staying and fighting for the people here." He looks up at me with those dark grey eyes. Underneath the sorrow and regret is a determination I've yet to understand. "If you're feeling up to it, please join me for dinner tonight. I'll send Jerome to escort you, but if you'd rather stay in your room, I'll understand."

He releases my hand, and the moment his warmth leaves my skin, an emptiness settles in my chest.

I watch him retreat down the hallway, unable to respond. I don't know what I'm supposed to do now, but at least I'm no longer consumed by irritation. Instead of questioning every aspect of what just happened, I choose to appreciate his attempt to relieve any ill-will between us.

Going back to my room, I decide to focus on the

things I can do, especially since Theo's given me permission to act as his queen. That thought sends a thrill through me, but I'm not going to examine that too closely right now. Though, because of it, I can do something for the pack, the shifters who've been shoved into the margins.

When I open the door to my room, Drea is there, perched on the edge of my bed with an expression of fierce determination that immediately makes my heart clench.

"Drea?" I say, closing the door behind me. "What's going on?"

She frowns, leaning forward. "I was going to ask you the same thing. Did Theo threaten you or something? Everyone's saying you're to be the queen of Selaris, that it's already decided."

I'm stunned but not entirely surprised. He did say I'm to act as one without the official commitment. While the me from last night—or even an hour ago—might've wondered if he had an ulterior motive, I can see why he did it. If we show a united front, the pack will have an easier time believing that positive change is coming.

"He hasn't threatened me," I tell Drea, offering her a smile before gesturing for her to come sit with me. "In fact, I think we may have just come to an understanding."

She takes a seat across from me at the dining table near the window. A slow smirk rises on her face. "And what kind of *understanding* would that be?"

"Not *that* kind." I tell her with a playful roll of my eyes. "I want to help the pack here and being in a leadership position will allow me to do just that while I figure things out. It doesn't mean I'm staying for good. I still need to know if I can trust Theo, but I do believe that he wants to see things change here. Sticking around to make sure that happens is as far as I've gotten."

She watches me closely, her gaze thoughtful. "So, you still don't feel the mate bond?"

My first thought is to tell her no, but that would be a lie, and with the back and forth of my emotions, maybe talking things out is exactly what I need right now. I recount my arrival at Theo's office and the flare of attraction, along with the other flickers of a connection, ending with the conversation I shared with him in the hallway.

Drea lets out a soft sigh. "Damn. I almost feel guilty about meeting Orion now. You could really use a wing woman."

I wave a hand in the air. "I can handle this. It just took me some time to wrap my mind around everything and see the situation in a way that seems more manageable. Yesterday, all I could focus on was not being able to accept Theo and how wrong this place feels. Now, I see that there's something to figure out between the two of us and that Selaris is worth my time. The shifters here deserve that."

A thought occurs to me as I look around my room again. "Was there a young girl in here when you arrived?"

She shakes her head. "Was there supposed to be?"

"There was." And I really don't like that Keera's disappeared without my knowing where she went. I get up and go to the phone next to my bed. As I reach for the receiver, I notice another note.

Dearest Princess Estee,
I know you asked me not to leave, but I have a friend that I left
behind at the church where we're staying. She needs me more
than I need to be here. I appreciate your compassion, and I
know you expected my acceptance, but I can't leave her like this.
Not even for the comforts you've so graciously offered.
Please forgive me.
Signed,
Keera

Oh, that child. All she had to do was tell me about her friend or any other orphaned children and I would've found space for them in the castle. Now, it seems I need to go on a little adventure, find this church, and bring the kids back here.

I glance at Drea and grin. "How do you feel about kidnapping?"

Her soft chuckle fills the room. "Under the right circumstances, I'm not opposed to it. Plus, Orion is busy at work. Might be fun to get into some trouble."

I knew she was my kind of people.

CHAPTER TWELVE

ESTEE

Before leaving the castle, I make a quick call to Jerome, and to my surprise, he treats me exactly as Theo said he would: like his queen. His tone is formal, his deference clear. There's no hesitation in his responses as I give my instructions. Rooms must be prepared immediately for any children we may find, with beds, fresh linens, and proper provisions. I emphasize the urgency of setting up a long-term plan for placement and that I expect to discuss this over dinner with Theo tonight.

Dinner. I wasn't sure I'd take Theo up on that offer—until now. Somehow, I hope the time with him will help piece together the mystery of Selaris and reveal the truth buried beneath the tension and secrets. I want to understand what Theo is hiding, and more than that, I want to know if I can trust him.

With Drea by my side, we leave the castle grounds. Past the stone archway, great double gates open before us, revealing the path that leads out into the heart of Selaris.

As we get closer to the market area, I feel several sets of eyes on me. And with those heavy stares, the curiosity, the suspicion, and the hope that swirl around this small kingdom.

Welcome to Selaris, I think, doing my best to square my shoulders and lift my chin. I need to be someone they can trust today, not just a visitor from a distant kingdom.

The town unfurls in front of me—homely yet worn by years of neglect from their king. The buildings are mostly stone, lining the narrow, cobbled streets. Shops have creaky wooden signs hanging above doorways—some brightly painted in shades of blue, green, and maroon, while others are faded by time.

Vendor stalls line the main street, their canopies creating patches of shade in the early afternoon sun. They offer everything from fresh fruits to woven fabrics and intricate jewelry. The scent of freshly baked bread mingles with that of earth and spices, reminding me of home, but different—more subdued, more distrusting.

"Stay close," I murmur to Drea. Though the town seems peaceful enough, there's an underlying edge that has my wolf ever-present. Her focused mind reminds me that with one wrong move, I might find more than I've set out to uncover on my own.

As we walk deeper into town, more people notice us, and murmurs spread like wildfire. "Princess Estee." Their whispers are hushed but eager. Some look on with expressions of interest, others with skepticism. One older woman meets my gaze with such intensity that I'm forced to nod in acknowledgment, and the briefest flicker of a smile softens her features.

Drea stays quiet beside me, her observant eyes scanning the crowd. "I get the feeling they don't know what to think of you yet," she says softly, leaning in closer. "Some look at you like you're their salvation. Others like you're just another royal passing through."

"I can't blame them." I look around, taking in every detail, every flicker of emotion that crosses their faces. "I wouldn't know what to make of me either if I were them."

We pass a tailor's shop, and there's a young woman sewing at the window, her fingers moving swiftly. She's so engrossed in her work that she doesn't even notice us. Further down the road, children chase each other, their bare feet slapping against the cobblestones, laughter ringing out in sharp contrast to the wary stares of the adults.

"Princess Estee!" A small boy suddenly darts out in front of me, eyes wide with excitement. He's holding a flower—wild, with delicate blue petals—and he pushes it up toward me, grinning from ear to ear. "For you."

I kneel, taking the blossom from his outstretched hand. "Thank you," I say, smiling. "What's your name?"

"Rory," he says proudly, rocking back on his heels.

"Well, Rory, this is a beautiful flower." I tuck it into the braid of my hair, and his smile widens.

"When do we get to call you Queen Estee?" he asks innocently, his eyes round with hope.

"I don't know," I answer honestly. "But I promise to do whatever I can to make things better even as a princess."

Satisfied, he gives a little nod and runs off, disappearing into the bustling market. I stand, my heart warmed by the simple exchange. But beneath that warmth, there's a chill, a reminder of why I'm here. There are children like Rory all over Selaris, some who are much less fortunate than him, and I intend to find them.

"Let's keep going," I say to Drea, and we move on, asking a few passersby for confirmation we're headed in the right direction. Some are reluctant to speak with us, but others are quick to help, eyes glimmering with a mixture of gratitude and uncertainty.

Eventually, we reach the edge of the town, where the stone streets fade to dirt paths and the buildings grow sparser. The air is thick with the scent of pine, and tall trees sway in the breeze as we approach the structure we've been directed to. A church at one point, but with its roof sagging, vines creeping up the sides, and doors hanging crooked on their hinges, I have a hard time calling it one still.

The place is abandoned—long forgotten by both gods and shifters alike.

"Is this it?" Drea asks, her voice hushed with disbelief.

"It must be." I step closer, running my fingers over the cracked wooden slats of the exterior. A chill seeps into my fingertips as I feel the neglect of this place, its ghostly silence settling around us.

I push open the door, the weathered wood groaning in protest, and we step inside. The space within is dim, lit only by rays of sunlight breaking through cracked stained-glass windows. Dust swirls in the air, and the floor is scattered with worn blankets, a few makeshift cots, and threadbare clothing. Though, I'm thankful to at least see open books and colored-on papers lying about. The scent of old wood and earth hangs heavy in the air.

It's clear that this church is a place of refuge—but one without the comfort and care that children need.

"Estee," Drea whispers, pointing toward the back. A group of children huddle together, wide-eyed and fearful, their clothes worn and faces dirty. They're clutching one another tightly, as if my presence is an omen they don't know how to interpret.

"Hey," I say softly, holding my hands out, palms up. "It's okay. I'm here to help."

One of the older girls, likely around ten or eleven, steps forward, standing protectively in front of the younger ones. Her face is set with a hard determination that doesn't belong on someone her age. "Who are you?" she asks, her voice shaking but resolute.

"I'm Princess Estee," I say gently. "I heard about this place and wanted to…" The words catch in my throat. How do I tell them I want to take them from their home, even if it's not a proper one? The last thing I want is for them to fear me. "I wanted to see if there was anything I could do to help. Can you tell me your name?"

She hesitates, glancing back at the others before looking at me. "I'm Neri," she says. "And we don't need anything from you."

"Are you sure?" I ask, my eyes drifting to the thin blankets and the hollow cheeks of the children. "Not even a warm meal or a place to bathe? Of course, you don't have to accept, and I don't intend to force you." Drea's eyes cut sharply to me, but I ignore her. "But I'll keep returning to check on you regardless."

Neri's fair blue eyes flash with defiance, but behind it

there's a fear of being betrayed, of promises broken too many times.

"What have you brought for us today, then?" she asks, looking pointedly at our empty hands. "Words don't mean anything to us."

"Understandable," I reply, offering a sympathetic smile. "Though, I'll be honest, I made the assumption that you were living in an active church." I look up at the rotting ceiling. "So, I've come unprepared with anything other than an offer to move all of you into the castle."

That has multiple growls echoing from the pups as Neri snarls. "We won't be slaves."

Gods, these poor children.

"And I wouldn't allow such a thing," I promise. "In fact, your friend Keera was sent to work for me, and I immediately relieved her of her duties and invited her to eat with me instead of serving me. I had hoped to provide her with a safe place to stay, but she left before I could follow through."

The silence stretches out between us, heavy with uncertainty. And in that moment, I realize that helping these children will mean more than providing shelter and food. It will mean rebuilding trust that has long been shattered—piece by fragile piece.

"I promise each of you," I tell them, slowly meeting each of their wide-eyed stares, "no matter what choice you make today, you will have food and proper places to sleep by the day's end. I'll have everything I can brought to you here if that's what it takes to make sure you're cared for, but I would also love to have you in the castle with me, where you'll have much more available to you, without the expectation of anything in return."

Neri turns to the others, and they huddle together. I could listen in if I wanted to, but I won't force their hand, even if it's for their own good.

I turn to Drea to give the kids some privacy, and there are tears in her eyes. "My heart has never hurt as much as it does now," she whispers. "Can't we just kidnap them like we talked about before?"

I force a tight smile, aching with the same desperation. "If we want this to work long term, taking them against their will probably isn't the best idea." I glance over my shoulder briefly to find they're still speaking in hushed whispers. "Patience is going to be our best option after whatever they've been through."

By my count, there are four of them. That doesn't include Keera—or, possibly, the one she came back for. Though, it doesn't matter how many we find. They'll all get the same love and care and eventually proper homes, even if I have to send them to Polaris to find new parents, considering the pack members here haven't already stepped up for the children.

Neri turns back to address me again, her chin held higher than before. "If you want to bring us things, we'll accept, but we don't want to move into the castle."

I shouldn't be surprised, yet my heart still constricts. "I can respect that. If you'll help me make a list of things you need most, I'll have them to you within a few hours."

"But I can't." Keera's voice comes from behind us.

Drea and I turn to find her standing there, still dressed

in the castle uniform, with a little girl clinging to her left side.

Keera frowns at me. "I'm sorry I left the way I did, Princess Estee, but if you'll take just some of us, the two of us would like to return with you."

"I'll take whoever wants to come and bring back supplies for anyone who isn't yet ready," I say loudly, making sure the children know it's not one or the other. I won't forsake those who need more time to trust me.

"Can I go too?" a little boy says from behind Neri, his eyes darting between me and her.

Neri's expression softens as she rubs a hand over his mussed blond hair. "If the princess is offering, I won't stop you."

He runs to Keera, clinging to her other side before popping a thumb into his mouth.

I look back at Neri, trying to convey all the compassion and strength she deserves. "I promise you," I say softly, "I will make this right for all of you."

She lifts her chin even higher, eyes guarded but resigned. "I look forward to seeing you try."

And I will. No matter what it takes—if I have to rebuild this church with my bare hands—these children will have a place to call home, full bellies, and all the love they deserve.

Anything less would be a failure I refuse to accept.

CHAPTER THIRTEEN

THEO

Stacks of papers lie spread out before me, their edges fraying from overuse, the ink smudged from my hands brushing over them repeatedly. Today, I've refused to let the piles gather more dust. Instead, I've combed through each document, hoping to make some sense of the kingdom's state. For too long, I've ignored my role as king—partly because of my doubts about being worthy of this crown, and partly because I've felt buried alive under it all.

Jerome, always reliable, was by my side the entire day, guiding me through the mess I've neglected. That is, until Estee called him away.

The way he smiled after speaking with her made me wonder what was going on, but he said it might be more impactful if I waited to find out until everything was done.

I can't afford to trust easily, not with everything that's happened, but something in me desperately wants to hope —to believe that Estee has a plan beyond just biding her time until she leaves. I've checked in with Jerome every hour to see if there's anything I can do to help, but he always brushes me off, insisting things are "well in hand."

The thought that this could all come tumbling down around me hasn't been far from my mind. It doesn't matter that I haven't felt *his* presence in over a day now. I know he's never truly gone and always watching. That's probably his favorite way to torture me, just keeping me on edge.

There has to be a way to assure my mother's safety *and* take my life back. I know there's a solution somewhere. I just haven't looked hard enough. King Asher would likely be my best ally, especially with Estee being my mate, but I don't want either of them to think I'm using her for my own gain. I didn't know she would be my mate before she arrived, but I know how it will look considering our bond is still only one-sided.

Gods, if only I could go back…

"Your Majesty." Jerome's joyful voice is a welcome disruption in my mind. *"You may want to come to the dining hall now."*

I glance at the clock. *"Dinner isn't supposed to be for another hour."*

"Yes, Sire, but Estee and her guests were hungry, and I think it would mean a lot if you joined them instead of waiting."

He doesn't have to tell me twice. Though I do wonder who her guests are, I don't take the time to ask as I grab my suitcoat from the closet in my office. I head out the door and close it securely before making my way down the hallway.

The dining hall is on the second floor and one of my

favorite rooms in the entire castle. The ceiling has open beams, taken from an old ship and recreating its base, only upside down. When I first moved in here, I used to spend hours in the hall, looking up and pretending I was anywhere else. Someone else.

Nearing the room, I pause, taking in the sound of laughter ricocheting off the walls that have felt so desolate for far too long. I almost don't recognize it. Warmth floods my chest, and before I know it, I'm striding forward again, eager to find out what's caused this unexpected spark of life.

When I shove the door open with a bit too much enthusiasm, the heavy oak crashes against the wall, the boom reverberating through the room like a crack of thunder.

The sound shatters the joy in an instant. Small bodies scatter and yelp, and before I can register what I've done, the room is plunged into fearful silence. Estee turns, and her glare hits me like a blade. Her fury is a palpable thing —radiant and furious, as if I've just burned down everything she's built.

"What is your problem?" she snarls through gritted teeth.

Beside her, a dark-haired woman—Drea, I assume—drops to her knees to comfort the frightened children, who've hidden under the table like trembling pups. I feel like a giant stomping through their world, bringing only terror with me. Jerome enters from the side door, his face stricken.

"Your Majesty?" His voice is calm, but I can hear the question underlying it. *What do you want me to do?*

I raise my hands in surrender. "I'm so sorry," I say. "I didn't mean to scare anyone. I was just—"

"You were just leaving," Estee hisses, closing the distance between us in a blink, her eyes burning with rage. "I promised these children they would be safe here. That means no slamming doors, no yelling, and no pissing me off. Do you understand?"

"No." I shake my head, tired of her believing the worst about me. "I'm sorry I *accidentally* slammed the door open, but I'm not leaving so you're going to need to find a way to be okay with that."

I move past her and walk toward the sound of the whispering children. Estee's wrath sears into me, but I ignore her. She needs to see I'm not the monster she's conjured in her head.

Drea backs up as I bend down to pull the tablecloth back. I kneel with a wide smile on my face before greeting each of them. "Hello."

Three young faces stare back at me. Two girls and one boy. The eldest is a teenager and the youngest maybe five or six. They're freshly cleaned and dressed well. Yet, I have no clue where they came from.

The boy with his thumb in his mouth burrows further behind the teenager, who watches me with hesitant eyes as she says, "Princess Estee invited us here."

"And I'm glad she did," I say earnestly, keeping my tone soft and light. "This big castle needs more people in it, don't you think?"

Before any of them can answer or I can apologize for scaring them, something warm and mushy hits me in the back of the head. I reach back and find mashed potatoes embedded in my hair.

The youngest, a little girl with curly blonde hair and big blue eyes, peeks out from behind the teenager, giggling nervously. I raise a brow at her. "Would you like some?"

She shakes her head frantically as her laughter spills out.

Glancing behind me, Estee stands not too far away, one arm crossed over her stomach and the other holding her potato-covered fingers up, an unmistakable smirk pulling at the corner of her lips.

An idea to turn this situation around begins to take root as I put my attention back on the children. "How about you help me get Princess Estee back?"

The boy brightens and sits up. "I'm on your team!"

The teenage girl, who hasn't said anything until now, speaks up finally. "I have pretty good aim."

That's all the encouragement I need. "Let's do this."

I catch the young boy as he dives for me then slip out from under the table with the small girl right behind us. When I stand, Estee and her friend Drea are shaking their heads.

"You don't want to do this," Estee says.

"I'm just finishing what you started, Starlight." I grab a handful of noodles and throw them at the two women just as the teenager stands up from under the table. Spaghetti sticks to her hair and her eyes widen at me then she runs to join the other ladies.

Estee finally cracks a smile.

I take the two littlest kids with me, motioning for

them to gather ammunition—brownies, mashed potatoes, and various bits of food on the table. "Get ready. We have to get them before they attack us!"

With our arms full, the three of us set up on the other side of the table, moving chairs to act as a wall at our backs.

"I'm Benji," the boy says, bringing one of the treats to his mouth.

"Well, Benji. That's our ammunition you're eating." I chuckle. "Are you going to let them overpower us for a bit of dessert or trust that I'll have all this food replaced once we've won?"

He shrugs and makes me laugh harder as he replies, "A little of both."

"I'm Addie," the blonde girl adds, filling her hands with dinner rolls.

"Nice to meet you both," I tell them with a friendly grin. "Now, let's show them why they shouldn't mess with us."

Both kids giggle, and the battle begins.

A well-aimed blob of pudding thrown by one of the kids splatters across Drea's cheek. She freezes for a moment, stunned, before laughing out loud. "Oh, it's on now!"

I throw a handful of shredded cheese at Estee, who deftly ducks out of the way, only to have them land on a snarling Drea. Estee's face lights up in surprise, and for the first time since meeting her, her defenses start falling away.

Estee laughs alongside the teenager—a genuine, bright sound—and it makes my heart swell. As much as I want to lose myself in that joy, I push it aside to focus on later and go back to the task at hand: getting them covered in as much food as possible.

"More ammo!" I yell to Benji, who's now tossing brownies across the room like they're throwing stars, while Addie, still giggling uncontrollably, flings spoonfuls of peas toward anyone who steps into her path.

The dining hall erupts into chaos—laughter echoing against the wooden beams of the ceiling, the sounds of children shrieking in delight, and the continuous barrage of food flying across the table.

Estee narrows her eyes at me playfully. "You think you're winning, don't you, *Your Majesty?*" she taunts, holding a serving ladle like a catapult, ready to launch a glob of gravy at me.

"I think I'm doing pretty well," I reply, dodging the incoming food, unable to stop the grin spreading across my face. It feels good to be in this moment—carefree, not thinking about my duties or the burdens weighing on me. Just living.

Estee, with an expression of mock determination, makes her way around the table. "You're going down!" she shouts, launching her gravy-loaded spoon at me.

I try to duck, but I stumble into one of the chairs, allowing the thick, brown liquid to catch me square in the chest. The warm goo slides down my shirt, and I can't help but chuckle. "You'll pay for that." I scoop up custard and fling it toward her.

It lands in her hair, making a mess of the dark strands. Estee gasps, her eyes wide, before she bursts into laughter. And it's beautiful—carefree and genuine, the kind that makes her eyes crinkle at the edges and lights up her entire face.

The children are howling with their own giggles, pelting whatever food they can find, and Drea throws herself deeper into the fray, smearing mashed potatoes onto Benji's cheek while dodging stray splatters of sauce.

The madness grows, and soon, the dining hall is a battlefield of laughter-filled war calls and feigned vengeance—a far cry from the solemn, silent place it usually is.

Estee locks eyes with me, still grinning, the custard now dripping down her face. And for just a moment, I let myself hope. That this lightness, this joy can stay—that she might stay.

"Truce!" I call out, holding my hands up in surrender, as I take in the mess we've made. "Truce before there's nothing left to eat!"

Estee raises a brow, looks down at the remains of the food then back at me. "Hmm," she says, smirking as she wipes her dirtied hands on her already ruined clothes. "But only because I'm starving."

Drea stands, brushing noodles from her dress, and the children come out from behind the chairs, snickering as they take in the state of everyone and everything. I step forward, offering Estee a hand to shake on our momentary peace.

When she takes it, warmth spreads through me—a hint of the connection that, for so long, I didn't believe I would ever have. However fleeting it is, it's real and worth fighting for.

And that's enough. For now.

CHAPTER FOURTEEN

ESTEE

I'm not sure I've ever been filthier. Bits of mashed potato and custard cling to my hair, streaks of pasta sauce splatter my arms, and breadcrumbs cling to my clothes. And yet, a joy pulses through me that I can't shake, a bubbling thrill that has me not caring about the fact that I'll probably be washing food out of my hair for days. A tiny part of me wants to hate this—the mess, this chaos, these ridiculous food-covered clothes. But the rest of me? I'm happier than I've been in years.

And that terrifies me.

When Theo scared the children, I'd let my fury loose without thinking twice and wanted nothing more than to see him gone. Then, when he stood up to me—refusing to cower like he had before—it shifted something inside me. Forced me to see him differently, to see strength I hadn't expected. I've grown a little too comfortable watching him hurt over his choices, and I'm not sure I like what that says about me.

But it's more than that. It's the way he brushed past

me, shoulders firm—every inch of him exuding a command I hadn't sensed before. I wanted to hate him for that moment of defiance, but more than that, I wanted to grab those shoulders and slam him against the wall in the least hateful way.

Then, when he teamed up with the kids, allowing them to have fun with all of us... Watching him let go, laughing, and embracing the chaos—it melted something icy inside me. The man could let his guard down, could be playful and kind. Could make me forget—just for a moment—every dark thought I've had about him.

The more I try to compartmentalize the new information, the more tangled my thoughts and heart become. Theo is a knot in my mind, one I can't unravel, and the more I pull, the tighter it gets. I still haven't forgotten that he's keeping things from me, but the more time we spend together, the easier that gets to overlook. Though, that's only temporary. We have to trust each other if we're going to make whatever this is work for any significant length of time.

After having filled a good portion of the day with the kids, I thought I would enjoy the quiet of my room after dinner, but I'm missing the distraction they gave me. Jerome offered them their own spaces as we got them settled into bed, but unsurprisingly, they've chosen to stay together for now.

Keera took charge helping Addie and Benji into their pajamas, then getting their teeth brushed, but that's something I also hope to change. She doesn't need to be a mother to these kids when she's still a child herself. While I don't intend to take that role from her, I plan to give her enough help that she no longer feels she has to parent them.

After showering, I put on underwear and a thick cotton robe then toss my hair into a bun. I should brush and dry it, but that's future Estee's problem. Tonight, I'm too damn tired. I want to enjoy my quiet time, maybe call Isla, and get a good night's rest.

My wolf paces in the back of my mind, hungry for the freedom of the wild. She wants to run tonight, I can tell, to stretch her legs and lose herself in the silence of the woods. And I understand that urge; the pull of the forest is always there.

Tomorrow, I promise her, and the steady drum of her restless energy begins to settle.

I collapse onto the mattress, staring up at the ceiling as a whirlwind of thoughts race through my mind. And then, just as everything starts to slow, a knock sounds at my door.

Theo.

I can't sense him like mates should be able to, but his scent is unmistakable. Over the past two days, the spicy, earthy aroma of sandalwood mixed with the perfect summer storm has become imprinted on my senses, enveloping me like a warm blanket with every interaction. And I'm not sure whether I love it or hate it. But I do know I'm beginning to crave it.

I walk lightly across the room, the cold wooden floorboards pressing into my bare feet. When I open the door, my smile is soft, gentle, but also cautious, as if I'm holding the slippery truce between my fingers and hoping it won't shatter.

Theo stands on the other side, the moonlight filtering through the hallway window casting a silvery glow on his face. His hair, damp from a recent shower, hangs over his forehead. He wears a white t-shirt and loose grey pajama pants, looking less like a king and more like a man who's just stepped out of a long day. His eyes are charcoal with a shimmer of something else, something that makes my breath hitch.

"Did I come at a bad time?" he asks, his voice a low rumble, and I catch the way his eyes dip to my chest for a split second before snapping back to my face.

I bring my hands up to cover myself, realizing belatedly that my robe is falling open. I tug the fabric tightly around me as heat rises to my cheeks. "I was just resting," I say quickly. "Did you need something?" I stay in the doorway, unsure if I should invite him in or if he'd even want me to. An uncertainty I don't like.

"I was wondering if we could talk." He glances behind me, into the bedroom. "Privately."

The deep timbre of his words curl around me like smoke, and I'm forced to grip the doorframe tighter to stay steady. The alpha power in his tone weaves through my mind, sending little shivers down my spine. Gods, it's hard to breathe when he's this close. Is this the bond? A fragment of what I've yet to understand? Until I do, I should say no—keep my distance, keep the questions locked away for another day. But I can't. Though I should at least be careful.

Do I really?

Damn that hungry voice in my head. I blame my wolf. She might not be able to talk directly to me, but there's no doubt she can manipulate my emotions to a certain extent. There's only so much of her pining that I can ignore when it comes to Theo.

Between that and seeing the other sides of him, this is going to get more complicated before there's a chance of anything making sense.

Even so, I step aside and welcome Theo into my room. "Come on in."

His eyes openly roam my mostly covered body, and suddenly, the puffy robe doesn't feel thick enough. "Thank you."

As he passes by me, just his essence has my shoulders shuddering.

He has to be doing this intentionally.

Theo makes himself comfortable in one of the two chairs across from my bed. I take the other one, purposely sitting with extra force so I can slide the seat another couple of inches away from him.

"Did something happen?" I ask, doing my best to ignore the breathiness of my voice. Gods, where is this attraction coming from? The unfolding desire doesn't fill the void where I expect there to be a connection if we're truly mates, but still, I can't help wondering if maybe I just have no idea what I should be expecting.

He nods slowly, his lips curling into a smirk that both infuriates and draws me in. "You moved children into my castle without my permission and threw mashed potatoes at me. Did you think we weren't going to talk about two of the best things you've done since arriving?"

"Excuse me, but you told..." My defenses go up so strongly the moment he says "without my permission" that it takes an extra few seconds to comprehend the latter part of what he's said. "Oh."

"Yes. *Oh*." His knowing grin has my stomach churning with butterflies. "So, what else did you do today that I should know about?"

"Jerome didn't tell you?" I expected that he'd be keeping Theo in the loop.

He shakes his head. "I wanted to hear from you directly. Jerome advises me on my role as king, not my role as mate."

My wolf surges to the surface so unexpectedly that I nearly lose control over my form. In those few seconds that her awareness is in charge, the connection that Theo has been so certain we share bleeds into me. At least I think it does.

A kaleidoscope of want, desire, and a sense of home consume me. Each emotion washes over me, cleansing my soul and preparing it for something that surpasses words. For a heartbeat, everything falls away. There's no castle, no politics, no regrets—just Theo and me, our souls entwining in a dance of longing and need. And I feel him—truly feel him—for the first time. The weight of his pain, the depth of his fear, but also the flickering hope that's fought so long to be free.

Yet, just as I start to process the deeper parts of him and before I can even breathe him in, the link I thought was forming breaks like glass.

It feels as though shards of him have been left behind, but the drive to heal him, to be the light in his life that he deserves is nowhere to be found. In its place is a desolation worse than any I've experienced in all my other lifetimes, made of raw edges and emptiness.

"Estee," Theo whispers, kneeling in front of me, cupping my cheeks as he uses his thumbs to brush away tears I didn't know were falling. "I'm so sorry."

"Why is this happening?" I need to understand. To know what could possibly keep that kind of happiness away from two people who just might actually be meant for each other. And then I need to destroy it.

He flinches, closing his eyes as if my words are knives against his skin. "It's complicated," he murmurs, his voice a plea for mercy.

"Then, uncomplicate it." I lean into his touch, searching his eyes for any shred of truth. "Because I won't stick around just to have a future dangled in front of me then ripped away. I can't live like that, Theo. I can handle a lot, but not this. I deserve better than that. I deserve the truth."

His heart beats so frantically that I can hear the rapid thumping clear as day.

"Whatever it is, just tell me," I plead with him.

Theo's shoulders slump, his eyes pinching shut as if every breath pains him. He stands and turns away from me, his back rigid as he walks to the window overlooking the castle's gardens. The moonlight casts silver streaks through his dark hair, and for a moment, I can almost see the man behind the crown—the man who's lived with a darkness no one else understands.

"I never should've been king," he says so quietly that I almost don't hear him. "I don't belong here, and the things

I've done to stay?" He shakes his head, still hanging in despair. "You'll never forgive me, Estee."

The pain in his voice keeps me in my chair. I'm afraid to go to him, of what he may admit. Maybe I don't want to know.

Yet, if there's any chance for any of this to be real, for Theo to be my mate, there can't be any secrets. Not even ones that could ruin us.

"Try me," I say patiently.

Slowly, he turns to face me, and when our eyes meet, it's like staring into a storm—fierce and chaotic, with a darkness ready to consume everything in its path. I don't flinch away. I hold his gaze, unyielding, demanding that he let me see the truth, no matter how ugly it might be.

"I killed King Airik," he finally says, each word heavy with a bleakness that fills the room like smoke. "I killed him and took his crown when it wasn't mine to take."

For a moment, I don't breathe. I can't. The world goes still around me, the air freezing in my lungs. I hear his words—feel the weight of them settle in my bones—but my mind fights accepting them as truth. This was exactly what I didn't want to hear, the one thing I might not be able to forgive.

My mate is a murderer.

CHAPTER FIFTEEN

THEO

Estee's eyes are sharp—clear and searing in their demand. They pin me down like a blade, cutting through every defense I've clung to for so long. There's nowhere to hide, no corner dark enough to bury what I've done, and the guilt of my secrets claws at me, threatening to spill out in a wild torrent. Her body trembles and she pulses with an intensity likely built from her need to hear my truth. I know that if I don't lay everything bare, I'll lose her. I might anyway, but at least I'll have done everything I could to keep her.

"Why did you kill him?" Her voice is rough, like gravel scraping against glass, filled with confusion and the unmistakable sting of betrayal. She wants to know, but she doesn't know what she's asking for.

My heart thunders in my chest as I struggle to breathe. The likelihood that she'll hate me for what I've done is high, and losing her will break me. I need her more than the air in my lungs, more than anything in this existence.

"Would you like the long story or the short?" I walk

back to sit next to her again. I didn't become king just by killing Airik. There were so many steps, so many things I could've done differently, that led me to this point. Though, now that I'm here, I can't quite bring myself to regret a single one of them. Not when Estee sits in the chair near me, my starlight plucked right from the night sky.

She adjusts in her seat, and I almost let myself believe that she's going to reach for me, but then she backs further away. "Tell me everything, and I swear, Theo, if you leave one part out and I find out later, I'll ruin you myself."

Despite her threat, I can't help but steady in her presence—the light in her eyes, the fire, the strength—and the noose I've felt around my neck for so long loosens.

"When I was young," I begin, my voice hoarse as I force the words to flow, "my pack was everything to me. They were my family, my world. We were small, close-knit, and lived far from this castle. We didn't need the kingdom or the politics, just each other. Eventually, I became the alpha without even realizing it, and I didn't think life could be any better."

Her brows pinch together. "How can you call yourself an alpha when there are only four packs? I can sense the power within you, but that alone doesn't make you a leader." Her tone isn't accusing, just curious.

"Just because there are only four recognized doesn't mean they're the only packs to exist," I explain. "Most aren't a threat, so it's easier to ignore us than attempt to force us to live where we don't want to. At least that was what I thought growing up."

Even three years later, having to remember that horrendous night makes my chest burn and my jaw ache with tension. Still, I continue to force the words out, with my voice low and choked by the pain I've kept buried for so long.

"But one night, they came for us—hunters who knew exactly where to find my pack. They killed them all, Estee. Every last member, young and old. My friends, my mother, everyone except me. I didn't understand why, and it took me a long time to learn the truth, and even after, it still doesn't make any sense."

Pity flashes in her eyes, but I can't let her softness stop me. I have to push through. "My mother was the last to go, crawling to me from her home next to mine."

As I continue to speak, I'm transported back to that night, reliving the nightmare I see every time I lie in bed.

"Son," she croaks and somehow manages to smile. "It's going to be okay."

I run to her. There's no one left to help, no bodies left to collect as the flames ravage the village. Kneeling, I press my hands over her stomach in hopes of stopping the bleeding.

"Don't look for me," Mother says, "I'm finally going to rest, and I want you to remember that you were meant for great things, my boy. Leave this place behind and start over. Find your peace."

I shake my head frantically. "No. Not like this. How am I supposed to..."

"You just are." She coughs and closes her eyes, leaning her cheek into my touch. "My time is done. I've taught you all I can, and I'm so proud of the man you've become. You're going to be okay. There's a reason you survived, and vengeance is..."

"Mom?" I grab her shoulders, shaking her more than I should, given her injuries, but I'm frantic, desperate. "Mother! Open your eyes. Please. Please, don't leave me. Not like this." The smell of burning flesh assaults me. "Please not like this."

But she never wakes up, never tells me what vengeance is. Not in any version of the nightmare.

"Gods, Theo." Tears fall freely down Estee's cheeks. "I'm so sorry that happened to you. How long ago was this?"

I have to wipe at my own face and clear my throat before I can speak again. "Just over three years."

"How did you end up here?" she asks. "Did you come seeking help from King Airik and he refused so you killed him?"

Gods, I wish it were that simple.

I shake my head. "I didn't find myself within the walls of this castle until the month before I was crowned. For weeks after the deaths of my pack, I was broken. But more than that, I was furious. Furious with the monsters who came from and fled back into the darkness, with the gods for allowing this to happen, with myself for being too weak to end my own misery."

She finally reaches for me, grabbing my hand and squeezing tightly. Though, I'm not sure if it's to comfort me or encourage me to keep going. "What did you do after the attack?"

"I went searching for the people who invaded my home. I had nothing to go on, but I still had to try. I didn't sleep for weeks, searching the woods around the pack for any sign of where they'd gone. Or come from. There was nothing. Nothing left of their presence, of my home, of the people I loved most in the world. After a while, I started to wonder if I'd imagined the whole thing. If I'd never had any of that joy to begin with."

The sorrow in Estee's eyes is mingled with something more. A burning resolve, like she wants to avenge every wrong done to me. Her wolf flashes in her gaze, fierce and untamed.

"And then someone found me," I continue. "He said he'd heard what happened to me and wanted to help." My body shudders with disgrace. "I didn't even question him. I saw a lifeline to finding some sort of peace and latched on with everything I had left. He said he knew where I could find answers and I blindly believed him."

"And did you? Find answers?" Her voice is breathless as if every word I speak could make all the difference in what she does next.

"I thought I did." I pull away from her and walk away, because I don't want to see the look in her eyes as I explain this next part.

I stop in front of the window. "I found the men this person told me were responsible. One by one, I went to them in the night, just like they did to my pack, and took their lives, following the whispers of guidance, trusting them without a second thought. Nights bled together, connected only by the screams of the fallen, until weeks had passed like this.

"By the time I was done, I no longer recognized myself. My hands were stained with crimson, and I didn't feel any better. In fact, I was at my lowest, more desperate for peace than I'd ever been. Then *he* returned to me, with a smirk on his face and more lies. Only this time, I began to see through them...yet I did nothing to fight back."

"Who is he?" Estee asks, standing much closer than I expected her to be and sounding ready for war. "And where is he now?"

My chuckle is dark. "He's a god, Estee. You can't touch him."

She huffs as if she knows something I don't, but if there was a way to kill Orix, I would've found it by now.

"And every time I gave into his magic, every time I willingly acted as his puppet, I became more tied to him," I admit. "He's linked to me in ways I don't understand. His voice and energy are a constant threat in my mind. One powerful enough to keep you from feeling the bond and to make someone commit murder. To ruin this kingdom just for fun. There's no stopping him, and I'm so sorry I've brought you into this mess."

I finally look at her again, expecting to see disgust on her face but there's compassion there and a determination in her strong stance that makes me hate myself even more.

"You should go," I tell her. "Go back to Polaris. I'll tell everyone I lied, that I was mistaken about you being my mate, and you can live your life without—"

"I wouldn't do that if I were you, Theodore." Orix's voice slithers through my thoughts. *"I told you that we needed her for the next phase of my plans and you're not going to let her go. You will make her stay or your mother will pay dearly."*

For the first time, I hesitate to put her life above all others. It's not just about my mother or me anymore. There could be consequences for Estee and—

"You're always worrying about the wrong things." Orix sighs. *"I thought this would be fun, but you're more pathetic than I already knew."*

"Why would you keep the bond from us if you want Estee to be here?" I ask, hating that I'm always too many steps behind him.

"Because I could." His chuckle is dry. *"Though it hasn't been near as fun as I'd hoped to mess with your emotions. So, let's move along, shall we? You're going to convince Estee to stay, she's going to know the two of you are mates, and then you're going to give me my heir. Only then will you be free."*

"No."

I can hear Estee's voice trying to break through to me, but I can't listen to her right now.

"No? Don't forget your place, Theodore. I've given all of this to you and I'll take it away just as swiftly."

When Orix told me he wanted me to find my mate and have an heir, I didn't believe he meant to take the child from me. Maybe that was foolishness on my part. I should have questioned things more, but the manipulation I've lived…it's broken me.

At least until Estee.

Whatever reason Orix needed me to have a child with my mate specifically, he just did me a favor because I'm finally thinking clearly.

"Go ahead, Theodore. Allow yourself to believe that you have the upper hand here. Try to stop me from getting what I desire and see what happens. I think I just might enjoy this game after all." His haunting laughter echoes through my mind, making my body recoil.

A stinging slap across my cheek jolts my consciousness and as my vision focuses once again, Estee is standing in front of me. Her golden eyes are wild with fury and she's breathing hard.

"Damn it, Theo. What is happening?"

Looking at her breaks my heart. I have to finish telling her everything and convince her to stay while also wishing she'd go because keeping her this close to that vile creature feels wrong. Yet, I know I have no other option. At least for the time being.

"I'm so damn sorry, Estee. I was only trying to protect my mother. I didn't realize what he wanted, what he was capable of and now…"

"What are you talking about?" she demands, her nails digging into my forearm as she glares up at me.

"Orix," I finally say his name. "He was just in my head. He's the reason you're here. He told me that if I found my mate and we had an heir that I'd finally be free of this mess. I didn't question why any of that mattered. I only focused on the thought of being free. Until I met you, you were nothing more than a means to an end for me, but everything has changed now, Estee. You have to believe me. I won't let him hurt you or our future child."

She shakes her head and frowns. Her gaze locks onto mine full of sympathy, but as the words leave her mouth, I know it's not the kind I'm hoping for.

"Theo, I don't think we're mates."

My hands tremble as I reach for her face. "Orix said he was blocking the connection. You are mine. I know it with all my heart."

"Are you sure?" she asks, her voice soft like I might break at any moment. "You've been through a lot and maybe he has been blocking me from feeling the bond, but he could just as easily be making you feel something that isn't real."

No. She can't be right. Estee is my mate. She has to be. My heart knows and my wolf...there's no way what I've felt these two days have been fabricated.

Yet, even as I think the words, I know she could be right. I just don't want to admit it, not even to myself.

"I'm sorry, Estee." My voice cracks and my heart shatters. "I don't know what's real."

I should let her go, but if I do, what will Orix do to her? Will her fate be even worse than being coerced into staying with me? I don't know, but I need to find my way through this mental upheaval and figure this out before it's too late for the both of us.

Though, it's like I'm standing in quicksand. Any movement I make just might be the end of everything I thought I knew. Up, down, right, wrong. Nothing makes sense any longer and I'm not sure what I'm supposed to do.

"This is where you belong and I want you to remember just how quickly I can break you before you get any grand ideas of trying to defeat me. All you need to do now is make her stay."

Orix's presence is gone just as quickly as it comes and when I focus back on Estee, more confused than I've ever been, her eyes are wide and she's gasping for air as she holds tighter to me.

"Mate."

The single word falls from her lips, just as I've been hoping it would, but there's no joy in my heart any longer.

Not when I know all of this might be a lie.

CHAPTER SIXTEEN

ESTEE

The bond—the one I've so vehemently denied regardless of my attraction to Theo—slams into me with the force of a tidal wave and once the surface breaks, the connection to this man that I've only felt glimmers of, roars to life. A part of me thought that maybe I'd never get this moment, that the fractured pieces I'd been teased with, were all I'd find with Theo. Yet, looking at him now, easily losing myself in his gaze, I know he's been telling the truth the whole time.

"I'm so sorry, Estee." The frown on his face is the last thing I expect after finally calling him mate.

"I don't understand." Instinctively, I step back, feeling as though I should protect myself from whatever he's about to say. "What happened just now?"

Except I can only manage a few inches of space between us before my wolf rises to the surface, demanding to be close to him. The need to soothe the hurt coursing through him is so strong that my hands tremble at my sides, making me unsure of what I should do.

The tether connecting me to Theo continues to pulse through my veins, tugging at my heart, but the fact that he's keeping a distance from me now has the rest of me terrified of what he's going to say next. Especially when it feels as though all the walls I've so carefully built up over the years have been torn down in an instant, and in their place, a flood of emotions crash into me—joy, fear, hope, but beneath it all, there's something deeper, primal.

Theo.

Every cell in my body screams his name, demanding to be close to him, to touch him in ways I haven't even dreamed of yet. I want to wrap myself around his warmth and never let go.

"Orix, the god I've somehow tied myself to..." Theo's body shudders as he seems to struggle for words as he meets my stare. "I'm sorry, Estee. I don't know if this is real or not. Hell, I don't even know what I'm saying."

"I don't know why I couldn't feel you before, but I do now," I promise him. "You were right about us being mates. Why are you questioning things now?"

Even now, the need to touch him is all-consuming. I can't fathom this being some sort of fabrication.

"Because Orix was just in my head and the things he said..." Theo grips the base of his neck as he looks away from me. "I don't know what to believe anymore."

Minutes ago, after he admitted to killing King Airik, I wasn't sure I could ever look at Theo the same, but now, there's no doubt in my mind that he's my mate. And after hearing what he's been through these last few years, I can't believe for one second that anything he's done to get to this point has been filled with malicious intent. Whatever this god is doing, I'm going to find a way to end the suffering he's attempting to inflict.

I might still need time to process all of this, but there's no more denying the truth and I need Theo to still believe because the pull I have toward him is stronger than anything I've ever felt. I know—deep down, in my bones—this is real. Theo isn't just some stranger I met a few days ago. He's my mate, and that truth crashes down around me, tearing apart the very foundation of everything I thought I knew.

The power of his scent—crisp yet earthy, like the woods after a raging storm—fills my senses, clinging to me like a comforting embrace.

I grab Theo's hands, holding tightly to him. "I may not understand everything you've been through or how Orix is connected to you, but he's not tied to me. I know what I'm feeling even if he's somehow made you question everything."

He leans into me, holding me close as his arms wrap around me. "This is what he does. He gives and takes and causes chaos. All for his own entertainment. I don't want this for you. You deserve better."

It's no wonder Theo seemed so broken when I first saw him. He's been through hell and there's no end in sight to his suffering. I might have seemed like a light for him, but whatever Orix has done to his mental state now, has just set him back.

My heart wants to be the strength Theo needs to overcome this darkness, but the more logical part of me knows this is something he has to do on his own. I can't fix this for him, not as his mate or even as an ally. But I can at least stop making things harder on him.

"We both deserve better," I say confidently. "Once you believe that, everything will change."

"Estee." His voice is an agonizing plea, branding my heart. His eyes—those deep charcoal eyes that hold more emotion than I can begin to unravel—search mine, and I can see the regret, the pain, the longing in them.

"It's going to be okay." I don't know how I know, but I do. There's no other option. Not after everything we've been through in our pasts.

"I don't want to hurt you," he says so quietly that I'm almost not sure if I've heard him correctly until he adds, "You should run as far from me as possible. Whatever is happening here will only get worse. Orix told me to find you. He said he needs an heir from me." Theo's voice cracks as he pulls away from me again. "I don't know what he meant or if he truly means to take a child from me that doesn't even exist yet, but without knowing how to stop him, I can't... I'm not strong enough to bear that kind of pain, Estee. And if something happened to you because of my choices, I'd never live with myself."

"Whether I stay or go is my choice," I tell him with a sharpness that I hope leaves no room for argument. "But if you need time to process whatever's happened here today, then that's different."

As his darkening gaze meets mine again, it's filled with agony and sorrow and fear. "I'm trying to be stronger for you, but what if I lost my mind the day my pack died? What if my spirit has been fractured and I'll never know what's reality and what's an illusion? I want to fight for us, but if *he's* always there, threatening to take it all away..." His head shakes. "I thought I could overcome this, but I don't know how I'm supposed to do this."

Nothing has ever made my heart shatter more than hearing the torment in his words. This is so much worse than I wanted to believe, but there has to be a solution. Orix can't have that much control, even if he is a god.

"Maybe the healer Elyn can help you." I can't believe I'm saying this given how crazy she seems, but I don't know what else to do. "She came to Polaris when my sister and I first returned. Her methods weren't conventional by any means, but they were effective."

"I'll have Jerome call for her and see what she thinks," he says, though his voice isn't as hopeful as I'd like as he meets my stare again. "I know I said you should go, but Orix threatened to hurt you if I didn't find a way to make you stay."

"I'm not going anywhere," I promise. "Not only because there's no way I'm willing to walk away from the bond I now feel just because some god thinks he can control you, but because we both deserve better than either one of us running from this."

The state of Selaris also isn't far from my mind, but I don't mention the pack to Theo. That's not something he needs to worry about right now. He can't help them before he helps himself.

His forehead presses against mine. "Thank you. Those two words don't seem like enough, but I meant what I said before. You are my starlight. Even now, when everything feels darker than it has since the night my family was killed. I might not have the drive to fight today, but I'm going to do my best to find my way."

I place my hands over his chest, feeling the beat of his tattered heart beneath my palm. "We're going to figure this out."

He nods, but then steps back and the distance is like ice piercing my heart, made worse when he tells me, "I'm going to go. Not because I want to, but because I have to." His eyes plead with me to understand his next words. "I need to know that I'm not going to hurt you, Estee. I need to be right in my head and that might take a few days. I have no right to ask this of you, but will you wait for me?"

The sorrow vibrating off him has the bond pulling, taut and trembling, like a thread that's both binding and fragile. A powerful reminder of what could be, and for the first time since laying eyes on him, I think I finally understand just how much is at stake.

"Take whatever time you need," I say earnestly. "I'll be here when you're ready."

He bows his head, seeming to succumb under the burden of his misery. "Thank you."

My wolf whimpers as I watch Theo turn toward the door, seeing himself out without another word. Before I do something like beg him to stay with me, I look out the window, focusing on the twin moons high in the sky. He needs me to be strong and that's what I'm going to be. The hurt over finally admitting that he's my mate, yet knowing there are uncontrollable obstacles in our way, is nothing compared to what he's already been through.

A few more days of space might be exactly what we both need.

The rumble from my wolf tells me she doesn't agree, and part of me doesn't either, but we're going to find out regardless.

CHAPTER SEVENTEEN

ESTEE

Patience is overrated. I throw the covers off me as I get up to a new day that already doesn't feel promising. I'm on day three since I last saw Theo and the only communication that I've had with him has been through Jerome. Something I'm trying to be understanding of since I know he's only trying to protect me, but damn it, how long is this going to go on?

I've done my best to stay busy, ignoring the way our bond now thrums wildly in my chest, but even caring for the orphaned children, all of which are now living in the castle, has done little to distract me. Though, I can't deny that having Neri finally agree to move in last night was a highlight I won't soon forget. Especially when she squared off with me, threatening that if any of this turns out to be a trick of some sort, she's not going down without a fight.

Just the fact that she's been through so much at such a young age and hasn't allowed life to break her makes me smile. Her feisty spirit is merely an added blessing that I've counted as I've gotten to know them all.

We've even begun looking for families for the kids, searching not only within Selaris but also the other kingdoms, wondering if a new start might be better. Jerome has been a big part of that, helping me to figure out how these children slipped through the cracks.

Even though it doesn't make anything right, apparently things in Selaris have been so bad that pack members were too afraid to stretch their resources, that by doing so, it would harm their own families. A fear that made it somehow okay to ignore pups living alone in an abandoned church.

After using the bathroom, I find a note on the floor near the door.

Princess Estee,
It might be time for you to go to King Theo. I don't mean to overstep, but I hate to see either of you suffer. I'll be busy with meetings this morning or I would have waited for you to wake.
I hope we can keep this between the two of us.
Signed,
Jerome Graves

I was planning to go see Drea this morning, but going to my mate after so much time apart isn't something I can ignore. Especially if Jerome is feeling the need to interfere.

Drea will understand. I thought her holding my hair while I vomited into a bucket was already more than enough to make me love her, but she's proven to be the friend I never knew I needed. I haven't been ready to talk about Theo with anyone—not even my sister. I only had to tell Drea that once and she hasn't brought it up again, lowering my stress. Something I've appreciated immensely.

As I rush through the motions of getting ready to go see Theo, my thoughts return to Orix as they have on many occasions since learning of his existence. I don't know how we're supposed to best a god who has some twisted connection to my mate, but there has to be a way to break the hold Orix has over him. If Theo doesn't figure one out, and agrees with my plan, then I'll be calling Asher later today. Well, Isla then asking to speak with him because I'd rather not have her trying to murder me if her mate finds out about all of this before she does.

Asher was able to reach the goddess Aurora, and while I don't want to deal with her and her erratic behavior, maybe we can get answers from someone who might be willing to help with this god, even if it comes at a price. There has to be something we can learn about him.

Growing up, we're all taught about our original creators, but it's mostly centered around the main three gods, the afterlife, and our choice in reincarnation. Even in death, if we choose not to be reborn, we're not supposed to be able to interact with the "higher beings", so why would we need to know about them? I guess now there's a reason.

My chest tightens, and I take a shaky, yet steadying, breath. I don't want to get worked up again. Theo needs me to be strong for him just as much as I need it.

I slide my damp hands over my black slacks then tug

at the end of my maroon sweater, giving myself another once-over in the mirror. The eyes looking back at me are a mix of my normal golden hue, but with darker brown flecks, telling me my wolf is right at the surface.

She's been silently supportive these last few days, but as I walk out of my suite and into the hallway, heading for Theo's office, I can sense her eagerness. At least now it matches my own.

"Where is my sister?" Isla's voice sounds through my thoughts, and I freeze on the stairs.

"Isla?"

She scoffs. *"Do you have* another *sister?"*

"Well, technically, back on Earth..."

"Seriously? We don't have time for this. Where are you?"

"I should be asking you that. How are you communicating with me like this from Polaris?"

Our telepathy had its limits and crossing to other islands isn't included in them.

"I'm walking through the front gates of the Selaris castle," she replies confidently. *"Now, come find me."*

"What the hell are you doing here?" I ask as I continue up the stairs instead of down them. I need to see Theo first. As much as I've missed my sister this last week, my plans aren't changing for the morning just yet. Not until I know he's okay.

"Did you really think after everything you have and *haven't told me I wouldn't come to you as soon as possible?"* She clicks her tongue, and I can easily picture the admonishment on her face. *"Honestly, Estee. You should know better. I don't care what crown I wear. You are family and you need me, whether you're willing to admit it or not."*

I love her more than I've shown her lately, and she might be mad about my next words, but I know she'll understand.

"I'm just walking in to speak with Theo," I say. *"I'll be down there soon, I promise."* She starts to object, but I continue. *"And thank you, Isla. I love you."*

Her voice is more subdued now. *"I love you, too. Take your time."*

I cut the connection and stop at Theo's office door. I close my eyes and look up at the ceiling, imagining the endless sky above me instead of the stone and rafters as I thank the Universe for bringing my sister to me. Her arrival tells me exactly what conversation I need to have with Theo, and for the first time since finding out I had to come to Selaris, I'm excited about what comes next.

My knuckles sweep lightly over the wooden door, and before I can take a step back to wait for Theo to answer, he's already swinging the door open. "Estee."

My name on his lips sends a jolt of warmth through me, and I inhale sharply, momentarily breathless. His eyes are pinched at the sides and he takes a step away from me. "You shouldn't be here."

"It's been three days, Theo." I move to step inside his office. "If time apart was going to solve anything, you wouldn't look worse off than when I last saw you."

His cheeks are hollow, his clothes wrinkled, and he hasn't shaved, but that means little to me now. Not when his warmth calls to me, draws me closer, making my fingers itch to reach for him.

I knew the bond was powerful. I knew there was a reason I was so confused about Theo calling me his mate and this was why. I might have been attracted to him from the start, but there is nothing that can compare to this *need*. To the desire to hold him and be whatever he needs so that he can come out of this mental war with the least amount of scars.

"Estee." This time when he says my name, it's more like a warning. One I can't find the want to heed. My chest rises and falls like crashing waves, and my mouth parts. His hand comes up, the back of his fingers ever so lightly grazing my cheek. "I've missed you."

"I missed you too." I lean into his touch, my eyes fluttering closed for only the briefest moments. "I know you need to find your way through all this on your own, but blocking me out completely isn't going to help either of us. Not now that our bond has been set free."

He looks away from me. "Maybe I was wrong. Maybe this is all a fabrication."

Since Theo told me I was his mate, the one thing I've feared most is being hurt by him. That if I allowed myself to let him in and things went wrong, that was a kind of pain I'd do whatever it took to avoid. Except now, drawing on the desire to be with the man before me, I know that no matter what happens, the risk is worth finding out the truth.

"But what if it's not?" I ask him. "Staying away from each other isn't going to keep either of us safe if Orix wants me here. I know you're trying to protect me, but if he's as vile as you say, then we're better off together. And if he's tricked us, then we'll sort that out later, but I'm not willing to give him anymore power over me. He's stolen enough already."

"Gods, Estee." He reaches for me and pulls me into a tight embrace. "I don't know how you're this strong, but I'm damn thankful for you."

"We're going to figure this out. I actually have a plan that I wanted to talk to you about." I pull back enough to see his face. "My sister's surprised me. She and Asher are here. At least I assume he's traveled with her." I guess she could have run off without her mate, but something tells me that isn't the case.

The lines around his face only deepen. "Asher called as a courtesy to tell me he was on his way. I assumed you knew, or I would've told you." He looks down as he continues. "I thought maybe they were coming here to bring you back to Polaris."

My head shakes. He really has been torturing himself. Theo's made mistakes—killing another king isn't something to be taken lightly—but even before the bond appeared for me, I knew he didn't do so maliciously. Theo's been backed into a corner for much too long and it's time for that to change. I might not know the man he was before his pack was killed, but I feel as though I've seen glimpses and that's enough for me.

"I'm not leaving you, Theo." My voice is firm yet full of understanding. "That's not even going to happen if you tell me to. We're in this together now. Even if the bond I now feel is nothing more than trickery, I've still been dragged into this with you. Orix targeted me. I'm not leaving you alone to deal with this. We're going to figure this out together."

His chin falls to his chest as he sucks in a breath and slowly lets it back out before meeting my eyes again. "I know I keep saying it, and I promise to give you more than words, but for now, thank you."

This time, I'm the one to pull him closer. We hold onto each other, the connection to him thrumming wildly within my chest. I stay silent, allowing our emotions to speak for themselves, and hoping that Theo will see his strength just as I'm beginning to.

"We're going to find a way to break the connection Orix has to you," I finally tell him. "Considering how you became king, you may not know this, but regardless of the how, you have a connection to the other gods that you can use to ask for help. Asher can show you—"

He shakes his head. "Jerome gave me books that explained some of those things, and I've tried, but the ceremony never worked for me. I'm not even sure I'm really an Alpha King. I know I have the gene. That was proven when I had my own pack, but I went for help and found none. The gods refused to answer my call no matter how much I pleaded."

He really has been alone in this. Knowing that sends a new wave of agony through me, but I'm determined not to give up. I also know that Asher won't either. With him and Isla here, we're going to find answers.

"If you're not actually blessed by the gods to be king, if Orix has somehow manufactured this entire situation, allowing you to be connected to the pack, but not the gods, then at least Asher is. He can perform the ceremony on your behalf."

Theo reaches until he's cupping my cheeks. "I'm sorry your family's been brought into this, and that you've been forced to accept the consequences of my choices, but I'm trying, Estee. For the first time in years, I have a reason to fight for those around me, and I'll do so until my last breath. Whatever has to be done to protect you, I'll do it."

I push myself up to be on his level and say something I know he needs to hear more than once. "I'm sorry I couldn't see how hard you were fighting before, but I do now and you're not alone any longer. I want to figure this out as much as you do."

He cups my cheeks, and my eyes flutter closed from the intensity of our connection, but I force them back open because I have to finish speaking, no matter how easy it would be to give in to the draw of his touch.

"I forgive your past choices, and I won't hold them against you now or in the future, but I also need you to understand that this isn't easy for me," I admit with a shaky breath. "Depending on anyone other than myself is something I've avoided for too long, but I'm going to do my best not to push you away any longer. Though, that doesn't mean I'm ready to go all in yet either. Being your mate means you deserve the best version of me, and I still have my own issues to work out. I need your grace just as much as I think you need mine."

He rests his forehead against mine and takes a deep breath as his eyes close. "You have it, whatever you need, Estee. Time, space, grace, my heart. You have all of it, regardless of what you decide. It doesn't matter to me, because the moment I saw you, you owned all of me."

Each word pierces the carefully placed armor around my heart, marking me in ways I won't ever be able to forget. For a moment, I let myself believe that everything is perfect. That there isn't a god screwing with our lives, that people haven't died, that an entire kingdom hasn't suffered. For just this moment, I'm Theo's mate and he's mine, nothing more, nothing less. I push up on my toes, lightly pressing my lips to his.

He gasps, his breath hitching as he tightens his hold on my face as if he's afraid I'll slip away. Yet, even though he's holding me like this, there's still a gentleness, a restraint, like he's waiting for me to lead—waiting to make sure I don't regret giving him this part of me. His touch is reverent, full of longing, but it stops just short of demanding more than I'm offering.

When he looks at me again, the flecks of light in his dark eyes are brighter than I've ever seen them, a mix of raw emotion and the kind of hope that stirs something deep within me.

I close the small distance between us, brushing my lips against his once more. This time, I linger, letting the warmth of his mouth seep into mine. I press my palms to his chest, feeling the steady thrum of his heartbeat beneath my fingertips.

His mouth parts, and I feel his breath, warm and inviting, mingling with my own. The tension that's been building between us finally detonates, and all I can do is lose myself in this moment, in him.

Theo slides his hands down from my face to cradle the back of my neck, pulling me deeper into the kiss. It's slow, deliberate—his lips moving against mine with a careful tenderness that makes my heart ache. He kisses me like I'm something precious, something fragile, and it's that softness that truly undoes me, that makes me realize how much I've needed this.

He tangles his fingers in my long hair, and I shiver at the sensation. I can feel the heat of him against me, a steady beat of our bond that pulses along my skin, burrowing deeper into me. My heart races with the thrill, and I'm aware of every single point of contact between us. Each one is intoxicating, dizzying, and I find myself leaning into him more, needing to close the distance between us entirely.

His lips move over mine with a kind of quiet yet commanding passion that leaves me breathless. I can feel the coiled tension in him, the way his body trembles with the effort of holding back to keep this moment from spiraling out of control. But there's something else too—a hunger, a need, just barely restrained, that mirrors my own.

I let out a soft sigh against his lips, and Theo responds by pulling me even closer, his fingers tightening on my neck. His breath is ragged now, matching the erratic rhythm of my own, and his body shudders with each inhalation. Every fiber of me is attuned to him, to the way he kisses me like he's memorizing the feel of my lips, the way his heart beats in time with mine, the way our bond ebbs and flows between us, undeniable and real.

When we finally pull back, my lungs heave. My palms are still pressed to his chest, and his heartbeat is steady, strong, and racing alongside mine. We stand there for a moment, gasping and staring at each other, the space between us crackling with energy. I look into his eyes, and I soak in the way he's looking at me—like I'm his entire world.

And just maybe, that will be enough.

CHAPTER EIGHTEEN

THEO

I leave my office to go quickly clean myself up before going with Estee to greet King Asher and Queen Isla. It doesn't take long before I'm back and we're headed through the castle. All the while, I can't help thinking what a fool I was for attempting to keep my mate at a distance.

Estee's kiss is a source of energy unlike anything I've ever known. The connection to her vibrates through me even now, offering a sense of calm that I've been longing for, and now that I have her, truly feel like I have her, I'm never letting her go again.

I'd thought I was protecting her by staying away, but I was only giving Orix exactly what he seems to want: me broken. I just don't know why. It's not often I've questioned his motives, considering he's told me time and time again that I'm his entertainment. I took that to mean the god was just bored and I was the unlucky wolf that caught his attention.

Yet, with Estee here now, I'm beginning to have these

moments of clarity where nothing seems to be adding up anymore. Orix wants to control me, but he also needed me to find my mate. A bond more powerful than any other in all the worlds.

Was that a calculated risk on his part in order for me to produce an heir? One he felt he could take since he can so easily mess with my head or am I missing something else?

I've spent the last few days holed up in my office, doing menial tasks for the kingdom while I've tried to think of any way out of this mess, but until Estee kissed me, the fight in me was gone once again. I thought I had what it took to overcome the darkness I've lived with on my own, but being alone made me realize that I can't do this on my own. I can't keep everyone at a distance any longer.

My wolf rumbles in agreement as his essence paces within me, more alive than he's been since losing our pack. We both needed this—especially before facing King Asher. I feel like a fraud compared to him. He was meant for his role, groomed to rule his pack. I was coerced.

Sure, I ran the small pack with no issues, but an entire kingdom has seemed farfetched since the moment Orix somehow convinced me it was for the good of the people.

King Airik might've been stealing from and abusing his people, but in the ways that matter, I haven't done any better. I've neglected them for far too long. At least that's finally changed. Since Estee's arrival, and with Jerome's help, I've met with dozens of pack members, made changes to food distributions, assigned care to elder shifters, and started to fix the small things that had been left to rot.

While my soul ached for Estee's company during our time apart, and I originally started trying harder in order to prove I was worthy of being her mate, I can't deny the satisfaction of seeing positive changes within Selaris. I should've been striving for this since I first took the crown.

Instead of feeling ashamed for my choices, I could've been making the best out of them. I didn't have to hide away, knowing what I'd done. I should've tried to be better from the start, but it's never too late. I've at least realized that.

Walking beside Estee now, in the quiet corridors, there's a warmth in the silence between us. It isn't the sharp tension that previously hung in the air, ready to snap at any moment. It's softer, but even still, I'm not sure where we stand.

She kissed me, but she also asked for my patience. I won't push her no matter how desperate I become to know more about her or how my hands twitch with the need to reach for her.

We approach the sitting room, and the echo of our footsteps is joined by the sound of our guests—Isla's laugh and Asher's deep murmur. I've yet to face the king of Polaris, but his strength is well-known, causing me to tense in preparation for the storm I assume is coming for me.

The moment we enter, any trace of Estee's regal bearing vanishes. She practically flies across the room to Isla, her sister's crown tumbling to the couch as they embrace, holding onto each other as if the world outside these walls doesn't exist. The bond they share is profound, like two halves of a whole being reunited. There's a pang in my chest—not jealousy, but something like longing.

I turn my attention to King Asher, who's watching me. He doesn't move as I extend my hand, his expression sharp and unyielding. For a moment, I think he's going to ignore the gesture, but then he accepts, his grip firm and full of unspoken challenges.

"King Theo," he says, his voice a blade, cutting through the space between us.

"King Asher," I reply, inclining my head respectfully. "Welcome to Selaris."

His sapphire eyes sweep around the room as if he can see more than just the decor and furniture, as if he's trying to assess everything I've done or failed to do. "Your people seemed happy when we arrived."

I can't tell if he means they were glad to see him or if he's noticed the small improvements I've made. Either way, I don't rise to the bait. "It's been an eventful week. Announcing Princess Estee as my mate and future queen has brought hope, and we've made strides in addressing some of the kingdom's more pressing needs." I glance at Estee, her smile lighting up the room as she seems to be having a silent conversation with her sister. "She's going to be good for Selaris."

"But are you?"

His words land like a blow, and I turn sharply to face him once more. There's no venom in his voice, just a bluntness that tells me we're getting straight to the heart of things. I expected this, but hearing the question still stirs something raw inside me.

"I wasn't," I admit, knowing there's no point lying to him. "But I can be. I will." It feels like a confession, one I'm not sure how he'll take, but I continue anyway. "I've made mistakes, and I'll probably make more. But I'm going to do whatever it takes to make things right. No matter what the future brings."

He watches me for a moment, his gaze unreadable. Then he glances briefly at the two women before turning back to me. "Listen, Theo. I'm not here to tell you how to run things. I'm not even here to challenge your role, but Estee is my family. She's everything to Isla, and when my queen worries, so do I. While I don't like the things I've heard of late, I'm here to help first and foremost, unless you give me a reason not to. You've remained secluded here, and if Estee's going to stay, that needs to change. For both our sakes."

A weight I didn't even realize I was carrying begins to lift from my shoulders, and the sudden urge to tell him everything nearly overwhelms me, but for now, I settle for, "Fair enough."

"Be careful, Theodore." Orix's voice pierces my mind, cold and invasive. *"I might've given you your bond, but that was for my benefit, not yours. If you step out of line, I will take it all back, just as I took your pack."*

The rage boils up so quickly, so violently, that I feel like I'm choking on it. *"You..."*

His dark laughter echoes through me. *"You pathetic excuse for an alpha. Did you think you were spared for your own sake? No. I needed you—broken, without hope. Now, as you've already admitted, you are mine to command. You're going to be the king I've created you to be, and Estee is going to give us an heir. There's no getting out of this. The two of you are mine now and I will get what I want. One way or another, even if that means impregnating your mate myself."*

I'm spiraling, lost in the darkness Orix has trapped me in, when I suddenly hear Estee's voice, fierce and unyielding. "Theo!" She shakes me hard, gripping my arms. "Wake up."

Her words pierce the fog, and I blink, the world coming back into focus, but I'm still paralyzed. Estee's face is inches from mine, her eyes blazing with concern and something else—something deeper, fiercer.

"I'm not above punching you, Theo," she warns, her voice shaking. "Fight whatever this is before I do it myself."

"I… I'm sorry," I finally murmur, my throat dry and voice hoarse. "It was Orix. He threatened to…" My gaze hardens and locks onto Estee. "I won't live like this anymore. We deserve better, and we will have better."

Orix has pushed me too far. Giving me Estee, taking her away, saying he's going to take my future child and if I don't cooperate, he'll take care of that himself as well? No more. I won't let him take anything else from me. Not when Estee gives me every reason to fight, to overcome the mess Orix has made of my mind and my heart.

I don't know how, but as my mate smiles up at me, believing in my strength, I know I have to find a way to move forward once and for all. Continuing to allow the darkness to suck me back in, taking all that I am with it, isn't an option any longer.

"Who is Orix, and what the hell did he just do to you?" Asher demands, looking between Estee and me.

I'm surprised Isla didn't already fill him in, but maybe Estee hasn't revealed everything I've done. I'm not sure if that's because she's ashamed of me or something else, but I'm done hiding.

"He's a god who sent a group of wolves to kill my pack," I admit to Asher. "That night broke me in more ways than one, leaving me susceptible to his lies. Something he took advantage of, but no more." I look up at my mate again and hope she can see the depth of my determination. "He won't take anything else from me."

Isla moves to take her place next to Asher and looks up at him. "We need to contact her."

"Absolutely not," he snarls. "Owing her one favor is enough. We won't owe her two when we don't know how she intends to collect."

"She won't let us through to any of the other gods and you know it," Isla presses. "They need us. We have no choice."

"There's always a choice," he grumbles but then looks at me. "Is Orix blocking you from reaching the other gods like Aurora is for me?"

I'd thought that maybe I couldn't reach them because of how I became king, but maybe it's been Orix this whole time. "Possibly. I've yet to be able to complete the ceremony."

Asher mutters something under his breath then nods toward the door. "Maybe we should take this conversation elsewhere. It seems we have a lot more to discuss than my mate saw fit to tell me."

Isla glares at him. "My sister only just told me how dire things are. Believe me, I've been screaming inside her head every second since she walked into this room."

Asher's lips thin, but I, for one, can't help being glad that Estee's kept what I've shared between us until she had no choice.

Still, Asher is right that we need privacy, so I grab my mate's hand without thinking, and when she doesn't pull away, I lead us out of the room and toward the stairs to go back up to my office.

She looks over at me, and for the first time since her arrival, I see pride in her eyes.

"You're going to regret this, Theodore."

No, I don't think I am.

Orix's presence is gone before I get the words across, but that doesn't make them any less true. I won't cower from his threats ever again. I can't.

CHAPTER NINETEEN
ESTEE

Between the shared kiss with Theo, my sister's arrival, and the looming challenge of facing Orix, I'm being pulled in too many directions. Exhilarated, nervous, determined—I don't know where to land. And yet, a quiet fear stirs beneath it all.

Not that I'm afraid of going against a god when there's every reason to stand up to him, but I'd be a fool not to acknowledge how dangerous Orix is—an ancient being of power beyond our understanding. That much, I can't ignore. We need to tread carefully. One wrong move, and the consequences could be fatal. Freedom from Orix's grip on Theo is the goal, but staying alive long enough to achieve it is just as crucial.

"I'm sorry I yelled at you," Isla's voice slides into my mind through our mental link. *"Seeing you with him now, I understand. I just wish I could have been here for you this whole time."*

"It's okay. We're going to figure this out." I normally loved

having a mental connection to my sister, but after I practically tackled her with my hug, she immediately began questioning me. I should have known I couldn't keep anything from her

Our gazes quickly meet and she grins. *"Yes, we are and I hope you know how proud I am of you right now. You might be the older sister, but you've always forged your own path, doing as you pleased. Seeing you already settling in here, making a difference with the people, it looks good on you."*

I chuckle and shake my head. *"You've been here less than an hour. How would you know what I've done?"*

"A fellow queen always knows." Her corresponding wink makes me laugh harder because while I already know she's an incredible leader to Polaris, she's only been in the role a month, yet acts as if this has always been her life.

"I've missed you."

She looks over at me and smiles brightly. *"Not more than I've missed you."*

We keep walking through the castle, the men not commenting on our silent exchanges that I'm sure they're more than aware of. I glance up at Theo and hope like hell that I can trust him. I have no doubt about his sincerity, but something I've tried not to think about since accepting that he truly is my mate is the fact that he's allowed himself to be controlled by Orix for the last three years.

I might understand how he got to where he is, but that doesn't mean it doesn't affect my decisions. I told him before that I also needed time, but not because I don't want to be with him. I just need to be sure that he isn't going to say one thing but wind up doing another. While I might believe he wouldn't *want* to hurt me, that doesn't mean he'll be able to prevent that from happening with a god linked to him.

He's been under Orix's thumb for years now, and I don't fault him for that, but that doesn't mean I won't protect myself from the potential fallout. I can't give him all of me if there's a chance he'll never be able to do the same with his heart. It's not fair to either of us, but it's the reality of our situation for now.

Something I've been trying not to think about while missing him over the last few days, but also it's a truth that I can't avoid for long.

"It's going to be okay." Isla's calm tone takes me by surprise. *"I'm your Alpha Queen. I can sense your unease even more than I could as your sister."*

Well, that I didn't think about, but I also shouldn't be surprised.

She continues, *"A mate bond is sacred, and I know why you've been hesitant, especially under the circumstances, but your walls are cracking and I don't want to see you sabotage yourself. Trust in your heart and in fate. At the end of the day, it doesn't matter what he's done. It matters how he treats you now and what he's willing to do to make things right for your future."*

Her welcome words chip away at my defenses, but before I can thank her for them, she manages to mentally throw a punch at me.

"We're going to figure this out, and you're going to be queen. Everything you didn't know you wanted is coming to you."

That reminder makes me stumble a little and has her chuckling. I've admitted to her many times how glad I am that it's her destiny to be queen in this lifetime and not mine. I'm sure this is a small payback that I'll continue to get for the foreseeable future.

Theo and Asher glance over at us, but neither say anything. Smart men.

It's not that I don't want to help Selaris—I've been doing that since I arrived. But to rule over an entire pack? To stand at Theo's side and bear the responsibility of a kingdom? That still feels like a future I'm not ready for.

I never expected to lead. Now, things are different. I have to wrap my head around this new path, but for today, we need to focus on Orix.

We arrive at Theo's office, and Jerome is waiting for us at the door. He bows respectfully to our guests then addresses Theo. "The room has been prepared, and a new cloaking spell has been laid, Your Majesty."

"Thank you, Jerome. I'll let you know when we're done." Theo enters first, his grip on my hand an anchor.

The office is different, rearranged for the visiting royalty. The two chairs aren't in front of the desk any longer. Instead, the only seating options are four throne-like chairs positioned on the left side of the space. Two of them are larger than the others, and that's where Theo leads us to sit, a statement of his higher rank since we're in Selaris.

"While you're here, this will be the safest place for us to speak," Theo says as the four of us get settled.

"How many of those cloaking spells do you have?" Asher asks, looking around as if he might find something amiss. "And where did you get them? They're not all that common these days with most of the other worlds not being as welcoming to supernaturals."

I glance over at Theo, who doesn't answer straight away, making me wonder if he's speaking telepathically with Jerome.

"My advisor tells me that we have about a dozen left and that they were stolen from a group of witches by King Airik's mercenaries."

Asher raises a brow. "Mercenaries?"

Theo's voice is steady, even though the subject has the potential to cause tensions. "The previous Alpha King may not have raised issues with the rest of the islands, but I believe that was because he preferred to be left alone to do as he pleased. I didn't reside here in the city before taking the crown. In fact, I lived as far from here as possible with my own pack. We knew things were bad, but it wasn't until I was coerced into killing Airik that I understood the full extent of his treachery."

Asher's growl is deep, reverberating. Isla places a hand on his arm, a silent plea for restraint, but the strain in the room tightens like a frayed bowstring.

"You did what?" Asher leans forward in his chair, his voice barely more than a whisper.

Theo meets Asher's intense gaze without flinching or shying away. He's no longer hiding his past indiscretions —a choice I deeply respect and that has me speaking up for him.

"My mate has done things he's not proud of, Asher," I interject confidently. "He's killed when he had no right to, and he's ignored his people, but for the better part of three years, he's been under the steady and tainted influence of a god. One more despicable than anything you may be thinking about Theo right now. Killing King Airik wasn't something he willingly did, but I also believe it ended up being what was best for Selaris.

"How is killing their ruler the best choice?" Asher demands then glares at Theo. "You could've come to us. We would've intervened once we knew."

Theo shakes his head. "No, I couldn't. Orix has had me under his thumb, using my mother's wellbeing against me. Even if I took a risk and tried to outsmart him, he's in my head. He has the power to break me and has done so more than once."

Isla and Asher share a look that doesn't bode well. Though, it's my sister who speaks next. "So, let me make sure we understand all of this since we're only now getting this information. Your pack was murdered. You were hellbent on vengeance, which Orix was eager to offer you. By accepting his help, you somehow tied yourself to him, which led to him being able to compel your actions and eventually bring you back here to kill King Airik for his supposed treachery, allowing you to take the crown. A destiny that was not yours to claim, but you took anyway because this god has been threatening the life of your mother, who now resides in the afterlife."

That has Asher's head tilting to the side. I'm surprised she didn't already share with him what I revealed earlier while he was talking to Theo, but before he can get a word in, Isla continues.

"Now, because of the true bond you share with Estee, you've found the strength to think for yourself and are trying to make things right. Not only for you, but my sister, the pack, and the future of this kingdom. Is that the sum of this entire mess?"

Theo's grip on my hand grows tighter as he nods. "Yes."

Now, it's Isla and Asher's turn to have a silent conversation, but I'm not nearly as patient in waiting to know what it is they're thinking.

"What is it?" I demand, staring at my sister.

"His mother isn't in any danger," Isla answers. "She never was."

Theo releases his hold on me finally and stands up. "What do you mean?"

"Did Estee tell you that our own mother had originally chosen not to be reborn after we were cursed to Earth?" she asks, and he shakes his head brusquely. "Well, she did, and she was living peacefully in the afterlife, but now, she's been returned to us as a favor. The memory of her time there is fuzzy, but a few times she's said things that don't make sense, and last week was one of them."

I grip the arms of my chair, my claws threatening to extend. "Is Mom okay?"

Isla nods and smiles brightly. "She's just as she was when you left, I promise. We have no fear of losing her, but I've noticed a pattern. When she wakes up, she's very groggy for a short time, and I believe she's dreaming so vividly that she's not actually getting the rest she's used to. I asked Dad to document anything she mentions, in case there was something to worry about."

That doesn't sound normal, but if my sister isn't worried, I'm going to try not to be either.

"So, what did she say that relates to what Theo shared?" I'm still not sure how this is helpful.

Asher answers me this time. "She told your father that she was reliving the moment she was brought back to us. Aurora didn't go get her. She somehow summoned Florence's energy, pulling your mother back to a body that we're beginning to suspect isn't actually her own."

Theo reaches for me, and I appreciate his support, but right now, I don't think this is about me and I'm not sure I like where this is going. "I didn't think the goddess actually got her hands dirty and decided to dig up our mother, reviving her corpse. So, what are the two of you getting at here?"

Isla looks more at Theo than she does me as she starts to answer. "Based on the things Mom has revealed, we've learned that gods don't walk among the spirits within the afterlife. At least not living ones. So unless this Orix god has the power of creation, like Bruess and his twins Ocules and Aurora do, or he's been lying and is actually Asiris, the ruler over the spirits, then he shouldn't be able to summon her spirit once she's settled into the afterlife."

Theo's grip on my hand loosens as the truth of that revelation seems to hit him. His mother—his reason for everything—has been safe all along. His face hardens with disbelief, then anger along with the crushing guilt of years lost to Orix's lies.

"I've done so many things," Theo whispers, his voice cracking. "And all for nothing."

My heart aches for him as I reach for my mate again, hating that he's going to live with this. "You didn't know, Theo. This isn't your fault."

He jerks away from me and shoves the chair back into the wall as he storms toward the door. "Don't lie to me, Estee. *I* made the choice each time I took a life, and I am most definitely to blame."

And just like that, he's gone, leaving behind only the whispers of his pain and the haunting echoes of a god's manipulation.

CHAPTER TWENTY

THEO

The moment the door slams behind me, the world collapses into a haze of fury. My breaths are quick and shallow, each one a battle for control as the boiling rage festers inside me. For three years, I've been Orix's puppet, dancing to his twisted tune, all for a lie.

Every life I took, every moment I spent drowning in guilt and shame—all of it for nothing. I was fooled. Worse than that, I let myself be fooled.

My fist slams into the unyielding stone of the castle wall. The impact reverberates through my bones, but it's not enough to calm the storm inside me. Pain blooms in my knuckles, but it doesn't compare to the agony of betrayal consuming me. I want to tear the world apart, rip it to shreds, scream until there's nothing left of this wrath.

"Gods!" I roar into the empty hallway, desperate for release. But the rage only grows. No answers come, no clarity. Just my own ire—boiling, seething, swallowing me whole.

I rush into the nearest room and throw open a window. I don't even know where I am, but I need to get out. To escape the suffocating essence of this castle, where there seem to be reminders of my failures at every turn. The air calls to me, and before I can second-guess my actions, I leap out the window, the three-story plunge nothing compared to the drop my soul has already taken.

I push my wolf forward as I free-fall, letting his power rip through me. The familiar sensation of bones breaking and reforming, the primal energy of the shift grounds me —if only for a moment. By the time I hit the grass, my wolf has taken over, and we bolt. His paws tear into the earth, propelling us forward, faster, harder, as if we might be able to outrun the pain, the guilt, the truth.

The forest rushes by in a blur of green and brown, but none of it distracts me. All that matters is the speed, the exertion. I need this. I need to feel the burn of my muscles, the sting of the wind against my fur. My wolf howls, and the sound echoes through the trees, raw and filled with the sorrow and anger we share.

I thought I was avenging my pack. I thought I was honoring them, protecting my mother. But now I wonder…did those men even know what they'd done? Did Orix play them just as he played me? Were they victims, too?

The questions make my chest ache, and my wolf pushes harder, but we can't escape the fear that nips at us: what if I'm no better than Orix?

"You're done controlling me!" I seethe within my mind, having no clue if Orix can hear me, but I hope he knows I'm no longer afraid. I'm done being played for a fool.

My wolf's claws dig harder into the dirt as we cross the forest, hunting for the unknown. His canines are out, ready for blood, but our enemy never appears as we run under the warmth of the afternoon sun.

Minutes pass, or maybe it's hours, before I feel calm enough to face Estee and her family. I still don't feel worthy, but I have to end this nightmare, to have my life back once and for all.

I've hidden for too long, and it ends tonight.

We circle back toward the castle, just as eager to return as we were to leave. Outside the back entrance closest to my office, my wolf relinquishes control, and I shift back to my human form, fully dressed. I walk into the castle with my head held high and push down the shame that attempts to choke me. I can't change the past, but I can do my best to fix the future.

My chest still rises and falls in ragged breaths, but not from rage, from determination. I've lived too long in Orix's shadow, let his control dictate my every move. No more cowering. No more running. He's taken nearly everything from me—my pack, my freedom—and now he's after Estee, too.

I won't let him have her. I won't let him hurt her the way he's hurt me.

I stride up the stairs two at a time, each step heavier, more purposeful. A war drum beats in my chest, my wolf pulsing with the need to protect and destroy. To reclaim all that's mine.

As I round the corner on the third floor, my mind racing with strategy and thoughts of vengeance, a familiar scent hits me like a shock to my system. Pomegranates and orange blossoms.

Estee.

My heart lurches in my chest, and I quicken my pace, the hallway narrowing in my vision as I focus only on her. She's coming toward me, her eyes wide with worry and something else—something that matches the fire burning inside me.

I don't stop moving. Neither does she. We collide halfway down the hallway, and before I can speak, before I can pluck the words from the storm within, her arms are around me and her lips are on mine.

The kiss isn't gentle or patient. It's fierce, desperate, full of promises we've both been too afraid to say out loud.

My hands tangle in her hair, pulling her closer. She responds with equal fervor, her nails digging into my back, her body pressed against mine as if she's trying to anchor me to this moment—to her.

"Estee…" I murmur against her lips, my voice broken with everything I want to say.

She pulls back just enough to look at me, her eyes blazing with passion. "You're not alone in this, Theo. I'm not leaving you. Not now, not ever."

Her words crack something open in me. The vulnerability, the raw truth of them, makes me feel like I could break. But instead, her presence and support steels my resolve. I cup her face, my thumb brushing over her cheek, and for a moment, all the anger, all the chaos, quiets. "Thank you," I say, my words rough but certain. "I won't fail you. Orix won't get the chance to hurt you. I'll die before I let him take anything more from us."

Her eyes soften, her lips parting as she searches my face. "We're going to fight him, Theo. We'll find a way to take him down, but," there's a pain in her eyes as she finishes, "you can't be involved."

I stumble back as if she's struck me. "I know I've messed up, but you can trust me. I'm not going to fall victim to him again. I can do this."

She shakes her head. "It's not that we don't trust you, but Orix is in your head. He already knows too much. Until your thoughts are safe, it's better if we do this without telling you everything."

Fury rises within me that this is just another thing Orix has taken from me, but this time my emotions feel controlled, lethal. He's going to pay for this. Even if I don't know the details, at least I know I can trust the people taking charge.

"Okay," I say quietly. "You, Isla, and Asher handle this. I'll focus on the kingdom and be here whenever you need me. Jerome is also available to you. He's the only person I've been able to truly count on since becoming king."

She smiles at me, and my chest hollows out. She's too perfect, too beautiful, too good for me and yet, she's all mine.

"Thanks for understanding," she replies. "I'm going to spend the rest of the afternoon with my sister and Asher then we can all have dinner together, if that's okay with you."

I take her hands. "If you're involved, it's always okay with me. That's all I want or need. You and me. Together."

I press my forehead to hers, the power of the moment settling between us as she closes her eyes and repeats, "Together."

The word feels like an anchor, pulling me back from the edge. Though I can't be certain Estee is truly ready to accept all of me yet, and I don't fault her for that. What matters most is that she's here and not running.

I kiss her again, slower this time, savoring the moment, the promise of what's to come. And as we pull apart, I squeeze her fingers lightly. "Go back to Isla and Asher. Do whatever you need to do. Just know I'll do whatever it takes to beat Orix. I'll give up the crown and everything I have—except you—as long as it means he can't interfere in our lives."

"I know." She gives me another of those radiant smiles then turns without another word, presumably to go back to my office.

I watch her walk away, captivated by the slight sway of her hips, the way her long hair falls in soft waves down her back, and how she holds her head up like the queen I hope she'll be one day.

Estee is everything—much more than I deserve—and I'm going to fight for her with all I have and then some.

Orix may think I'm weak, but he's about to learn just how wrong he is.

CHAPTER TWENTY-ONE

ESTEE

Walking back into the office feels like slamming my face into a brick wall. Isla and Asher are standing as if they're ready to leave, and that's the last thing I need right now.

"What's wrong?" My gaze fixes on my sister, a demand in my voice I can't hold back.

She hesitates. "We have to go."

I close my eyes, inhaling deeply to brace myself then look at her again, hoping for some way to change her mind. "Why?"

"Jerome came by while you were looking for Theo," Asher says, his expression grim and a deep crease between his brows. "We received a call from Malimorte. There's been a threat against our kingdom—against Isla, specifically. I have to get her back and keep her safe. As much as we want to stay and help you, being here leaves Polaris vulnerable."

"What kind of threat?" I ask, my tone sharper than I intend, but the idea of someone targeting Isla sends a surge of protective fury through me, especially as she remains much too still beside Asher.

The two of them share a look, and she nods just before he answers. "Pictures of Isla were delivered to the castle, including ones of us getting on the ship, with a note stating they're watching her every move, can find her anywhere, and it's only a matter of time before they do."

My stomach roils, and I close the distance between me and Isla, wrapping my arms around her. As much as I need her, my sister's safety will always come first. "I'm so sorry. Don't worry about me here. I can handle a pesky god. Everything will be just fine."

She nods over my shoulder but doesn't speak out loud. *"I want to be here for you, I swear. I wouldn't have come all this way to tease you, but the pictures...there were private ones, ones nobody should've been able to take."*

I shudder, trying to imagine how she feels having her privacy violated like that, but the more I let my imagination run wild, the more worked up I get on her behalf.

"Go home, find the bastard, and cut his balls off." I pull back, forcing a smile before I glance at Asher. "I'll figure this out. Just take care of my sister."

"Once we're home and I've cleared the castle myself, I'll reach out to Aurora as planned," he replies. "In the meantime, lie low and stay in contact with Malimorte. He'll relay everything to me when we return. The most important part is keeping an eye on Theo to make sure he doesn't do something he's not supposed to."

"Of course." I step back, hating that they have to leave already, but more than that, I appreciate that they've come all this way.

Asher's arm wraps around Isla as she continues to stay silent. "I told Jerome that if he wasn't sure about something, to ask me instead of Theo, assuming the king's on board with leaving himself in the dark. I've also suggested that he reach out to the queen of Alcaris. Sloane might be willing to come here and assist."

I tilt my head. "Why not King Aeson? Don't get me wrong. I like Sloane, but doesn't Aeson have more combat experience?"

"He does," Asher says. "But that isn't what we're looking for unless Aurora says otherwise. We need someone who can think outside the box. Sloane's kingdom has been dying for decades, but she's somehow made her land survive much longer than any of us predicted. Plus, I trust her more than Aeson."

"Fair point." I go to Isla again. Her face is pale and her stare distant. I squeeze her shoulders. "I'll come see you just as soon as things are sorted here. I love you."

"I love you, too," she says, but doesn't meet my gaze.

I look up at Asher, glad to still have my pack connection to him, so she doesn't have to hear what I'm about to say. *"I know you'll protect my sister with your life, so I won't bother threatening you, but if anything happens to her, I will be out for blood. One tiny scratch on her, and I'll murder this son of a bitch. And if those pictures get out? Asher..."*

"I know."

I have no doubt he does. We both love Isla more than anything else in the world. Just in different ways. If I didn't believe that, I wouldn't be letting her out of my sight right now.

"We'll talk soon." I hug Asher, grateful to have him as

part of my family. "Tell Mom and Dad that I love them and I'll see them soon."

He nods and leads Isla out of the office.

Once the door closes behind them, I take advantage of the magic soundproofing within the room and let out a scream. My fists are clenched and my heart races as I yell into the abyss, thankful nobody can hear me. I need this moment. I need to scream and cry and plan a few murders, because if I don't, I'm going to lose my damned mind.

My throat is raw by the time I'm done, but I feel marginally better. Time is of the essence, so that's all the breakdown I'll allow myself. Instead, I look around Theo's office, hoping to find something he's overlooked that will be helpful. Nothing holds my attention long except for his desk.

I sit in his chair and peek at the stacks of papers on the desktop. There's nothing unusual for a king: orders for repairs, transfers, amendments, and so on, along with meeting requests from his advisory council. Interesting. That currently only includes Jerome. I'm not sure if that's a good thing or not.

It makes me sad that there isn't anything personal here. Not a trinket or picture or even a rock. Everything is here out of necessity, nothing to remind him of love or family or a happy time in his life.

Theo's done unthinkable things, but hearing his story, knowing that Orix has been screwing with him since the moment he sent mercenaries to slay his pack... I can't help feeling sorry for my mate.

I keep going through his drawers, but there's still

nothing of consequence. Maybe Jerome will have more insight for me…or maybe I should spend the rest of the afternoon with Theo, not worrying about any of this and getting to know him. He just found out that his mother was never in danger. Even without a completed bond, before he stormed out of the office, I could taste the smokiness of his despair, of the regret I'm sure will plague him for years to come.

He doesn't deserve to be alone right now, and I should've realized that before.

It's time for me to leave this office and find my mate. With that plan firmly in my sights, I'm finally looking forward to what happens next.

When I enter the hallway, it's eerily quiet. A heaviness hangs in the air, pressing in on me to the point that I'm tempted to go back into the office for some relief. Reaching back, I twist the handle and almost step back in before someone calls my name.

"I've been looking for you everywhere," Drea says with a bright smile. "Benji was jumping on the bed and…" She looks me up and down. "What's wrong? Did Theo do something?"

Considering how much I've already told her, I'm tempted to divulge the latest happenings, but this is so much bigger than her. I have no doubt I can trust Drea, but there are some things she shouldn't have to worry about. Going up against a god is one of them. At least for now.

"Theo's actually been great," I tell her with a genuine smile. "I'm just going to find him, but what about Benji? Did he get hurt?"

She shakes her head, still eyeing me. "No, but his hard head put a hole in the wall. He hid under the bed for nearly an hour before Jerome came and made everything better by taking one of the paintings from another wall and hanging it over the hole."

I'll have to thank him for being so welcoming of the children. After all they've been through, the more adults who show these kids love and understanding the better.

"I love that," I tell her then frown. "Thank you for checking in on them today. It's been busy, and I haven't had time yet."

"I heard your sister and King Asher are here." I can hear the question she's not asking.

"They were, but they're probably back on the ship already, headed to Polaris again," I say. "Isla is a little over-protective of me and had to see for herself that I'm okay. It was a short visit."

Gods, I really hate not telling her the whole truth. At least I'm not technically lying to her.

"Well, okay." She glances at the ground, avoiding my gaze. "I'll be around if you need me."

"How about dinner tonight?" I suggest then remember I'd just mentally committed to spending the rest of the day with Theo. "Or breakfast tomorrow morning. We could order food in, my place or yours."

Drea's gaze brightens. "Breakfast is perfect, and defi-nitely in your room. Orion has a hard time going off to work when he knows I'm going to be home. A good and bad problem to have." Her cheeks flush. "That beast of a man can't keep his paws off me."

My heart twinges with jealousy. While I'm happy that

she seems to have this incredible mate, I won't lie and pretend I don't wish for the same. Not to say Theo can't be the same given the chance, but if things could be as simple for us as they seem to be for Drea and Orion, I wouldn't complain. At least, I'd like to think so.

"I'll see you around seven tomorrow then?" I confirm so I can go find my mate.

"Absolutely." She turns to walk away then pauses to look back at me. "If you need me before then, I'm here for you. Don't forget that."

"I won't, I promise."

I head toward Theo's bedroom. I haven't personally been there, but Jerome made sure to point out its location when I was avoiding life last week.

Turning left, I see the painting of a stunning woman in a yellow dress. She's wearing a diamond crown and sitting on a throne with a wolf at her feet. I don't know anything about her, but I imagine she was a powerful queen and one I'd love to know.

I continue, daydreaming about having grown wolves lie at my feet and start to chuckle...until my vision goes black. I can't see, and then, before I know it, I can't hear anything either. I reach out for the wall and open my mouth to call for help, but no sound comes out. At least as far as I know.

"Hello, my little queen," a man's raspy voice says in front of me. "I thought it was time we officially met."

Oh, gods. This is bad. So, so bad.

"I'm Orix."

He doesn't need to say the words. I already know and I

want to punch him in the face, but I can't even form words, let alone lift my arm.

He's closer now, his breath warm on my cheek. "Don't panic, my pet. At least not yet. I'm still undecided about your future. You see, I thought about keeping you as my prize, but you've not done as I hoped since summoning you here. If you quit causing me so much trouble, that's still a possibility."

It's probably a good thing I can't physically vomit right now. I'll never willingly be his *prize*.

He squeezes my shoulder, sending unwelcome shivers down my spine. "I've decided you being in Theo's life isn't the motivation he needs to please me. Until I say otherwise, you won't be able to move or speak. You are mine to wield now. Just like Theo is." He chuckles darkly. "He might think you've saved him from me, but that's the furthest thing from the truth. He'll see that once he realizes you're gone. Hmm, yes, this is going to work out quite nicely. Now, let's get you somewhere safe."

"Isla?" I call for my sister, but she's already too far away. Our connection is gone, and I'm left defenseless against this bastard.

Orix's fingers dig deeper into my flesh, forcing me to move with what feels like chains around my body, each step moving me further from freedom. I can't see him, can't see anything, but his presence wraps around me, suffocating me. His power slides through my mind, rooting itself in every corner of my being, controlling my movements with effortless precision. I'm his puppet now, blind, mute, and defenseless.

I never imagined things could get worse. I thought

we'd seen the darkest depths of this nightmare. But now, as I'm dragged into the unknown, I realize how wrong I was. Each step echoes in my mind, pounding with the fear that no one will ever find me, that I'll remain trapped under Orix's control, hidden from those I love, for as long as he allows me to live.

My heart pounds, and the dread coils tighter, sharper, with every silent scream. This isn't just fear. This is a hollow, consuming terror—a fate that chills me to my core.

A fate worse than death.

CHAPTER TWENTY-TWO

THEO

It's been hours since I last saw Estee. Hours of restless pacing, of my wolf clawing at me from the inside, of an itch beneath my skin that refuses to settle. I've asked Jerome about her more times than I can count, but she's remained locked in my office since Isla and Asher left. I hate that she's working on this alone, but I hate it even more knowing that I can't help her myself.

Still, every time I try to leave the new and temporary workspace I've set up, someone else appears, needing something from me. Repairs to housing, trade disputes, complaints from vendors—it's endless. I've ignored this kingdom for too long. There are months of work ahead of me to undo the damage, and I can't even begin to touch the surface without confronting my mistakes. But I'm grateful the pack is allowing me to try to redeem myself, just as she is. I'm not sure I deserve this chance to prove I'm worthy, but I'm accepting it anyway.

As dusk begins to swallow the bright sky, and there's

no one else waiting to speak with me, I escape and make my way back to where I assume Estee is—in my office.

After the time I've already spent apart from my mate and the whispers of our kiss still lingering on my lips, I'm desperate to have eyes on her. She's the only one who can lessen the unease currently stuck in my throat.

My wolf rumbles in agreement from within, and my stride lengthens. Each step echoes in the castle halls, and I take the stairs three at a time, my heart pounding faster with each foot forward. A pressure surrounds my chest, tightening with a suffocating grip.

This is insane. I shouldn't be losing myself so completely after an afternoon away from my mate. Yet, I am, and I'm beginning to wonder if there's a reason for my increasing distress.

That thought sends another wave of dread through me that doesn't ease even as I get closer to my office. In fact, it only gets worse when I realize her scent isn't getting stronger, like she hasn't been here for quite some time.

Something *is* wrong.

I start to run.

It's as if poison seeps into my lungs with each breath, filling me with a cold, acidic fury. I break into a sprint, my vision narrowing, blood roaring in my ears. My mind races through possibilities I can barely stomach, each one twisting the knife deeper.

Where is my mate?

The door to my office looms ahead, locked. I don't waste time fumbling for keys; I kick it open with a force that splinters the wood, the shards biting into my skin, but I barely feel the sting. My gaze sweeps the room, wild and desperate, but she's not here. The faint traces of her linger, but they're stale, hours old. My wolf howls within my mind, a primal cry for our mate, as I call for Jerome.

"Yes, Your Majesty?" he replies immediately.

"Lock down the castle," I demand. *"Hell, lock down the whole damned island. Estee is missing."*

"Sire, might I suggest we don't alarm the pack and—"

"I don't give a damn about the pack right now!" My fury lashes through the link like a whip, blazing. *"I need to know where my mate is. Something's happened to her, and I will tear this place apart stone by stone if I have to."*

There's a short pause, followed by a determined, *"Yes, my king. I will initiate the lockdown."*

The connection snaps, and I let out a roar that shakes the surrounding walls, echoing back at me, a sound of unbridled anguish. Estee wouldn't disappear without a word, not after this morning, not after the promises we made. She wouldn't just leave me, not like this. The thought of her abandoning me claws at my heart, twisting it until I can hardly breathe.

For a single, horrid moment, doubt slithers through my mind like a snake. *Could she have left with Asher and Isla? Were our moments this morning a farce?*

The idea hits me like a blade, sharp and brutal. If she left me here, if she abandoned me to face Orix alone… I don't know if I'd survive it. I don't know if I'd want to.

But no. I force the thought aside, burying it beneath a rising tide of rage. She wouldn't do that. Not the Estee I've only just begun to know, not the woman so full of passion earlier. And if she's not here, there's only one other explanation. One that has a dark shadow tightening around my heart like a noose.

Just the thought of *him* has my mind turning venomous and foul, a reminder of every twisted manipulation and lie he's spun. If he's taken her, if he's laid a single hand on her—

I will sacrifice whatever I must to get her back. No price is too high to pay for my mate.

I storm from the office, fury surging through my veins like wildfire. Jerome rounds the corner, his face pale, breaths coming in short, nervous gasps. "I've searched all the lower floors for Princess Estee, Sire," he says, voice losing confidence. "But there's no sign of her, and her room has remained untouched since this morning."

Even though I already dismissed this idea, I still have to ask. "Could she have left with King Asher and Queen Isla earlier?"

He shakes his head then frowns. "She certainly *could* have, Your Majesty, but I don't believe so. When the king and queen of Polaris departed earlier, it seemed Queen Isla was quite ill, and King Asher made a point of speaking with me about certain things before boarding his ship home. Topics that made me believe I would be working with Estee within the walls of this castle. He even asked me to call upon Queen Sloane to come and assist Princess Estee since her sister is unable to."

There are plenty of questions I could ask about all that, but finding Estee is far more important.

Relief mingles with fury, a volatile mix that only sharpens my resolve. She didn't leave me willingly. She's here, somewhere, hidden or taken.

"I'll search the castle myself," I say, barely holding back the growl in my voice. "Then we'll scour every corner of this cursed island if we have to. She *will* be found."

As Jerome nods in understanding, the energy of my wolf tingles along my skin. He wants to hunt, and I'm not going to stop him, not even within the walls of the castle.

My back starts to arch, and a loud rumble reverberates from deep within me as a fierce determination soothes my frayed nerves. At least until Drea begins shouting from down the hallway.

"Where is Estee? Why is there a lockdown?" she demands, barreling toward me, eyes blazing, fury etched into every line of her face. She's flanked by one of my guards, who looks as if he's trying to restrain her without much success.

"I don't care who you think you are," she adds before I can even entertain answering her question, "I will make your life even more miserable than it already is if you don't take me to Estee right now."

The threat is laughable, but there's a fire in her gaze, a loyalty that *almost* makes me admire her. Still, my wolf snaps, snarling as I let some of his rage bleed into my voice.

"Watch your tone," I growl, low and dangerous. "One word from me, and you'll find yourself in the dungeons."

Drea falters, but she doesn't back down entirely. "Estee said she was going to see you," she insists, trembling with barely suppressed fear and anger. "She was hiding something from me. She didn't trust you, and neither do I. Lock me away if you have to, but I won't stop trying to find her while I can, no matter the consequences."

I narrow my eyes, letting the weight of my presence bear down on her. "Estee never came to me this afternoon," I say, each word a cold, hard truth. It infuriates me to know that she was trying to find me but never succeeded. "If you know anything about where else she might've gone, I suggest you tell me now."

As much of an annoyance as this woman appears to be, she clearly cares for my mate. Maybe I can use that to my advantage.

Drea barely manages to shake her head, and I glance up at the waiting guard, whose name I can't recall. "Take this woman and allow her to keep watch for Princess Estee, but only from within the castle. We don't need two of them missing."

Her eyes remain clear as she takes in my words, seeming to weigh their truth. "She really never made it to you this afternoon?"

"No." The word burns through me.

Drea looks back up at the guard. "We have to find her, Orion. She's," her voice cracks, "she deserves better than what she's been through."

That was something we could agree on.

The guard bows, keeping his eyes low, before speaking to me. "I will keep Drea from causing any trouble, Your Majesty, and if we find any sign of Princess Estee, you'll be the first to know."

"I'd expect nothing less."

When I step away from them, my wolf rushes to the surface, and I don't stop him this time. His snarls echo through the hallway as he makes his powerful presence known. He sniffs at my guard and Estee's friend then shakes his head, seeming satisfied that they know nothing more than they've shared.

"Estee was coming to see us," I tell my wolf. *"We have to figure out why that never happened."*

He makes a harsh noise as he tears through the corridor, going in the direction of my bedroom. But when he turns the corner, he comes to an abrupt halt, his claws digging into the wooden floors.

His snarls grow louder, but there's nothing here. I don't even sense Estee. At least not at first.

A low, feral growl escapes from my throat, my wolf's rage blending with mine until there's no separation, only a single, burning wrath. I close my eyes, inhaling deeply, and the horrifying scent solidifies—a twisted blend of Estee's essence and the vile taint of that god.

He was here. He has my mate.

The realization ignites a maelstrom of fire within me, a violent need to hunt, to reclaim what's mine.

Hold on, my Starlight, I vow, my wolf's roars vibrating through me. *I'm coming for you.*

CHAPTER TWENTY-THREE

The world around me is nothing but shadows and silence, an endless void where time seems irrelevant. My limbs remain as heavy as lead, immovable no matter how hard I will them to obey me. My voice, too, stays locked within me, a prisoner alongside my body. The only sound is my heartbeat, steady and sure, and the constant hum of my wolf—a calm, grounding presence in the dark. She's with me, solid and unyielding, and thanks to her, I'm not afraid.

Orix took me from the hallway and, based on the energy shift, created a portal to this place. He's at least given me my sight back, but the room where he's left me has only the faintest layer of ambient light. There are no windows, and I can't tell what the walls are made from, but considering the coolness of the room, I'd assume an earthy material of some sort.

I've been left on a rough, stone platform without physical restraints, just the crushing influence of Orix's power holding me still. It's here, in this pit of despair, that he finds me again.

He enters with a predatory grace, his lean frame swathed in darkness, his presence filling the air with malice. I suppose he expects me to tremble, to beg, to show even a hint of terror. Hell, I probably should. Yet, the longer I'm here, the less afraid I become. I give him nothing. Not an ounce of satisfaction.

"You know," he drawls, his voice a twisted thread in the stillness, "considering how you treated Theo upon your arrival in Selaris, I expected something a little more… theatrical from you, Princess." He steps closer, his face inches from mine as he bends lower, causing his oily, black hair to brush my cheek. The sensation mixes with his sour breath on my skin as he presses my stomach lightly. "Maybe we need to make this game more interesting. I could share a secret with you if you decide to finally participate." His eyes, nearly black with a hint of poisoned blue, glint with a sinister amusement.

Yet, all I feel is the barest flicker of disgust, masked beneath this unexpected calm. I want to laugh, to let him know just how little he intimidates me. In my mind, I give voice to my defiance: *A game you'll surely lose in the end.*

"Do you know why you're here, Estee?" he purrs, his tone silky but laced with spite and a power that seems to seep into my throat.

The invisible barrier there, the one binding my words, lifts, finally allowing me to speak. "You want something." The sentence slips out like daggers, sharp and cutting.

His smile widens, revealing stained teeth. "I don't want something, dear Estee. I want *everything*. I want your soul, the kingdom I stole you from, and all the others in Lunara. Even better, thanks to your mate, I'm so close to reclaiming that which was taken from me. I just need him a bit more focused on the task at hand."

"And you think stealing his mate is going to make him *focused*?" If I could roll my eyes at this imbecile, I absolutely would.

His sinister chuckle sweeps over me, sending a shudder up my spine. "Now, you're worried about poor Theo? Interesting. Though, don't fret. I'll only let him suffer for the day. Once I feel he's learned his lesson, I'll tell him how he can get you back."

Great. More threats, more decisions Theo will feel he has no choice but to make.

Orix presses harder on my stomach as his sharp, hooked nose moves across my forehead, inhaling. "Tell me, Princess. What would you do to save your own life or that of your future child?"

I scoff, wishing I could turn away from him. "Nothing that would interest you."

"Not a single thing?" His tongue clicks. "I find that hard to believe."

"Unless you care about your own death, I don't see the point of this conversation."

His fist slams down next to my head, the stone beneath me cracking. "When will you accept that you've already lost? My demise isn't happening, much to the dismay of others."

Interesting. Who else has tried to knock this god down from his flimsy pedestal? Something that makes me wonder...

"Who hurt you, Orix?" I say, pretending to care about his seemingly hurt feelings. "Did the other gods not play nice?"

He wraps his hand around my throat, and his voice lowers into a growl. "Don't act as if you know me, wolf. I'm a god, and I can end your existence with the snap of my fingers. Do you understand that?"

My eyes narrow in defiance, daring him to follow through. "Then do it. Kill me now. As you pointed out earlier, my arrival in Selaris has only hindered your plans. Make this less complicated for both of us. Squeeze the air from my lungs and be done with this."

I'd rather be dead than his prisoner. At least then I'd be free to be reborn and find a way to kill him later.

His grip deepens to the point I'm sure there will be marks, and as my throat begins to burn, I realize I'm truly not afraid of this death. Except as my vision begins to dance with spots, the bastard releases me.

"It's not your time yet," he hisses, removing his cold touch from my neck before shoving away from me.

Those five words tell me all I need to know and confirm that I've been right not to be afraid since arriving in this dark room.

Orix needs me, but why? I have royal blood, but there are plenty of others out there who do as well. What's so special about me? Is it because I'm Theo's mate? Maybe, but I feel as though I'm missing something that's right in front of me.

My wolf snarls, and her presence spreads through my core, warming my...stomach.

But what can he do with a child that a wolf shifter

carries? Technically, because of my and Theo's bloodlines, the baby will have the right to a throne, but again, that's not a rare thing.

"What if it was never my time to die?" I ask Orix before he leaves me alone in the dark again. I can't see him any longer, but I sense him close enough to have heard me. "Gods live forever. If I help you, couldn't you make that happen for me?"

A rumble echoes through the small, shadow-filled space. "You are not worthy of my power."

"But Theo is. That's why you've tied yourself to him. He holds a strength within him that you need."

I don't know how I ever saw my mate as weak. He's made poor choices, but even now, when it shouldn't be possible, his energy is reaching for me. He's determined and loyal and filled with more love than anyone I've yet to know. It doesn't matter what happened in his past. His actions don't make him less worthy of redemption than anyone else. Something I wish I'd seen long before now.

"Theo's nothing more than a pawn." Orix sneers, coming back to me. "It's the future heir who'll hold the power you should fear."

He glares down at me, his godly power slithering over my cold skin and pressing in on my body. Pinpricks of agony poke along my limbs until my blood begins to burn, as if actual flames are building within me.

As my lungs ache, I remain unmoving, watching him watch me. He expects a reaction. Anger, fear, and pleading, I'm sure. Yet I give him none of it. Not out of pure stubbornness, but because there's only a rebellious calm left for me to hold onto.

My wolf's presence remains strong, a steady heartbeat in the back of my mind, her unwavering loyalty and confidence merging with mine, along with the energy I can only identify as Theo's, bringing with it a peace.

It doesn't matter what happens here, we're going to be okay.

Orix's expression hardens as he searches my face, irritation etching into his gaze. "You're testing my patience, Princess," he snarls, his eyes flashing with something dangerous. "Perhaps I need to show you the consequences of your defiance."

"I thought you wanted to play games," I tell him, my voice hoarse from the tension still riddling my extremities. "I was merely trying to give you what I thought you wanted."

"Let's see just how true that is." His palms push against my temples, and he closes his dark eyes. In the shadows of the room, he looks more ghostly than godly, but before I can stare for too long, he jumps back, his face somehow even more ashen.

"That's not possible." He steps forward again, grabbing my throat. "Did you bond with Theo without my knowing?"

I can't speak thanks to his grip, nor can I move more than my eyes, so I settle for blinking rapidly.

"Answer me!" he shouts in my face, releasing his hold as he paces next to me.

"No...bond," I manage to croak.

"Lies." His bellow fills the room, echoing off the cool stone walls, a thunderous sound that reverberates through my bones. Before I can respond, he moves with a vicious, lethal grace. A dagger materializes in his hand, its edge catching what little light exists, gleaming with a sinister promise. In one swift, brutal motion, he drives it into my stomach, the steel piercing flesh and muscle, straight into my core.

Pain explodes—sharp, blinding, an agony that sears through the numbness, breaking past every wall I'd built around myself. My vision blurs as a cry rips from my throat, the sound broken, desperate, and filled with a torment I'd never thought possible. He twists the blade, and the suffering intensifies, consuming me, until I feel as though I'm made of nothing but ash.

Orix leans over me, his eyes shining with devious intent. "You won't win against me, Princess. I've been at this longer than you can imagine, and I will get what I want. I might have been... Well, that doesn't matter now. Fight all you want, nothing will change. Theo will do as I command and so will you. Death won't free you from this fate. Nothing will. The sooner you accept that, the easier this will all be."

"Death won't free you from this fate."

Tears of frustration begin to fill my eyes. He's wrong and I won't give up. I can't, no matter how hopeless my surroundings are. I have to hold onto the rage. It's the motivation that will get me through.

His laughter sweeps over me as he wipes at my falling tears. "Good girl. Maybe you'll be more than I expected after all. I was looking forward to watching the life bleed from you, but if you cooperate, maybe I'll let you live long enough to raise my...the child. He won't be of use to me until he's grown, but don't worry. I already have a plan to speed that process up."

The renewed hatred boiling within me feels almost tangible, a fire that burns away the pain, sharpening into a blade of its own. *Like hell he will.*

I might be trapped, I might have even been a fool, but one thing is certain now—I will never, ever let him have my future child.

Not in this lifetime or any other.

"You may think these tears are a sign of weakness, but that's the furthest thing from the truth," I rasp, my voice filled with a rebelliousness that builds from the depths of my soul. "But even gods can bleed. And no matter what it takes, I will make sure that's the last thing you ever do."

The flash of anger in his eyes is my only satisfaction as he steps back into the shadows, and I hold onto it, letting this moment fuel me. I may be broken, bleeding, and helpless right now, but he's just made a fatal mistake—he's shown me his weakness, his arrogance. And I'll find a way to use it against him even from here.

CHAPTER TWENTY-FOUR

THEO

Each step forward feels like a war within me. The bond that ties me to Estee pulls taut, a visceral ache that digs deep into my chest, but I push through it. The castle lies behind me in quiet disarray—a reflection of the chaos I've been battling since realizing she was missing. The wreckage doesn't matter. None of it does, not when Estee is still out there, somewhere, waiting for me.

The beast inside stirs restlessly, demanding action, demanding blood. My hands tremble with the urge to tear down every barrier in my path, but I hold firm. This isn't who I want to be anymore. Not for Estee. Not for the kingdom.

Jerome's attempts to calm me had only sparked my frustration earlier, but now his words echo faintly, urging me to think beyond my pain. I let the pulse of rage simmer beneath the surface instead of letting it consume me. My control is fragile but deliberate as I approach the first house in the pack's village in search of my mate, or anyone who might have seen anything that could tell me more.

"Alpha King Theo," Zane greets me at the threshold, his stance rigid but his tone measured. He doesn't flinch, though the tension in his shoulders betrays his apprehension.

I meet his gaze evenly, feeling the weight of my authority and the eyes of my people behind me. "I'm looking for Estee," I say, my voice steady despite the wild storm within.

"You won't find her by tearing through your own pack's homes," he replies, standing firm in the doorway. "My daughter is asleep inside. She doesn't need to see her alpha like this."

I glance past him, seeing the small figure curled up on the couch, her tiny chest rising and falling peacefully. The sight strikes me in a way I don't expect, piercing through the haze of my desperation.

Zane continues, his voice softer now. "I know what it feels like to lose someone you love. My mate's mind became broken, and before we could get her help, she disappeared. It almost destroyed me, but Sadie was only a few months old. I couldn't let the beast win. My daughter needed me, and I needed to be strong for her."

His words hit with the punch of truth that I can't ignore. I see myself reflected in the window behind him—not as the alpha I aspire to be, but as the monster I fear becoming. The shadows around my eyes, the unbridled anger in my stance... I'm so close to breaking, just as Orix wants. I can't let that happen. Worse, Estee wouldn't recognize this man. She wouldn't want him.

I take a breath, steadying myself. "Thank you for your words," I say, stepping back from the door.

Zane nods, his expression softening. "Find your mate, Alpha, but don't lose yourself in the process. Your people need you whole—not broken by your own fury."

His words stay with me as I leave, weaving through the village, to go back to the castle. I already know I won't find answers out here. Coming to search the houses was merely a way to feel as though I was doing something to get me closer to Estee, instead of accepting that I have no damn clue what I'm supposed to do now.

Still, I need to be better. Not only for myself and Estee, but for the people who look to me for strength. The beast inside me howls for destruction, but I silence it with a single thought—Estee needs a man who can lead, not a monster who destroys.

She's out there somewhere, and I *will* find her. And when I do, she won't see the wreckage of a broken king, but the mate she deserves—the one she believed I could be.

I'm almost at the edge of the village when another figure steps out of her home, this one wearing a smile and cackling. "Oh, *King* Theo. Have you learned nothing? Put your claws away and come inside."

It's Elyn, the elder wolf, her gaze sharp, assessing. Her voice is a mocking caress, a challenge wrapped in silk, and I can feel my wolf stir, his irritation bristling beneath my skin.

"I've learned plenty," I tell her as I keep walking toward the castle. "I don't have time for your nonsense,"

But then her voice stops me cold, slicing through the

air with an authority that sends a chill down my spine. "If you want to know where your mate is, I'd suggest you make time, young wolf."

I whirl to face her. "What did you say?" For her sake, she better not be playing with me. The control I have over my wrath is fragile. As much as I don't want to lose myself to this fury, I can only handle so much.

Her grin deepens as her eyes gleam with something dangerous. "You heard me." She steps back, her silhouette framed by the dim light spilling from her doorway.

Feeling as if I have no other choice, I make my way toward her home, hoping this won't be a waste of my time or that she won't push me over the edge. Yet, as I step into her doorway, a hidden force traps me within her threshold, and that sends my wolf spiraling.

I can't move and the sense of loss has my inner beast attempting to force a shift on me. My bones begin to crack, but in the next second, I can't feel anything. Not physically or even emotionally. The wrath that was surging within me is stolen away, replaced with a nothingness that's even worse.

"What did you do to me?" I ask, my voice lifeless.

Elyn sits at her table across the room and shrugs. "I'm protecting myself. You might think you've hidden yourself from the people, King Theo, but I've known exactly who you are since the moment you stole the throne."

While I glare at the wrinkled woman, I see that glint in her lavender eyes—the look of someone who knows more than she should. More than I've ever hoped anyone to know about me.

She stirs something in a mug sitting in front of her.

"I've been waiting for you to pull your head out of your ass, or at least out of Orix's," she says with a chuckle. "It's been…entertaining, especially with Princess Estee's arrival, but it's time for change. Though, it's funny how things work out. I gave her a new chance at life, and now I have the opportunity to do the same for her mate."

A snarl rises in my throat. My wolf is furious at the calm arrogance in her tone, but my body refuses to act on my mental commands.

She takes a long pull of her drink, slowly picks up a cloth napkin to dab at the corners of her mouth, and then stands before addressing me again. "Are you ready to be free, Theo?"

"Of course I am. I need to find Estee."

She shakes her head. "Stubborn alpha. I should've known you'd make this difficult. Now, I'm going to release you from the doorway, but you still won't feel any emotion too strongly. I need you to hear everything I have to say—some of which you won't like—and I won't have you destroying my home, you hear?"

"I was keeping myself in check just fine before you baited me," I say, feeling breathless and weak. "Just tell me where she is."

She flattens her lips as she walks toward me. "Forgive me for not believing you after all I've seen." Her light purple eyes never leave mine, and she reaches for a small bag that's tucked into the pocket of her long black skirt. I watch carefully, still unable to move, as she takes a pinch of something then flicks the powder at my feet.

With a heavy breath, my body slumps forward, and I stumble, but as Elyn said, I still can't feel much, not even the pain of missing Estee. The urgency to find her is still there, but the emotions behind the need are muted.

"For you to save your mate, we need to go back to the beginning, when Orix first sank his claws into you," she says, stepping around me to close her door. "Come have a seat, and I'll pour you some tea."

"What are you?" Even though I want to refuse, I still find myself heading toward the table.

"I'm the pack healer, an elder wolf, and someone you want on your side. Beyond that, *who* I am is none of your business."

She busies herself in the small corner kitchen, reaching for a blue kettle to fill a second cup.

"How do you wield the magic you do and still call yourself a shifter?" I've used spells myself plenty of times, but I've never known another wolf to be able to trap people or control someone as Elyn is with me.

She pats my head as she sets the steaming mug in front of me. "I'm a full-blooded wolf shifter. I merely choose to make friends with those who can elevate my reach. I was born with the power and mind to help heal those who can't do so themselves. Once I mastered that, I grew curious about what else I might be able to do."

"And what did you discover?"

She settles into the chair across from me. "King or not, as I've already mentioned, that's none of your business."

A growl echoes from me, making her raise a brow. "I knew your wolf was powerful, but seeing him this close… It's a waste you've yet to realize his potential after all this time."

"What do you mean?" Even my confusion seems

dulled, yet my inner animal still paces right beneath the surface.

"Did you think Orix just happened upon you, picking you for no good reason?" Her eyes peer into me, making my chest constrict with how much she might actually know.

"How do you know I'm tied to him?" I pause, filled with shame. "How *long* have you known?"

Her laughter is soft, but it does nothing to lessen my unease. "I've known you were compromised since the moment you stepped foot in that castle you now call yours. I could smell the tainted god on you." Her nose scrunches. "His shadows can't be hidden from those who are looking."

"Then, why haven't you ever said anything? Why did you stand up for me in the market if you knew I was compromised?" My words and heart still feel so flat, yet this conversation is nothing of the sort.

"I've lived a long time," she muses. "Sometimes an old lady just wants some entertainment. Plus, it's not as if you've done anything terrible since doing me the favor of killing Airik. Well, not overtly. You've allowed the people to begin to come together. The only thing that hasn't gone my way since your crowning has been the orphaned children, but it seems your mate is taking care of that."

Gods, she knows everything. I don't know how and I don't presume she'll tell me, so I don't waste my breath asking.

"Where did Orix take her?" Maybe now that everything is out there, we can get back to the task at hand.

She waggles a finger at me. "As I said before, you need

to go back to the beginning first. Do you even know who you are? In any of your lifetimes, have you ever truly known yourself?"

This has my wolf snarling again. "We need our mate back."

Elyn reaches across the table, the warmth of her palm covering my still-clawed hands as she locks eyes with me. Her gaze is intense, unwavering, grounding me in a way I haven't felt in years. "I will show you how to get your mate, wolf, but this is important. Be patient." Her words are a balm, seeping through the storm raging inside me, urging calm where there's only been chaos.

For the first time since I last saw Estee, a sliver of relief settles over me. My body begins to relax, my claws retracting. It feels like surfacing after being submerged in dark, cold water—a shuddering breath of clarity. I nod, signaling my willingness to listen, and Elyn's expression softens, a brief glint of satisfaction in her eyes.

"Now that we're all willing participants in this conversation," she says, clapping her hands once, a sharp sound that slices through the tension, "let's speed things up. You, Theodore Northcroft, come from a long line of alphas. Your soul has been reborn across lifetimes, carrying the essence of each set of parents, each ancestor, and each wolf that has built the power inside you. I may not have known you in each lifetime, but I know what I'm sensing now."

"And what is that?" I expect her to call me out on any of the many things I've done wrong over the last few years, but instead, her words become the next blow to my already fractured psyche.

"What you've yet to figure out on your own is that you're more god than wolf, Theo."

Shock fills me, spreading like wildfire through my veins, igniting emotions I haven't allowed myself to feel in what seems like forever. But before I can let myself hope that this information might help me get my mate back, I need to know more.

"What does that mean exactly?"

She tilts her head, her tone soft but firm, one that leaves no room for doubt. "The answer to that is meant for another day, when we have more time to unravel the intricacies of your heritage. For now, you just need to know that by not understanding who you truly are, you were left susceptible to Orix," she replies, her words cloaked in a quiet urgency. "He was a lower god, a bastard with no family, and that left a chip on his shoulder. Instead of creating a legacy of his own, he chose a path of terror, lashing out, spreading misery like a disease. For thousands of years, he manipulated, broke, and devastated those around him. Until the other gods had enough. They stripped him of his power, banishing him to the shadows, a place between realms where only darkness resides."

I shake my head, the information swirling in my mind, trying to find a place to settle. "No, he's still plenty powerful. He's in my head. He appears to me whenever he feels like it. Whatever the other gods thought they did, they failed."

Elyn remains steadfast. "No, Theo. They succeeded. They stole his power, and he's been tied to the shadow realm ever since—that's where lost souls reside. Unfortunately, as powerless as Orix is, he's just as cunning. He knew of your existence and targeted people to ruin you so that your soul would come to him. He broke you so he could attach himself to you, stealing your power for himself."

My shoulders slump under the weight of her revelation, the gravity of the truth pulling me down, grounding me in the depths of my own failure and ignorance. How could he have been taking my power—a power I never even knew I possessed? Though as Elyn's words sink deeper, my denial fades, replaced by a cold, steely acceptance, a dark melody that resonates with the pieces of my soul I'd long since buried.

The hold on my emotions shatters, and I'm left exposed, raw, drowning in a storm of grief, rage, and vengeance that threatens to consume me. I grip the edges of the table, my knuckles whitening, as a single, burning desire takes hold.

Elyn's gaze sharpens, her voice a challenge that cuts through the chaos within me. "Are you ready to reclaim your power, Alpha King Theo?"

I nod, the motion small but filled with determination as I try not to focus on everything I've lost. Instead, my thoughts race with all that I'm prepared to do to take everything back.

A slow, knowing smile curves her lips. "Good," she says with satisfaction. "Because I have a plan. One your wolf is going to love."

CHAPTER TWENTY-FIVE

ESTEE

Theo, where are you?

Orix left me to suffer alone, and while I thought I had him right where I wanted, the passing hours have begun to blend into an agonizing haze. Before there was only silence when he was gone, now the emptiness is punctuated by the howls of broken souls that haunt the darkness around me. Their mournful cries echo, filling the quiet with despair.

They sing a melody of suffering, a reminder that I'm as trapped in this misery as they are, alone in a way I never thought possible. Their grief tugs at something deep within me, tempting me to surrender, to sink with them. There's a twisted beauty in it, a fragile, haunting allure to simply giving up.

Maybe it would be easier. Easier than hoping. Easier than waiting, clinging to the fraying thread of a bond I don't even know if Theo can feel while I'm here. A darkness as thick as death presses in around me, and I'm so, so tired. My strength seeps away with every drop of blood that drips from my body, pooling onto the stone beneath me, swallowed whole by this wretched realm.

The pull of oblivion is so strong that I begin to give myself over, sinking deeper into that endless void. But just as I'm about to let go, a spark flares within me, fragile yet defiant—a glint of light in this suffocating darkness.

Theo.

That tether, faint and almost indistinguishable, flickers within my mind, a pulse of life that refuses to extinguish. The bond I'd once doubted and pushed away now feels like my only salvation, my only reason to hold on. I can't explain it, I don't even fully understand it, but I feel him— somewhere out there, searching, desperate, determined. It's a weak, unwinding piece of thread, but it's real. It's *him.*

With a shuddering breath, I reach out, pouring every ounce of strength I have left into that fragile bond. My silent plea becomes a scream in my mind, aching and desperate.

Please, Theo. I know you can find me. I'm right here. Don't give up on me.

CHAPTER TWENTY-SIX

THEO

It's as if I've been blind all my life, and I'm only now seeing the world for what it truly is. My wolf is calmer than he's ever been, even in our happiest moments, a steady, silent guardian within me. And the fear that once controlled me—the terror of losing Estee— is gone. There's only the certainty that I will have her back. Orix can't and won't keep her from me. Not now that I know where she is, and not once I reclaim the power he's stolen from me.

A part of me knows this won't be easy. But that dread of failure has faded into resolve. The only thing that concerns me now is taking back what's mine.

"Don't be greedy, boy," Elyn snaps, as if reading my thoughts. Her sharp eyes pierce me as we stand in my office, back at the castle. "The shadow realm isn't your playground. You're not strong enough to fight him there. Find Estee and return as quickly as possible. That's all you're supposed to do."

That's what she's told me already, but if I get the

chance to sink my claws into Orix, I make no promises that I won't. Though, I don't admit that to her.

"My mate is always my priority," I state, having to force myself to keep the bite out of my tone. "I won't put her at risk for selfish gain."

As protective as I feel over Estee, I can't help the images that float within my mind. Ones of Orix attempting to stand in my way and me taking back every piece of myself, one savage act at a time.

Still, as salivating as that scenario is to both me and my wolf, we know what needs to be done. Our mate will be safe above all else.

"More god than wolf."

Elyn's earlier words whisper through my thoughts again. They're my beacon to the future, the hope I'd believed Estee had brought me, but I can see now that it's not on her to provide my happiness, to show me forgiveness. That's something I must do for myself, and I'm going to. No matter what it takes.

Outside my office, I can feel the murmur of the pack. Even at this late hour, the kingdom is restless, their energy vibrating with anticipation, confusion, and a hint of fear. They're waiting to see if their king has finally lost his mind. Maybe I have. But when I return with Estee, I'll show them who I truly am. Selaris will become a sanctuary, a place others yearn to be. I'll make this kingdom something to be proud of—something Estee can look at with pride.

"The shadow realm is infinite," Elyn says, her voice laced with warning. "I know you're feeling invincible but let me remind you: you have very little of your god power left. The darkness there will affect you. Don't linger. Don't speak to anyone. Don't touch anything."

I place my hands on her shoulders, squeezing gently, a rare smile tugging at my lips. "I've got this."

Her eyes narrow, her lips pressing into a thin line. "I'm not sure if your newfound confidence will be our salvation or our damnation. Just remember, Estee won't have much time left now."

A cold dread coils in my chest, making my fingers tighten involuntarily on her shoulders. "What do you mean?"

"Did you think all those warnings I just gave applied only to you?" She jerks back, freeing herself from my grip. "Estee's been in there for nearly twelve hours. She's going to be weak, believe she belongs there with the trapped souls, and basically useless to you until we cleanse her. There's still a chance, but you need to hurry."

She doesn't have to tell me twice. The urgency claws at me, my wolf snarling in agreement. Estee is in danger— not just of physical harm, but of losing herself to that wretched place. I double-check my pockets, fingers grazing the daggers and throwing stars tucked within both sides.

It's time to get my mate back.

"Not so fast, King Theo." A voice, silken and sharp, snakes through my mind before echoing in the room.

A striking figure materializes in front of me, her presence stealing the breath from my lungs. She strides toward me, each step brimming with the confidence of someone who's never been refused.

Her eyes, a mesmerizing shade of violet, gleam with an

ancient, unyielding power. Dark red lips curve into a smirk, and strands of sleek hair fall to her waist, the color a blend of fire and shadow. Charcoal fabric covers her yet it's almost as if she wears nothing at all.

She stops beside Elyn, casting a radiant smile at her. "My child. So full of power."

The elder wolf bows deeply, her wrinkled skin beginning to glow with a faint luminescence. "Aurora. It's a blessing to see you again."

The goddess chuckles softly. "Of course it is. Now, why have I been disturbed to deal with mortal wolf problems? The delicious King Asher mentioned you've made enemies with another god."

Her presence pulls at something deep within me, an intoxicating draw I can't ignore. My hand instinctively reaches for hers, craving her touch, her power. She swats me away with a laugh, wagging a finger in my face. "Down, boy. I don't give my energy freely. If you want something from me, you'll have to give me something in return." She sniffs the air, her face twisting in disgust. "Why does *Orix* linger on you? What sort of loathsome entanglement have you created?"

My voice catches in my throat as her power presses down on me, rendering me momentarily speechless.

Aurora's hand is still raised toward me, but her gaze shifts to Elyn. "Explain."

"Orix found a way to attach himself to Theo. The god has been siphoning Theo's god energy ever since, and I believe he plans to do something with the next crowned heir if we don't stop him."

"He also stole my mate." I manage to find my voice

once more, needing to share what's most important about all of this.

"I thought I was coming here for…" The goddess sighs deeply and drops her hand. "Never mind. I'll still get what I want. Now, as amused as I am that Orix is attempting to make a comeback, I don't have time for this, nor do I have any desire to step foot in the shadow realm. Lure him back here, and I might decide to help you, but that nuisance is nothing more than a pest to me. Even if he manages to transfer his soul to your child, which I presume is his intention if he's still as shrewd as he once was, he'll never be a threat to me."

This has my wolf surging to the surface, a ferocious growl ripping from deep within me. "*That's* why he wanted me to produce an heir? So he can claim his body?"

Aurora shrugs, her hair floating around her as if caught in an invisible breeze. "What else is a child good for?"

The casual cruelty of her words sends a chill through me. Now I understand Asher's reluctance to involve her.

She chuckles, as if sensing my thoughts. "Asher is merely afraid of our connection, but thankfully for him, I'm not easily offended." With a sly smile on her lips, she comes closer to me. "And because he dared to ask me himself, I will grant you one gift." She moves so gracefully that her body seems to glide over the floor. She lifts her arm and places a finger at the center of my chest, her grin turning wicked. "This will hurt."

My body tenses, my shoulder curving inward as my chin drops submissively. Each of my fingers bend painfully as a jolt of pain explodes through my chest. Her energy stabs into me, tearing through my flesh, forming a barrier that settles around my heart and mind, a searing shield that makes me grit my teeth against the agony.

"I can't break the bond Orix has formed," she says, voice like honeyed venom. "But this will block him from your mind, preventing him from toying with your emotions."

She pulls her hand away and shakes it off, as if touching me has left a taint on her skin.

"How do I sever the bond entirely?" I rasp, my body still throbbing.

Her laughter echoes through the room, sharp and mocking. "*You* can't. So, don't get ahead of yourself, pet. Let's see if you can survive the shadow realm first." She looks down her nose at me, a final dismissal, before addressing Elyn again. "Your time is drawing near."

The elder wolf bows her head once more. "Yes, but I'm not afraid."

The goddess's smile is almost tender, a seemingly rare hint of affection. "Of course you're not. You're my creation. You might even be my greatest yet. Though, I'm not quite done with you." Aurora presses her palm to Elyn's forehead, and light blue power radiates from her skin before transferring to Elyn, flowing freely between them.

The old wolf's wrinkles begin to smooth, and her long grey strands take on a vibrant white hue. When Elyn opens her eyes, I can still see the centuries of knowledge within them, but there's a youthfulness about her that shouldn't exist any longer.

"This is a gift I won't take for granted, my goddess," Elyn whispers reverently.

Aurora lifts Elyn's chin with a single finger, smirking. "I know." Then, she turns back to me, her gaze sparking with a dangerous promise. "Don't mess this up, or I'll end you right alongside that cockroach."

She begins to dematerialize from my office, but before her essence has fully left, her voice sweeps through the room one last time. "I'll be back."

The threat in those three words is clear, but if all goes as planned, it will only be one for Orix to worry about.

CHAPTER TWENTY-SEVEN

THEO

My wolf prowls within me, restless, eager to enter the shadow realm. It doesn't matter that the world there is full of darkness. I've been living without light for years now. I won't let this place take that from Estee.

She is too good for that fate.

"When I open this portal, the spell used to create the doorway should take you close to Estee, but that doesn't mean you'll find her easily. The souls there will be drawn to your life force. They'll want to attach themselves to you, taking whatever they can from your essence. You'll need to—"

My inner beast snarls, and I face Elyn, still not used to her younger appearance. Her eyes are a deep purple now, and despite her lack of wrinkles, her age is evident by the wisdom in her harsh stare as I cut her off.

"I need to bring Estee back. Nothing more, nothing less," I grumble. "I won't speak or touch the shadows. I won't go after Orix. I just need to get my mate out of that hell."

Her lips flatten, and she shakes her head. "Interrupt me again and see what happens."

The elder wolf pauses, but I say nothing. My frustration may be returning, but there's at least a part of me aware that Elyn is a little too much like Aurora. After their exchange, I know I need to be more careful with both of them.

"Much better," Elyn says. "You'll be tested when you arrive there. The shadows will try to break you, and you can't allow yourself to believe what you see. The visions will feel real, but the moment you actually find Estee, her warmth will be different than anything else there. Until your bond confirms that you've found her, don't trust anything, or you'll both be lost to us."

"I won't lose her," I vow, my voice a growl.

There's been too much loss in my life. Before Estee, before her light, I would've gladly succumbed, but not now. The drive to be more, to be better, for my mate and the future I so badly need with her, that's what I need to focus on.

Me and her. Us. Now and always.

"When you're ready to return," she says, pulling a vial of glowing blue liquid from her coat pocket, "drink this. The magic will bind you to the portal, and I'll reopen it. But only when you're certain. I can't send you there a second time. This is your only chance."

"One is all I need."

Elyn reveals a matching potion and murmurs what I assume to be some sort of activation spell for the portal.

The air in front of me shimmers and distorts, the fabric of reality tearing open to reveal a gaping cavity. The portal hums with a low vibration, pulling at my very core as though it knows what I seek—and what I'm risking. My wolf growls low in my chest, both a warning and a promise. *We're ready.*

Without hesitation, I step through.

The instant I cross the threshold, the temperature drops. The air here is thick and oppressive, alive in a way that feels wrong. Each breath scrapes against my lungs, the shadows already pressing close, their presence suffocating.

The ground beneath me shifts, soft and uneven, like ash that clings to my boots. Every step echoes in the silence, but it isn't empty. The sound is wrong—distorted, layered—as though something unseen moves with me. Watching. Waiting.

This darkness isn't an absence of light. It's a force, sentient and malicious, its whispers piercing my ears. They weave lies and half-truths, promises and accusations, trying to find a crack in my resolve.

I keep moving. My claws dig into my palms, the momentary pain grounding me.

"Estee," I murmur, the bond in my chest flickering faintly, like a distant star in an endless sky. It's there—fragile but real. I press forward, following its pull.

I can't see anything distinct around me as if I'm blind to everything except for the ominous forces and my desire to find my mate. There is nothing significant to tell me if I'm above ground, under the earth, or what kind of terrain I'm dealing with. Just a bleakness filled with dark seams that create something I'm unable to identify.

The harder I try to make sense of where I am, the blacker the air becomes until the shadows begin to shift, and suddenly, I'm not in the void anymore.

I'm back in Selaris. The throne room stands before me, grand and imposing. But it's not as I left it. The once-pristine stone floors are cracked, the banners torn, the air thick with the metallic scent of blood. My mother stands at the center, her figure distorted, her eyes hollow.

"Why did you let this happen?" Her voice is rasping, broken and accusatory. "You were supposed to protect us. Instead, you destroyed us."

"I…" My voice falters, my mind racing. I know this isn't real. Elyn's warning is still fresh, but the guilt of my mother's words burrows deep, cutting parts of me that I've tried to bury.

"You let me die," she continues, stepping closer. Her form twists, her face contorting into something monstrous. "You let them kill me. And for what? A crown you don't deserve? A mate who'll never forgive you?"

"Stop," I growl, but my voice trembles. My wolf scratches from within, urging me to move, to fight, but my feet feel rooted to the spot.

"You can't save her," she hisses. "You can't even save yourself."

Something inside me snaps. This isn't real.

With a roar, I lunge forward, my claws slashing through the illusion. My mother's twisted form bursts into dust, the throne room dissolving into darkness.

I stagger, my breaths ragged, but there's no time to recover.

"Estee." Her name falls weakly from my lips as I step toward her. She's lying in a bed, her back to me. I can't see her face yet, but I know without a doubt that this is the other half of my soul.

With heavy feet, I push through the shadows. I'm only focused on Estee, on picking her up in my arms and getting the hell out of here.

Whispers crawl over me, each one cutting, but none of them stronger than the protective need to retrieve my mate.

"You did this to her."

"If you'd never forced her to come to Selaris, she'd be safe."

"She's better off without you."

"You'll never be worthy of her."

I shake my head, trying to physically push the murmurs from my mind, but when my fingers curl around Estee's shoulder and I pull her toward me, I know they're right.

Her dead eyes look up at me with little emotion and her hands settle over her protruding stomach. "He gave me something you'll never be able to."

"No." The word leaves me, deep and broken. "No, Estee. Don't do this."

Her stare turns black as she smiles up at me. "I didn't. You did this, Theodore. You killed us. Just as you've done to everyone else you've ever cared about."

The howl that builds within me tears from my throat, turning into a roar of agony. Grief, cutting and cold, slices through me. Each death I've ever been responsible for creates a new mark on my soul, reminding me of all that I've done, even when I was only trying to protect them.

I drop to my knees, my head in my hands. "This can't be happening."

"It already has, Theodore. She's forever mine now. You've failed."

My eyes close, and the world around me slows like quicksand, drawing out my demise. I have nothing left to fight for. Without Estee, I'd rather die. The shadows can have—

Something changes. The more I cut myself off from the darkness, crawling back into my own mind, the worse the guilt becomes, but there's something more, waiting and ready.

A flicker of hope. The connection is faint, but the more I search for it, the easier it becomes to grasp.

The bond. My Starlight.

I keep my eyes closed, shutting out the illusions that nearly overtook me. I focus on the tether, on the glow that is Estee. Slowly, the burden of these visions start to dissolve.

With renewed determination, I stand, still keeping my gaze away from the shadows. As I move forward, the trapped souls press in harder now, angry that I've defied them. The air grows heavier, the whispers louder, but I keep walking. With every blind step, Estee's essence grows stronger, pulling me forward like a lifeline.

There's a groan of pain, one that pierces the center of my heart. *Estee.*

Without thinking of the consequences, I open my eyes,

only to be caught in another trick. This one far from painful. Tempting in ways I'm finding hard to ignore.

I'm standing in a field, the sun warm on my skin, a relief after the shadow realm. Estee is there, her laughter ringing out as she runs through the tall grass, her hand resting on her rounded belly.

A child bounds into the picture, his laughter joining hers.

They both turn toward me, beckoning me forward, to be with them in this euphoria. It's a perfect dream, one I never thought I could have. This life, this opportunity calls to me, wrapping around me with soft tendrils of hope.

"Is this what you want?" a voice whispers. "It can be yours. All you must do is let go of the outside world. Release your soul, and you'll have everything you've ever dreamed of."

Release my soul…it sounds so easy.

"Tell me you want this, and it's all yours," the whisper promises.

I hesitate. This can't be real. No matter how much I yearn for this future, it's not right, not like this.

"You don't want me, Papa?" The young boy, whose eyes are a mirror of my own, looks back at me, breaking my heart.

Still, I don't give in, but…*Am I supposed to?*

"Yes, Papa. Come with us."

The idea of what could be settles over me, and I'm ready to give in, to release my soul and go to them, but the moment my thoughts begin to change, the child smiles at me, showcasing sharp, predatory teeth.

This isn't happening.

His laughter swiftly turns into a shriek as he leaps toward Estee, ripping into her throat, painting the field crimson.

"No," I snarl, shutting my eyes once more, allowing the real bond with Estee to grow brighter, cutting through the illusion again. The warmth of her essence is undeniable, pulling me back to reality. I push forward, the darkness recoiling as I focus on her, on our truth.

I have no idea what I'm walking through as the air grows heavier and thicker around me, but I don't dare look. Not until the connection I share with Estee becomes blinding and the scent of pomegranates and orange blossoms replaces the stench of ash.

"Estee," I whisper, my voice cracking.

The bond between us pulses wildly, a desperate, aching rhythm. My heart clenches. She's here, slumped on a stone platform, her body pale and weak. Blood pools around her, yet before I can lose myself once more, I see the faint rise and fall of her chest.

She's alive.

I rush to her side, my hands shaking as I cradle her face. Her eyes flutter open, her gaze unfocused but soft.

"Theo," she whispers, her voice barely audible.

"I'm here," I say, my heart breaking at seeing her like this. "I've got you. I'm taking you home."

"I knew you'd come." Her lips curve into the faintest smile before her eyes close again and she goes limp in my arms. Not wasting another second, I reach into my pocket, pulling out the vial Elyn gave me. I drink it in one gulp, the liquid burning down my throat as the magic binds me to the portal.

The air shifts, our lifeline beginning to form behind me, but then the room grows colder, the shadows around me thickening. A presence looms, dark and oppressive.

"You can't have her," Orix growls, his form materializing from the shadows. His black eyes burn with malice as he steps closer.

I glance behind me; the opening back to Selaris hasn't completely formed. Now that I have Estee, so dependent on me in her weakened state, it's not hard to ignore my need for vengeance, but as Orix comes closer, I get the sense that's not a choice I get to make any longer.

Urgently, I place Estee on the ground to keep her as far from Orix as possible, my lips grazing her cool forehead. "He won't hurt you ever again." I stand, taking a step away from my mate. "Try and stop me."

His laughter is menacing. "You're bold, Theo. But you're nothing without me. Remember that."

Orix lunges, his strike fast and brutal. Pain explodes in my side, where a dagger has left a gaping wound across my ribs. Still, I don't fall. Not even when I sense the bastard trying to get inside my mind again. Instead, I call on my wolf, ready to shift and rip his head from his shoulders. It might not kill him, but as long as I keep him away from Estee, that will be enough for now.

Just as my wolf starts to surge forward, a lavender energy seeps from my injury, stitching my skin back together. I ignore it, but Orix stumbles, his gaze narrowing as he sneers. "*Aurora.*" His voice drips with venom as he steps back, his movements unsteady.

The god's energy presses around me again, but for the first time in three years, he can't enter my mind. He can't steal the information he seeks or manipulate my thoughts. Not with the goddess's essence pulsing within me, a shield he can't penetrate. His hesitation is all I need to get my mate to safety.

I turn and lift Estee, her weight barely registering as I carry her toward the portal. "She'll never be yours, and neither will my heir," I tell him, my voice steady as the energy drawing us back home clings to my skin.

"You'll regret this!" Orix roars, the shadows around him writhing, but he doesn't follow.

We've escaped...but that doesn't mean we've won anything. Not when I get back to my office and find Estee completely slack in my arms, her face pale and lifeless, the rest of her bloodied.

CHAPTER TWENTY-EIGHT

ESTEE

My body is cold, but I don't shiver. This is a soul deep freeze like death itself has crept into my veins. A frost that lingers, unyielding.

Then, a familiar presence stirs within me, providing not just hope, but a sliver of warmth. *Wolf.*

Her steady energy moves through me, calming and grounding. She's with me. We're not dead. Then again, maybe that would be better.

"Estee?"

My heart soars at the sound of his voice. *Theo.* Not Orix. Not the shadows. The memory of him showing up replays in my head, but I can't remember leaving that hell. Gods, please don't tell me we're both stuck there.

I try to open my eyes, but my body doesn't budge and when I try to tell Theo as much, the words don't make it past my lips. *What's wrong with me?*

"I told you," a woman says, her voice smooth and

measured, "she needs rest. What she endured should've killed her. The fact that her heart's still beating is all you need to concern yourself with." Though her voice sounds familiar, I can't tell who she is.

Theo growls in response, a deep, guttural sound full of raw frustration and pain. "She's been *resting* for two days." The ache in his words cuts me deeper than anything Orix could've done. I want to reach for him, reassure him that I'm still here, and the fact that I can't, only increases my frustrations.

Then, I feel him. His warmth breaks through the cold, his hands cradling mine as if they're his lifeline just as they are mine. His heat chases away the frost inch by inch, thawing the parts of me that still seem stuck within the shadow realm.

"Please, Estee." His voice cracks. "I need you."

The tether between us, erratic since the moment I stepped foot in Selaris, flares to life. The bond glows, faint at first, but steady. Its energy spreads through my chest, pushing through the lingering cold and extending into my core, my arms, my legs.

"Don't let go, Theo," I tell him, even though he can't hear me. *"Don't ever let go."*

I picture his charcoal eyes, the silver flecks that appear when he's happy. I remember the way my chest pounded the first time he kissed me, the gentleness in every touch, the way he's been so patient, even when I didn't deserve it.

I imagine a future with him, not running, not hiding, but living for our highest good. Together. The thought fuels me, bringing me back from the edge of oblivion. The more I focus on my mate, the harder I pull on our connection, anchoring it to me, the easier it is to accept that there's no reason to be afraid any longer.

Theo is mine. He's the other half of my soul, and he won't ever hurt me. He couldn't even if he tried.

The knowledge that he would die for me, that we would die for each other and that we never have to be alone again fills me with strength. Not one forged out of a need to survive but a force made of love and compassion.

A bond that can't be broken.

"Mate." The word is garbled in my mind, and I'm not sure I've even spoken until Theo's hold on my hands becomes almost painful.

"Estee. Can you hear me?" His voice is full of hope, trembling with emotion. "Oh, Gods. Please say something else."

"Here." The word is barely a whisper. I struggle to open my eyes. They burn, but I blink through the pain. I need to see him. "Theo."

Carefully, he leans over and slides an arm under me, holding me against his chest as he strokes my back. "I thought I was too late."

"Never," I promise him. "I knew you'd find me."

He presses his lips to the side of my head, his body shaking against mine. For several minutes, we just hold each other, soaking in our nearness while the bond pulses with barely restrained power that seems to be bringing my energy back.

"Well, as fun as this *isn't* for me, I'm going to go," the woman says from behind me.

Theo doesn't lighten his hold on me. "Thank you, Elyn. I owe you my life."

Elyn? The smooth voice doesn't sound anything like the elder wolf. But before I can figure that oddity out, a door bangs shut.

My senses begin to return to me. I can feel the softness of the mattress beneath me, the heat from my body being retained by a thick comforter, and the steadying beat of Theo's heart, soothing any lingering worries.

He finally pulls back, and my vision is clear once again. Theo's eyes are tense and darker than they should be even though he smiles lovingly at me. "Are you okay? Do you want something to eat or drink? Drea washed and dressed you, but I can start the shower if you want one. Or I can call for—"

I place my hand over his, stopping him mid-ramble. "I don't need anything other than what I have right now." As I sit up, my head spins a little, but there's at least no pain.

When I glance at my stomach, searching for the wound Orix inflicted, it's nowhere to be found. "I expected there to be a scar."

Theo's fingers brush over the smooth skin. "Thanks to Elyn, there shouldn't be any trace of that hell left in you, but you might still be tired. You were filled with dark energy when I got you back here. I thought it would kill you, but Elyn said that's what was actually keeping you alive."

Once again, I find myself indebted to that wolf and I'm not sure how I feel about that, but that's something for me to figure out later. As my heart races, I know the only thing I need right now is Theo. Well, and maybe a few answers.

"How did you get me out of there? Did you have to

fight him?" I give him a once-over, but there's nothing of immediate concern.

"He came after us, stabbed me, but thanks to Aurora's essence, Orix became distracted," Theo explains. "I didn't waste a second getting you out of there once I had the chance. I'm so sorry I let this happen to you."

His eyes pinch closed, and I lift my hand, cupping his cheek. "This is just as much my fate as it is yours. You couldn't have stopped this from happening even if you knew he was going to take me."

"He wouldn't have taken you if you weren't my mate." Theo's head drops further, agony in every line of his face.

"Would you rather I wasn't your mate then? Because that's the only way I might've been safe," I challenge, but I still let him hear my compassion.

That finally breaks his self-reproach and has him holding tightly to my arms. "There isn't anyone else in all the worlds that could be more perfect for me. I just hate that you've been put in danger because of my choices."

"Without those choices, good or bad, you wouldn't be who you are right now," I tell him sincerely, holding his stare. "That would be worse than anything else. I know I did my best to push you away and maybe even make you feel like a failure over the state of Selaris, but I see you now, Theo. You've always done what you thought was best, and nobody should fault you for that, least of all me."

He takes a shuddering breath, his body shaking as he draws me close. "I thought you'd hate me for this."

"I might have wanted to, but that had nothing to do with you and everything to do with my own fears," I say, steady and sure. "I finally feel you, us. What we can and will be."

Theo breathes me in, his lips grazing my neck as his shoulders drop. "I've been dying to hear that since the moment I sensed your arrival."

I lean back, needing to see his face again. The strong lines of his jaw, the deep care in his eyes, and the love he exudes even when he doesn't realize it. My strength is returning with every shared touch.

"I'd say I'm sorry that we were robbed of that moment, of us realizing at the same time that we're mates, but I'm not." I offer him a smile. "We've each been through hell in our own ways. Our story wouldn't be ours if it was easy, and now, I can appreciate you even more."

He blinks, his head seeming to shake with awe. "My Starlight."

We push toward each other, my need to taste and touch my mate growing more insatiable by the second. Theo's urgency seems to match my own as he fumbles with the buttons of my silk pajama shirt.

He nips at my neck, and his low growls send shivers down my spine, all the way to my toes and back. "Are you sure?"

I'm already tugging at his pants, but I stop to look into his eyes, holding his gaze. "I've only ever counted on myself. It's been me against the world for centuries. Even with Isla, I've felt alone." I place a light kiss on his lips and settle my hand over his chest. "Being in the shadow realm, I wanted to give up, but then I thought of you, and there was only peace. I knew you'd come for me, but more than that, I needed you to. Not just to survive, but so that I can finally live. You are mine, Theo Northcroft. There are no more doubts, no more waiting. It's just me and you, now and always, if you'll have me."

He wraps his fingers around mine and nods. "Always. For now and every lifetime after this, it will always be us. You'll never be alone again."

Our mouths crash together, and even though our bond can't technically be completed without a ceremony for the gods, our connection grows brighter with every shared touch. Our energies reach for one another with desperate need, just as our bodies do.

We strip free from our clothing, and I fall back onto Theo's bed, a place I've never been before but suddenly have no desire to ever leave.

He starts to lower himself, kissing his way down my chest, and as much as I know every part of him will likely make the stars explode behind my eyes, I need him inside me before I shatter.

"I've waited too long for this moment," I say breathily, bringing him closer for another kiss.

Without needing more explanation, he slides his hand between us and his fingers part my center, making me jump from the feather-light touch.

Gods, this is going to be quick.

"You're utterly divine," he whispers, his stare staying on mine as he guides himself toward me.

I reach up, cradling his face and holding him close while he pushes forward. My hips come up, meeting him in the middle, and my legs fall open, needing him as close as possible in this moment.

Theo kisses me, a gentle demand. He inches into me,

stretching and filling me completely. I suck in a breath, adjusting to him, my moans of pleasure the only sound in the bedroom.

His teeth scrape over my neck, causing me to clench harder. "I could stay here forever," he whispers in my ear.

I slide my hands over his back, encouraging him to move again. As much as I agree with that statement, I might also combust, and not in a good way, if we stay still.

His chuckle makes my heart swell. "As you wish, mate."

Our hips move together, slow and purposefully at first. The glow of our bond pulses within my mind as our bodies collide, and I almost expect a blast of magic to ignite between us, but no such luck.

Delicious tension starts to make my toes curl as he moves over me, kissing every inch that his mouth can reach without breaking our closeness. The coiling of my muscles travels slowly up my legs and around to my spine before striking deep in my core.

I meet his thrusts with renewed eagerness that Theo easily matches. He stops kissing me, his full attention on my face, his eyes staring into mine. "I love you."

Those three words detonate the last of my restraints. My nails dig into his shoulders and my back arches, pushing my chest into his. My heart feels as though it might break through my skin at any moment.

My lungs work overtime to catch their next gasp of air and spots fill my vision as I blink rapidly, desperately needing to see my mate's face once again.

When he comes back into view, I give him the biggest smile I'm capable of considering my current state and say what my heart was feeling long before I was ready to admit it. "I love you, too."

He lightly pushes my hair back, and his grin matches my own. "My mate."

"As it always should've been."

He brushes his lips over the tip of my nose. "As it always will be now."

CHAPTER TWENTY-NINE

THEO

Dawn breaks, the golden light filtering through my heavy drapes, softening the shadows that clung to the room last night. The air is quiet except for Estee's steady breathing. She's resting once again, her chest rising and falling in a slow rhythm that soothes the storm inside me.

I lie beside her, not touching her, though the pull of our bond makes it almost impossible to stay still. I don't want to disturb her. The faint pink on her cheeks is proof that she's healed, but the image of her pale, broken form in the shadow realm lingers. It's burned into my memory, as though Orix left his mark on me as well.

She stirs slightly, her body unconsciously shifting closer to mine, and my heart constricts. I focus only on her, my gaze tracing the lines of her face, the softness of her lips, the curve of her cheeks. She looks peaceful, and I wonder how long it's been since she's truly felt safe. Even when she arrived in Selaris, there was an edge to her. A hardness that refused to shatter, but one that provided her with a strength that acted as a barrier between her heart and the world. A place that constantly let her down.

I've spent years running from my mistakes, from the lives I failed to save, from the promises I never fulfilled. I thought that by keeping everyone at arm's length, I could avoid hurting them. But I see now that all I did was damage them in a different way.

My eyes fall closed, and I let out a shaky breath. With Estee's presence beside me and the bond that now flows freely between us, waiting to be solidified, each is a reminder that I still have time to make things right. She's given me a chance I might not have deserved before, but I won't waste this opportunity. Not for me or Estee.

I'll earn her love, not through words but actions. I'll rebuild Selaris, not for the crown, but for the people who've been waiting far too long for a leader to rise.

As if she senses the shift in my thoughts, Estee stirs again, her eyes fluttering open. Her gaze meets mine, and for a moment, the weight of my guilt lifts. She smiles, a small, sleepy curve of her lips that ignites warmth in my chest.

"Good morning," she murmurs, her voice soft and laced with exhaustion.

I brush a strand of hair from her face then rest my hand against her cheek. "Good morning, Starlight."

She leans into my touch, her trust in me clear. A quiet determination settles over me as I hold her gaze. My past will no longer define me. Each of my choices, whether right or wrong, will guide me, shaping me into someone better.

Because for the first time in years, I believe I can be better. And that belief starts with Estee.

"There's something different about you. I saw it last night, but I was a bit distracted." Estee's cheeks flush. "Your presence is even stronger now. Did something happen while I was gone?"

I run the back of my fingers lightly down the side of her face and momentarily lose myself in her golden eyes. "Several things happened, actually. Some not so great, but others were better. I nearly lost my mind when I realized you were gone, but I knew I had to stay strong if I was going to find you."

Her gaze hardens. "He took me from inside the castle. I was on my way to you, intent on spending the rest of the day with you, when Orix showed up. He took all my senses from me until I woke up in that cave."

I rub a hand over the tension gathering in her shoulders. "He won't ever hurt you again. I know what I need to do now."

She sits up further in bed, her brow lifting. "And that would be…?"

"Taking my power back." My wolf stirs at the reminder. "Elyn revealed several things the night I went to get you, including that Orix has been stealing god energy from me."

Estee's hand settles over my chest. "Did you get it back? Is that what I'm sensing now?"

"Just as I was ready to enter the shadow realm, Aurora showed up."

The growl that escapes from her makes me smile

almost as much as her jealousy. "She better not have touched you."

I lean over to kiss her forehead. "No, Mate. She didn't. At least not in that way. The goddess seems to have a thing for Asher, which I'm sure makes Isla react as you've just done."

"If she hadn't brought our mother back to us, I'd have been helping my sister plot Aurora's death." Estee grimaces then looks back at me. "What did she do to you?"

"It's actually what Elyn said and what Aurora did that's given me clarity." I reach for her, intertwining our fingers. "Well, them and having you back. The elder wolf told me that I'm more god than wolf thanks to my ancestry. Because of that, I was able to become the alpha of my own pack before coming here, but that's also what drew Orix to me."

I explain his banishment and the conclusions I've come to based on what's been revealed over the last few days, and ending with what Aurora said about Orix needing our heir to one day be free of his ties to the shadow realm.

She doesn't seem as surprised as I expected. "I took a risk while I was there, trying to get him to reveal whatever his intentions might be. He brought up our future child and how he intended to claim him, but I didn't realize…" Her eyes darken and she vibrates with determination. "That god won't ever touch our child or any other."

I brush my fingers over her cheek, my touch seeming to calm her slightly. "No, he won't. Orix might still have my power, but he won't ever be able to control me again. Aurora's block seems to have made sure of that, and I'm going to find a way to get the energy he stole from me back. I won't let him grow stronger or escape the prison he deserves to be in."

Estee's hold on me tightens as she nods. "*We're* going to find a way. You're not alone anymore, Theo."

"I know." I pull her into a hug, holding her close as I breathe in her sweet scent. "And neither are you. We'll do this together, starting with apologizing to the pack. I need to make some announcements, and I'd love it if you were by my side for them."

She leans back until I can see her brilliant smile. "You won't find me anywhere else."

A promise I won't ever take for granted. Not now or a thousand years from now.

CHAPTER THIRTY

ESTEE

I don't think I've ever been more at peace. Theo gets up to order us breakfast, and I take a few minutes to simply be in this moment. To soak up all that's happened since I woke up yesterday, and even more so, since I arrived in Selaris nearly three weeks ago.

I went from disliking Theo—believing him lazy and cowardly—to knowing my heart will never belong to another. And now I see that most of his choices, even the questionable ones, were only for the benefit of others.

We spent all evening and well into the night wrapped in each other's arms, exploring one another and enjoying the free flow of our bond—which I hope to have finalized today. I know that as king and future queen, there's supposed to be a big ceremony. Nothing about our situation has been typical, though, and I don't think either of us wants to wait.

Theo plans to address the pack, and I want our official mating to be one of the topics. While this is a private matter, it's also symbolic. The people deserve to know that we're making strides toward stability for Selaris.

Gods. I'm going to be queen.

I chuckle to myself. Oh, how things have changed. I arrived here hellbent on hating every second before my swift return to Polaris, and now, I don't ever want to leave this island.

Well, that's a lie. I haven't forgotten the recent threats to Isla. If anyone so much as harms a hair on my sister's head, I'll hunt them to the ends of every world in existence. And I'll have Theo by my side as I do so.

Thinking of her has me reaching for the phone, but before I can pick up the receiver, there's a soft presence in my mind: Drea.

"I know you're resting, but I just need to know you're okay." Her worried voice whispers through my mind, a bit of a shock since that's not something she's done since we became friends even though we're part of the same pack, but also not surprising considering all that's happened.

Sensing her outside of Theo's suite, I slide out from under the thick maroon comforter. *"I'm coming to let you in."*

"I thought we were going to eat breakfast in bed." Theo's pout is adorable as he walks toward me, wearing only loose black pajama pants.

Grinning, I reach for his robe and cover myself before we can get distracted with one another again. "We have forever to laze in bed all morning, but our responsibilities have come knocking."

Theo glances toward the front room of his suite, his

brows furrowing. "Drea?" he guesses. "I can't remember exactly, but I might not have been kind to her before."

I pat his chest and kiss his cheek. "Considering the circumstances, I'm sure she understands. I'm going to show her I'm okay, then I need to call my sister. Does Isla even know I was taken?"

Theo's eyes widen. "I'm so sorry, Estee. I never thought to call her. I was so focused on you that I didn't consider your family."

I grab his shoulders and offer him a sweet smile. "It's okay. Honestly, with all they have going on in Polaris, it's probably better she didn't know. At least Asher was able to reach Aurora for you."

He sighs with relief as he leans in to kiss my forehead. "I'll go shower so you and Drea can catch up. Extend an apology for me, if one's needed." He starts to walk away then turns back to me, his heady gaze traveling over my barely dressed body. "I've also already reached out to Jerome. He'll be coordinating moving your belongings to this room." Theo leaves no room for negotiating, turning to enter the ensuite bathroom before I can respond.

His assertion leaves a warmth in my chest, and I walk out of the bedroom grinning.

Everything's going to be okay. Hell, it already is.

I open the door for Drea, and before I can say a word, she launches herself at me, wrapping me in a tight hug. "You have no idea how good it is to see you."

Returning her embrace, I laugh lightly. "I missed you, too."

She pulls back then studies me intently, her gaze sweeping over me as though assessing every inch. "Are you okay? I probably should've asked before assaulting you, but I couldn't help myself. I've been going mad with worry. Theo never left this room, so I couldn't get any updates. I spent hours pacing the halls, waiting for any sign you were going to be okay."

Taking her hand, I lead her to the couch, shutting the door behind us. For the first time, I get a proper look at Theo's suite. The walls are painted in deep grey tones, accented by ornate silver detailing that exudes regality. A plush navy-blue rug softens the dark wood floors, while a stone fireplace crackles quietly in the corner. The space is understated yet undeniably luxurious—a reflection of Theo himself.

"Thank you for worrying about me," I say as we settle onto the cushions of the dark leather couch, sitting close together. "I'm fine now. Maybe better than I've ever been."

Doing my best to condense everything that's happened, covering the things I'd originally kept from her, I finally fill Drea all the way in.

By the time I'm done, and back to happier topics, such as accepting Theo as the other half of my soul, Drea is squealing, her knees bouncing with uncontained joy. "You deserve this, Estee. In case you didn't already know, I hope you do now. And it's good to hear that the king isn't as much of a monster as we both thought."

Laughing, I shake my head. "Not even close. I almost wish I'd kept an open mind before, but everything's worked out the way it was supposed to. I feel confident about that. Now, we just need to make sure Orix can't ever hurt anyone else again."

Her expression hardens, her eyes darkening. "He won't

get away with this. God or not, he'll pay for what he's done."

"That he will."

There's a knock at the door, and my stomach grumbles at the unmistakable aroma wafting into the room. *Bacon.*

Drea shakes her head at me playfully and stands. "I'll leave you to your breakfast. Thank you for seeing me and sharing. I know we haven't been…friends for long, but I promise you can trust me."

I get up and hug her tightly. "If I didn't already believe that, you wouldn't be in this room right now. And we *are* friends. There's no need for hesitation. I also hope you'll consider staying in Selaris with Orion. I have plans for us that include all kinds of mischief if you're interested."

There's a twinkle in her eyes that I'm sure matches my own. "Those kids already made that choice for me. There's no way I can leave them."

A pang of guilt strikes me. How could I not have asked about Keera and the others?

"They're doing okay?" I press before she goes. "Did you tell them I would have come to see them if it was at all possible?" Panic claws at my throat and my hands start to shake. Gods, I hope they don't think I've forsaken them.

Drea steadies me with a firm grip on my arms. "Calm that mind of yours. I told them you'd fallen ill and didn't want to get them sick. Keera doesn't believe me, but she also caught a glimpse of Theo's wolf running through the castle. She knows something happened, but it seems making sure the younger ones have a home is what matters most to her."

Of course it is. There's so much to be done but making time to visit the children just moved to the top of my list.

"Thank you for taking care of them," I tell Drea as she opens the door to leave.

"It's been my pleasure."

In the hallway, one of the staff members waits with a cart of food. I exchange goodbyes with Drea as he brings it in.

Theo comes toward me, fully dressed and commanding the room like the king he was always meant to be. His finely pressed white dress shirt clings to his broad shoulders, the tailored black slacks accentuating the effortless grace with which he moves. His strides are measured, deliberate, and every inch of him radiates authority.

My stomach aches with a hunger that's no longer for bacon.

I barely register the quiet coming and going of the staff as Theo prowls toward me, his stormy gaze locked on mine. Each step carries an unspoken promise, and by the time he's standing before me, I'm breathless.

"Mine."

The singular word comes from deep in his chest, his voice filled with possession and devotion. His hands find the lapels of my robe, and with a swift tug, he jerks me forward until we're flush against each other.

Heat pools in my chest as I reach for him, my fingers curling into the crisp fabric of his shirt. There will never be enough moments with this man. I'll never tire of his presence, his strength and determination, his love.

The tray of food sits forgotten behind us as I rise onto

my toes, seeking his mouth. His scent—crisp yet earthy—wraps around me, intoxicating my senses. I decide right then that devouring him will be all the sustenance I'll ever need.

That is until his need-filled growls turn harsher, more frustrated. His fingers tighten around my waist and his sigh of disappointment tells me reality has come crashing back into the room.

"What is it?" I ask, staring into his loving gaze.

"Queen Sloane is here," he murmurs. "As much as I'd prefer to stay in this room with you, we shouldn't ignore her."

He's right. I forgot Asher said to send for her, and her arrival serves as a reminder that there are still things to be done. Our days need to be reserved for responsibilities. Night will fall soon enough and then we can lose ourselves in each other all over again.

"I'll go back to my old room to get dressed while you greet her," I tell him, taking a deep breath to calm my libido.

Theo leans in, and what I expect to be a brief kiss quickly steals the air from my lungs. His tongue sweeps against mine, his lips coaxing a response I have no power to withhold. By the time he pulls back, I'm dazed and clinging to him for support.

"I'll go with you," he declares, his tone leaving no room for argument. "Jerome's already bringing her to my office. We have time to eat first and then we'll go get your clothes."

"You don't have to—"

He cuts me off, his eyes darkening. "I'm not ready to let you out of my sight."

I can't blame him there, and truthfully, I don't want to. "Then don't," I say softly, lacing my fingers with his. A smile pulls at my lips.

It doesn't matter what awaits us or what's to come, as long as at the end of every day I get to lie next to this man. Nothing in all the worlds can take that from us.

Not even a banished god with a chip on his shoulder.

CHAPTER THIRTY-ONE

ESTEE

Jerome awaits us outside Theo's office, a picture of composure marred only by the exhaustion on his face. His grey slacks and maroon three-button jacket are immaculately tailored, as always, but the dark circles beneath his eyes tell me he hasn't slept in days.

He bows slightly as we approach. "Your Majesty. Your Highness."

I step forward before Theo can respond and lightly grab Jerome's elbow, softening my tone but remaining firm. "Take the rest of the day off, Jerome. Go home and rest. If you return to work before sunrise tomorrow, you'll be relieved of your duties for even longer."

He blinks, visibly startled, before glancing at Theo as if seeking confirmation.

Theo nods in agreement. "Estee's right. You haven't stopped since she went missing, and I've relied too heavily on your support. Go home to your family. If something urgent comes up, I'll contact you."

Jerome hesitates, his loyalty evident. "Sire, I don't mind—"

Theo shakes his head, silencing him. "You've done more than enough for both of us and for Selaris. That's an order, Jerome."

Finally, he bows deeply. "Yes, my king. Princess Estee." He turns on his heel and walks away, his steps measured but heavy with fatigue.

Once the advisor goes around the corner, Theo turns to me. "Thank you for seeing the things I don't. I should've sent him home long before now."

"We're more than just mates," I tell him with a smile. "We're partners who are going to balance each other out for many years to come."

He kisses my forehead. "Yes, we most certainly are. Now let's greet our guest."

Theo opens the door to his office, and we enter together. I've yet to meet Queen Sloane, and when I find her lounging in Theo's chair as if it were carved just for her, I'm not the least bit disappointed by her commanding presence.

She exudes authority without effort, and her icy blue eyes are razor-sharp as they assess us. The faintest curve of her lips could almost be called a smile, but there's a sharpness to her expression, a silent challenge that accompanies her grace.

"King Theo. Princess Estee," she says, her voice smooth as velvet, carrying an undertone of strength. "It's a pleasure to finally meet you both."

As she rises, her movements are deliberate and fluid, like a predator surveying its domain. Her ebony hair cascades past her shoulders, glinting under the light. Atop her head rests a silver crown, its intricate twists forming seven distinct points that glimmer without the aid of jewels. Her gown, a deep purple masterpiece of silk, clings to her nearly-six-foot frame, accentuating her regal presence.

I accept her outstretched hand, the warmth of her palm contrasting the coolness of her gaze. "The pleasure is ours. Thank you for coming all this way."

Her eyes flicker to Theo, narrowing slightly. "When Jerome reached out, relaying King Asher's suggestion that our two kingdoms collaborate, I found myself intrigued. Especially when so few details were offered."

"Allow us to fill you in." Theo gestures to the four chairs still in his office.

I nearly expect Queen Sloane to take the bigger of the options, but she shows her respect by selecting the smaller one.

We settle in across from her, still holding hands, remaining a united front as he speaks, recounting his history with Orix, hopefully for the last time.

Queen Sloane gives nothing away as she listens, and when he's finished, she stands as if to leave, keeping her hands poised in front of her and face devoid of emotion. "The gods are fickle beings. Even trusting Aurora is a calculated risk, one I wouldn't take lightly." Her lips flatten. "For centuries, our kingdoms have fought separately for survival." She pauses, her gaze meeting mine and Theo's as we wait for her rejection. "I think it's time that changed."

Relief floods my chest, though I keep my emotions in

check. Not that I believe we *need* her help to end this nightmare, but with everything Theo's just shared, I wouldn't have felt good about her walking away with that new information either.

"This god that's tied to you. Orix," she continues, remaining standing. "He was banished from the god world, made to feel less than for who knows how long, and it seems he now seeks not only retribution but acknowledgement of his power, yes?"

"He's mentioned wanting to rule all of Lunara," Theo confirms. "So, yes, I'd agree with that."

"Then deny him the very thing he craves," she says as if that will be the easiest thing to do. "Show him that what he's done has no effect on you any longer. That you're living your best life, thriving regardless of what's been done. You need some sort of grand gesture, a celebration of what's to come. Maybe the crowning of the new queen would be sufficient."

"What about a grand ball?" I suggest as an idea begins to form. "Not that my crowning shouldn't be celebrated, but if we put on an event to commemorate defeating Orix, I bet that would more than ruffle him."

The visiting queen offers us a wicked grin as she points at me. "Now that is an excellent idea. There's still a battle to be won, but your escape from the shadow realm is a victory to be thrown in his face. Lure him back here, where he relies on the energy of others to be strong, and take back what's yours."

Theo remains quiet a beat longer before he nods in agreement. "The last time I addressed some of the pack,

I'd mentioned a ball to welcome Estee as future queen. We can use that, combined with her safe and triumphant return, to invite the pack into the castle for a celebration, but their safety needs to come above all else. We can't put them at risk."

Sloane takes her seat again, still grinning. "I've been fighting men like him for over two hundred years. His eyes will be on the prize of power. Your pack, even present in the same room, will be of no consequence to a monster like Orix, as long as they're not attempting to be a threat. Command them to stand down, and they'll be safe."

She talks as if she's spent a lifetime not only ruling as queen but as a warrior. Suddenly, I find myself especially eager to get to know her.

I have a feeling I can learn more than strategy from her.

OUR TIME WITH QUEEN SLOANE PROVES MORE PRODUCTIVE than I anticipated. Discussions flow easily—strategies, contingencies, and ways to ensure the pack's safety take precedence. Sloane speaks with an authority that demands attention, yet there's a genuine concern in her words, especially when the topic shifts to the people of Selaris. By the time we've finalized our initial plans, I'm struck by her ability to command and inspire.

Theo and I escort her to the guest wing, where she'll be staying during her visit. I can't help but admire how he guides her through the halls, his movements purposeful yet respectful. When we reach her quarters, I realize my old room—apparently, the second-best in the castle—will serve as her temporary accommodations. All my belongings have already been moved, so we leave Queen Sloane to rest after her long journey and head back to our room.

As much as I'd like to seclude myself with Theo, I have to make a phone call that's long overdue.

He kisses my forehead as I sit near the phone. "I'll be in the next room, dealing with a few other matters I've ignored of late."

I grimace. He's once again disappointed his people, this time because I was missing. We're going to have plenty of damage control to do later, but until tonight's pack meeting, I'm going to focus on the things I can do something about.

The phone operator connects me to Polaris castle, then to Isla and Asher's room. When the voice on the other end of the line isn't either of them, my stomach drops.

"The royal suite, how may I help you?" a woman says.

"This is Princess Estee," I tell her. "I'm looking for Queen Isla."

She clears her throat. "Of course, Your Highness. She and the king are in the observatory and have asked not to be disturbed."

"Oh." Part of me wants to have them interrupted, but if anything with Isla has worsened and she's finally having a moment of peace...

"Unless you called," the woman quickly adds. "If you

don't mind holding, I'll make sure to let them know you're waiting."

"Thank you." I grip the phone. "I'll hold as long as it takes."

Suddenly, I realize how much I miss my sister and how worried I should've been about her these last few days. There's no telling if the person sending the threats is someone right under their noses. Someone who could've been on the ship with them or anywhere within the castle the day they got back.

I nibble on the inside of my cheek and pick at my manicured nails as I wait for someone to come back to the phone. Minutes tick painfully by, and I regret not putting an urgency on the handmaiden that answered to get Isla on the line.

At least until I hear my sister's giggle and the deep timber of Asher's murmurings just before she says, "Hello, my dearest sister. Were you too busy plotting a war yesterday to care about my safe return to Polaris when I called in the morning?"

That's why she's not worried about my previous silence. I didn't consider the time it would take them to get home. She has no idea anything happened to me, and hesitation chokes me. She sounds happy, a far cry from when she left Selaris several days ago, but when she ultimately finds out, she'll be furious with me if I keep it from her.

"I was, well, unconscious for a decent part of yesterday and didn't know you called," I say sheepishly, while trying to make light of the situation.

"What?" The sharpness in her voice snaps through the line. "Explain. Now."

I glance at the door separating me from Theo, drawing strength from his proximity before I answer, my words coming out rapid fire once they start. "Orix kidnapped me the day you headed home, and I was in the shadow realm with him for over twelve hours before Theo rescued me, but by the time he got to me, I was in a bad way. Elyn fixed me up, and after a couple days, I woke up, accepted my bond with Theo, and everything's on its way to being okay again. So, nothing to worry about here."

Asher groans in the background as Isla snaps at him. "I told you we should've gone back. Leaving her alone was a mistake. Get the ship ready to sail again."

"Don't you dare put yourself at risk," I tell her with more authority. "By the time you get here, this will likely already be over. Plus, we have plenty of help. Queen Sloane showed up today and according to Theo, when Aurora made her brief appearance, she gifted Elyn with so much energy that the elder wolf looks like she's in her thirties, instead of on her deathbed."

Asher mutters, "That goddess shouldn't be messing with our wolves," but that seems to be the least of Isla's worries.

"You were kidnapped, and *nobody* called me?" Her snarls echo through the phone so loudly that Theo must hear because he's at my side by the time she finishes her next sentence. "I'm your sister and the queen of Polaris. How dare they keep this from me? I'm going to be there in two days, and when I arrive, I expect—"

Theo takes the phone from me. "I owe you an apology,

Isla. I meant no disrespect. I was so out of my mind with fury that I wasn't thinking clearly. Then, when I got her back and she didn't wake right away, I was scared to leave her side for any reason. I should've asked someone else to notify you. There's no excuse, but it wasn't the least bit intentional."

I listen carefully for Isla's response, but it seems my mate has rendered her speechless, which isn't something that happens very often and has me grinning.

"What's most important," I say, "is that Theo did bring me home, I'm okay, and at some point today, we're going to be officially bonded."

This isn't something I've actually discussed with Theo yet, and the shock on his face makes me laugh, which only gets louder as my sister stumbles over her words.

"You're…the two of you…how did this…what now?"

"If it makes you feel better, Theo didn't know until just now either." I reach for him, holding his hand tightly as I speak to my sister. "Everything is clear now. I know being kidnapped by an insane god shouldn't be a good thing, but I can feel the bond with Theo, and I know what I want now. What I'll always want, and that's him."

I'm saying the words to him as much as to Isla. I need them both to know that I'm all in and there are no doubts in my mind any longer. This is where I was always supposed to be. Where I'll stay.

Asher cuts in. "What your sister means to say is that she's happy for you and wishes we could be there, but we understand your urgency and know that everything's going to be perfect for the two of you."

"Yeah, that," Isla adds with a bit more enthusiasm.

Though she doesn't let us completely off the hook. "But I'm still pissed, and I expect a two- week visit from the two of you when this mess with Orix is dealt with."

"Consider it done," Theo says, still keeping his bright stare on me. "Have the threats there been dealt with?"

Isla sighs heavily. "I think so. We have a lead on who might've sent the notes. If we're right, there's nothing to worry about, but we're being cautious until we're sure."

I want to ask more, but Theo cuts in again. "Great. We're going to get bonded now. Estee will call you tomorrow. Or in a few days, if I have my way."

"Seriously? I still have questions, like—"

Theo hangs up, and I shake my head, my heart never happier. "She's going to kill you for that."

"She'll have to get through you first." He throws me over his shoulder, heading for the door. "Cecil is making preparations. He'll get Sloane to perform the blessing, since we need an alpha and I can't do it myself. We'll be bonded within the next half hour."

My light-hearted laughter echoes through the room as I dangle upside down. "Are you afraid I'll change my mind?"

The air whooshes out of my lungs as I'm jerked back to my feet, suddenly standing in front of Theo. "Am I rushing you? The way you looked at me and what you said... I thought..."

I reach up, holding his face securely between my palms. "This is exactly what I want. Me and you, now and forever. Let's do this."

"Oh, thank gods." This time he grabs my hand, and we exit the suite together, practically running through the castle to get back downstairs. I'm not sure where we're going, and I don't bother to ask.

Theo not only has my heart already, but he has my trust. Whatever happens next, it doesn't matter as long as we're together.

CHAPTER THIRTY-TWO

THEO

The moment Estee said that she wanted to be officially bonded today, my mind went into overdrive. Jerome being unavailable wasn't ideal, but I'm getting better at remembering that I'm not ruling this kingdom alone. I have people who can and even want to help. Cecil was my next thought, and I reached out to him. He's almost always around the castle, overseeing the staff, which might actually make him perfect for what I've asked of him.

After, giving him instructions and asking him to prepare Sloane for the ceremony. I'm not the least bit nervous about what comes next, only eager to never let my incredible mate leave my side again.

With Estee seeming fully on board, we race through the castle, and I take her through one of the back exits. Cecil has only had minutes to prepare, but I haven't asked for much, so I hope he's ready.

Outside, the sun is high in the sky, its warmth

spreading over my skin as if Lunara itself is blessing this moment.

Estee beams up at me as we rush across the expansive backyard. "Are you going to give me any details? Should we at least have changed clothes?"

I pause momentarily, glancing down at our outfits. While they're presentable for day-to-day activities, she's right. I'm rushing this. Not thinking all the details through. My enthusiasm just might ruin everything.

"We can go back and do this later," I tell her, frowning. "Spontaneity isn't the same as special, and you deserve a day you'll never forget."

She shakes her head and squeezes my hand. "I don't need perfection, Theo. I just need you. I was only curious and because of a twisted thought that had me wondering if the gods will be displeased that we aren't making this a spectacle for them. But the answers don't really matter. We're doing this now, and if for some reason, they don't approve, we'll go through the ceremony as many times as it takes until they do." Her intense gaze holds me hostage as she finishes. "I will never give up on us."

I draw her closer, breathing her in. "Thank you. I promise I'm going to be the mate you deserve. I'll be strong and sure and protect you with my life. I just never want to disappoint you."

"Save the mushy stuff for the ceremony," she says lightly, pushing my chin up as she looks at me again. "We have a bond to solidify."

This time, Estee takes the lead, and I merely point her in the right direction. We pass the old gardens and through the stone gates to the spot I've chosen—one I've grown fond of over the last year.

The tree before us is ancient, its roots spreading wide into the earth like veins carrying life to the island. Its trunk is impossibly large, with bark marked by centuries of growth and wisdom. The canopy of leaves gently sways in the breeze, casting fractured light over the red petals I've asked Cecil to have scattered over the grass.

The air hums with energy here, a vibrant peace that resonates deep within my chest. Each time I've come to visit this place, I've felt anchored to Selaris. Now, I hope it will be the same for Estee.

Cecil comes around the other side of the tree with Sloane not far behind. They wait for us by the small table stand that's been brought out here, on it waits a bouquet of tiny maroon blossoms, native to our home.

"This is," Estee looks up at me again, her eyes glossy, "everything I could've asked for."

I kiss her forehead, smiling as any fear of disappointing her finally leaves me. "Are you ready?"

"More than." She wraps an arm around my waist, and I tuck her into my side, keeping her close as we approach Cecil and Sloane.

"Your Majesty," Cecil greets us first, looking pristine in his grey suit and red tie. "I hope everything is to your liking."

I nod. "Just as I knew it would be. Thank you."

"You're most welcome, Sire." He bows once more. "I'll work on notifying the pack of the meeting taking place next."

As he leaves, I make a mental note to speak with

Jerome about adding Cecil to my advisory council—one I haven't actually had since becoming king but could certainly use.

Queen Sloane steps forward, her regal presence commanding attention. She's changed into a gown of shimmering silver that matches her crown. Though, even her powerful energy can't tear my gaze from Estee's for long.

"You two continue to surprise me," she says, her face managing to hide her emotions almost too well. "Now, let's see what the gods think, shall we?"

"Please," Estee says. The bright rays of the sun make her golden eyes sparkle, and the longer she stares at me, the more confident I am that every day after this will only be better than the last.

Sloane glances around and grins. "Normally, there's an audience to speak to when I'm doing this ceremony, and I have more time to plan, but this might actually be better." She clasps her hands together and stands taller. "Gods, we come before you, accepting the fate that has brought these two shifters together. King Theo Northcroft and Princess Estee Blackwood wish to accept the gift they've been given and ask for their souls to be bound together, now and for all eternity."

There's a pause, and my shoulders tense, waiting for any sort of sign that we're being heard. When there is none, Sloane proceeds.

"This bonding will not only strengthen these two individuals but will also bring unity to Selaris," she declares as if she knows more than we've shared. "This moment is more than tradition. With your blessing, this will be the beginning of a foundation on which to build this kingdom's future. One that will bring peace to many."

Sloane's words hold significance, the power behind them pressing in and around us, but my focus remains on my mate. Our eyes stay locked as we hold each other's hands, the intensity of our connection growing bright within my chest as the seconds pass.

Wind kicks up around us, swaying the branches above our heads. The ground vibrates with energy that feels as though the ancient tree is offering her approval of the vows being spoken.

"Do you feel it?" Estee whispers, the rapid beat of her pulse calling to me.

I forget her question nearly as quickly as she asks, lost in the depths of her golden eyes.

"I believe he does," Sloane answers for me with a wry grin before continuing. "Your bond is sacred. Through hardship, through love, through the trials that await you, this connection will be your home. It is your responsibility to treat it as such, showing one another the respect and care you need. Now it is your turn to speak your vows not only to your mate, but to let the gods bear witness to the commitment you make."

I draw a deep breath, the words having formed in my heart long before they ever leave my lips. "Estee, my Starlight, from the moment you arrived, you turned my world upside down. You've challenged me, changed me, and made me better. I vow to protect you, to fight for you, and to love you as you are and as you will be, with every part of who I am, from this moment forward and for every lifetime after."

Estee's smile widens, her cheeks flushed as she clears the emotion from her throat. "Theo, in our short time together, you've shown me what it means to trust, to believe in something greater than ourselves, and to open my heart. Most importantly, you've been my light in the darkest of moments. I vow to stand by your side, to protect this kingdom alongside you, and to love all parts of you with all that I am, now and always."

My chest tightens, and the tether that leads from my heart to Estee grows hotter as the energy that draws me to her becomes blinding.

Sloane wraps her fingers around our joined hands, her touch surprisingly warm. "Do the gods bless this bond? Do you accept that the promises made here today by these two beings will be upheld for the rest of their lifetimes?"

We wait with bated breath, the only sound for several seconds being the hum of power radiating from the tree beside us. Estee holds onto me tighter, but I don't lose focus. We belong together, and after all that's happened, I have to believe that the gods know this to be true.

Her lips part, but then the air cracks with thunder. We look toward the sun and mesmerizing light rips through the sky, striking the ground where we stand.

Energy explodes within my body then the sweetest sound floats through my mind.

Estee's voice. *"Theo?"*

"I'm right here."

She throws her arms around me, and I hold her just as tightly as a sense of peace seems to surround us, tying us together with a bond that will forever remain unbreakable.

Estee is mine, and I am hers.

No god or power will ever be able to take that from us. More importantly, we won't let them.

Sloane steps back, pride on her face. "It seems the gods approve. Congratulations."

Howls echo around us. Even though the people of Selaris aren't here to bear direct witness, they already appear aware of what's happened.

"I'll leave you two to handle the pack," Sloane says. "That was one of the most power-struck blessings I've ever been part of. I would be ready for Orix to make an appearance at any time. With an energy like the one you now share, he'd be a fool to allow you more time to prepare for whatever he has planned."

I take note of her warning, knowing she's most likely right, but before I let any darkness into this day, I lean forward, capturing Estee's lips in a kiss that feels like a vow all its own. She grips my arms as she pushes higher up on her toes, deepening the kiss.

With the pulse of our bond complete, her love radiates through me, showing me that while her words of promise and love mean the world to me, feeling them is something I'll never take for granted.

And I'm going to make sure that doesn't happen by first taking back my life. Estee deserves all of me, and no matter what it takes, that's what she's going to get.

CHAPTER THIRTY-THREE

ESTEE

My skin hums with electricity, a live wire I want to hold onto for as long as possible. The bonding ceremony was exactly what I didn't know I needed. The original plan had been to tell the pack first, but this was so much better, and I know they'll understand. If we'd waited, allowed those around us to make a spectacle of the whole thing, it wouldn't have been for me and Theo.

But beneath the ancient tree, just the two of us with Sloane, who held no judgement nor expectations, it was as if the universe was in perfect alignment. Energy flowed freely between us, reaching and pulling for one another, and wrapped around me like the world's greatest comforts.

For the first time in my life, I felt utterly connected—to Theo, to Lunara, and to myself.

Now, standing in our royal suite, the storm of emotions within me has settled into something calm and grounding, yet powerful. A force ready to be unleashed when the time is right.

Theo places my hand over his heart, his warmth radiating through my palm. His eyes—those deep grey pools flecked with silver—are filled with something I can only describe as reverence. "I thought I could feel you before," he murmurs, his voice low and intimate. "From the moment your ship docked, there was a pull, a draw to find you, to understand you. But I was wrong. I've only ever felt a fraction of what was possible between us. This," he presses my hand tighter against his chest, where his heart beats steadily beneath my fingers, "this is what I've been waiting for."

I rise onto my toes, my lips brushing over his as I whisper, "Wrong has never felt better."

The kiss starts soft, tender, but even the slightest connection sends a jolt of power through me, sparking a need that pulls us closer. My hands glide over his chest, savoring the strength beneath his clothes. His chest vibrates with a deep growl, the sound moving through me and waking my wolf.

But before we can get carried away, there's a knock at the door.

"Jerome's back already," Theo says, his tone a mixture of amusement and resignation. "The pack meeting has been brought forward. Everyone's eager to see the two of us together and hear what's going on."

I squeeze his hand, offering him a confident smile. "Then let's go."

Jerome enters with Cecil beside him. They both bow respectfully, but Jerome speaks first. "Your Majesty. Your

Highness. I know I was told to go home, but you also assured me that I would be made aware of anything significant happening. I believe the two of you bonding qualifies as such an event."

Even though it's been less than half a day since we sent Jerome home, he already looks better. There are no dark circles beneath his eyes and exhaustion no longer surrounds him.

"We only told Cecil," Theo assures Jerome, "and we would've said something to you, but there were only minutes to prepare. Plus, we wanted it to be private and wouldn't have been talked out of that."

I expect Jerome to show some sort of disappointment, but he surprises me when he smiles. "Just as it should be, Sire. There is no discord about your decision. Not from me or even the pack. Only curiosity. Everyone is merely pleased to know that the princess is one step closer to becoming queen."

Relief washes over me, and for the first time, the mention of me "becoming queen" doesn't make my stomach twist with nerves.

Cecil steps forward, his hands clasped in front of him. His emerald-green eyes meet Theo's with quiet respect. "The hall is prepared for your announcement. Every member of the pack, young and old, has a seat, and there's a staging area for you, the princess, and Jerome."

Theo nods then pauses as an idea seems to strike him. "Add another chair next to his," he instructs, motioning toward Jerome. "Cecil, I want you to join the advisory council. It's something I should've made happen long ago and one of the more immediate changes I plan to implement. The people deserve to know that their voices are being heard by more than just their alpha."

He's right. The advisory council wasn't just created as a resource for the king. It was first meant for the people. A group of non-royals who would ensure that the pack was always treated fairly. Something tells me that even if King Airik had his own council before, the shifters weren't at the top of their priority list, but they will be now.

Cecil drops to a knee in front of his alpha and lowers his head. "I would be honored to serve you in this role, my king."

When he stands back up, Theo shakes his hand and grins. "Then consider it done. We'll meet tomorrow and make a list of who else might be qualified to join until we have five of you. Does that sound fair?"

"Yes, Sire."

Jerome lightly clears his throat. "Shall I give permission for the pack to be let into the hall, Your Majesty?"

"Please." Theo looks over at me and interlaces our fingers. "Officially introducing my mate to the pack and having a pack run sounds like the perfect way to spend the rest of our evening."

My wolf hums in response, rising to the surface as my gaze stays locked on our mate.

"I see you, little wolf," Theo's voice whispers through my mind. *"You'll be free soon."*

If it was physically possible for me to melt into a puddle where I stand, that's exactly what I'd be doing as Theo looks at me, managing to see past who I am, going deeper to *what* I am, offering my wolf a sense of peace I've never had the opportunity to give her. A sense of home that not even Polaris nor my own family has been able to provide us.

Not until him.

By the time I come out of my trance, we're alone again, and Theo kisses my forehead. "Do you need anything before we go? Food, water, rest?"

He's always thinking about my needs and while I know that's nothing to complain about, it's harder to accept than I thought it would be.

I've spent so long relying only on myself that the thought of depending on anyone sends a tendril of panic through me. Yet, the moment I refocus on our bond, I know there's no one I'll ever be safer with.

"As long as I have you, there's nothing else I need," I tell him sincerely. "And you? Do you need to grab your crown or change before making your speech?"

He frowns, considering my words. "If I'm addressing them as their king, I should look the part, right?"

I squeeze his hand. "It's not the crown or the clothes that make you a king, Theo. It's the way you hold yourself, the compassion in your words, and the honest intent in your eyes. But if proper protocol calls for it…"

"Then that's what I'll do." He grins, more confident than I've ever seen him.

"That's what *we'll* do," I say, pulling him toward our bedroom. "We're in this together."

His light laughter settles over me. "Is it bad that we're getting more dressed up for a pack meeting than we did for our bonding ceremony?"

"Not at all," I reply, going to the closet. There's a silver gown that will be perfect for the meeting. "That was for us. This is for the people of Selaris. We got what we needed. Now, it's their turn."

He nods, his smile softening. "Yes, it is."

As he pulls out clothes, brushing lightly against my back in our now-shared closet and sending love through our bond, I have no doubt that today is the start of something extraordinary—not just for us, but for the kingdom I now call home.

NOT EVEN AN HOUR LATER, WE'RE STANDING BEFORE THE pack. Over two hundred shifters fill the hall, their voices hushed, their anticipation palpable. Despite the circumstances, there isn't a single trace of animosity in the air when Theo and I step onto the stage.

The room buzzes with anticipation, their murmurs fading into silence as Theo takes his place with me beside him. The air is charged, thick with unspoken emotions, but Theo stands tall, his presence commanding.

He looks every bit the king he was meant to be, wearing his crown and a tailored suit. His grey tunic covers his shoulders, every stitch and seam perfectly sewn. The maroon sash across his chest is adorned with medals and there isn't a hair on his head out of place.

Before he speaks, he reaches for me, our fingers twisting together as a steady flow of assurance passes between us.

"Thank you all for joining us tonight," Theo begins, his voice booming through the hall, resonating with strength and sincerity. "For too long, I've been an absent king. I know the efforts I've made over the last few weeks don't erase the years of neglect, but I hope you will see that every decision I make moving forward is with you—the heart of Selaris—in mind."

He pauses, scanning the room as if waiting for someone to challenge him. But the pack remains silent, their focus unwavering.

"As many of you already know, Estee was kidnapped, but what you don't know is why, and I believe it's time I finally told you the truth."

"*Theo*," I warn him. My first thought is that he's about to tell them how he became king, but he does exactly what he should. He remains honest without giving them the details that can no longer be changed.

"I was not chosen by *the* gods to be your king. I was chosen by just one of them—a being I thought was an ally but have since learned his intentions are anything but noble." He looks down at me, smiling brightly before turning his attention back to the people. "I lacked the strength and motivation to fight him as I should have, and I sincerely apologize for that, but that all changed the moment I met this incredible woman.

"Estee and I held a private ceremony today where the gods blessed our bond, forging us into one. I know it's something the pack normally bears witness to, but we needed this for us, and we hope you understand and respect our decision—one made with the kingdom in mind, because with Estee by my side, we're going to be stronger than ever."

Murmurs move through the room, and I tense, part of

me expecting some sort of outburst, but as the voices get louder, the cheers begin. They throw flowers onto the platform we stand on and chant for their king and queen.

My heart swells, not in the way it does for Theo, but for these people, who will soon become my responsibility. Each one, young and old, will need our care and respect, and providing that to them might be the greatest purpose in all my lives, including the ones I've yet to live.

Theo raises his hands then lowers them slowly, signaling for the pack to quiet. A pulse vibrates through the room even when the voices subside. One that has my wolf ready to break free and run with her people.

"I've said my piece," Theo's voice sounds in my mind. *"It's your turn. They want to hear from their queen."*

I expect my stomach to churn or my palms to sweat, but as I stare out over the crowd, there's nothing but gratitude flowing through me.

"Thank you for your kindness and understanding," I tell them first, knowing they still have every right to be furious. "Since arriving here, Selaris has pulled me in and found a special place within my heart, giving me a new home. I promise to bring only joy to our kingdom, and as our first step toward unity, I'd like to start with a pack run."

The crowd's renewed excitement buzzes through the hall, encouraging me to continue.

"Tonight, the skies may not be filled with the full moons of Lunara, but we can fill them with our howls of strength. We will run beneath the stars and show not only ourselves, but the world that we are stronger together."

"Invite them to the ball," Theo inserts. *"Tomorrow night."*

I glance at him. *"We'll be ready by then?"*

He nods, his gaze sure and steady, and I give my attention back to the people, their excitement still palpable. "To celebrate this next chapter, we are inviting you all to a ball tomorrow evening. A chance for us to come together as a pack, to honor our past, to celebrate our win over the god who stole me, and to look forward to the future as one."

The cheers that follow are deafening, the pack's energy profound. My chest tightens with emotion, and as I glance at Theo, his pride shines brightly.

He pulls me against his side and presses a kiss to my temple. "I can't wait to make you my queen."

I try to be as enthusiastic as everyone around me, forcing a smile as I look up at Theo, but the mention of the party sends a chill down my spine. I'm thrilled to see the pack coming together like this, but Orix is still out there, possibly watching us and waiting for his chance to strike. While I won't let that knowledge ruin what's still to come, especially when his showing up is exactly what we're hoping for, I can't dismiss the feeling that tomorrow might bring the fight of our lives.

CHAPTER THIRTY-FOUR

THEO

S omething's off with Estee. She smiles at the pack as they file out of the hall, their faces lit with hope and anticipation, but unease whispers through our bond. Though subtle, it's enough to raise the hairs on the back of my neck.

I tug gently on her hand, urging her toward the royal suite where we can talk, but she stays rooted to the stage. She waves and offers confirmation that she'll be seeing everyone shortly for the pack run. When Drea comes toward us with Orion trailing her, I resign myself to being patient.

"You did so good up there," she exclaims, wrapping Estee in a tight hug. "I've never been more interested in a royal speech in my entire life."

Estee blushes, her shrug modest. "Thank you. It wasn't much, but as long as the people of Selaris are safe and happy, so am I."

Drea's gaze shifts to me, sharp but not unkind. "Apologizing to the people was a nice touch, King Theo."

"I owe you one as well," I say, my tone genuine. "You were trying to help, and I dismissed you. I hope you can forgive me."

The last thing I need is for my mate's closest friend to hate me. Even if I'm not entirely sorry for my actions that day, I know Drea needs this just as Estee does.

Drea's spine straightens, her demeanor shifting. "I guess I'm sorry too. I shouldn't have accused you of hiding her and pretending someone else took her. And I shouldn't have called you all those names."

I raise a brow, slightly confused by her apology.

She shrugs. "Not everything was said to your face, but in case it gets back to you, just know I'm sorry."

Estee's laughter fills the hall, the sound rich and warm, and I find myself smiling. Each time I'm around Drea, I understand more why she and Estee are such good friends.

"You'll be joining us for the run, right?" Estee asks, glancing toward the exit.

Drea looks up at Orion, and he answers. "Of course. Selaris hasn't had an official run like this in years. I don't think there's a single shifter here who will miss it."

Guilt slithers up my throat, but I push it aside. I've already promised to do better, and I can't be the best version of me if I'm still stuck in the past, on the things I can't change.

"While I still hope everyone comes tonight," I say sincerely as I extend my hand to him, "this will be the first of many moving forward. I assure you of that."

Orion's grip is firm. "I look forward to seeing you keep that promise."

"See you out there." Drea waves then she and Orion make their way outside.

I keep Estee close, not ready to rejoin the pack yet.

My eyes find hers as I lightly grip her waist. *"Are you okay? Something was bothering you right after the speech."*

Her golden eyes meet mine, her smile radiant but tinged with something I can't quite place. *"I'm glad to be here and to do these things for the pack. It just surprised me that we're having the ball so soon. I thought it would be something we talked about more."*

"I'm sorry, Estee." Gods, how could I not consider her feelings about this? *"I quickly asked Jerome as you were speaking how soon he thought we could host the party, and when he said tomorrow, I agreed. I just want to get this over with...but I should've confirmed with you instead of forcing that information on you like I did."*

She squeezes my hands, her touch grounding me. *"No, you're right. The sooner the better. I just want to make sure we're prepared. That we can keep everyone safe."*

"After the run, we'll go over what we talked about with Sloane and if something feels off, we'll postpone," I promise. *"This is going to work, whether we do it tomorrow or a week from now."*

Estee leans into me, wrapping her arms around my neck, and it feels as though she's anchoring herself to me. *"I believe you."* When she pulls back, the pulsing through our bond takes my breath away. *"Now how about we go and let our wolves run together for the first time?"*

Mine howls within my mind, confirming what I already know.

Nothing could be better.

As we walk outside, hand in hand, I look up, taking in the twin crescent moons and the billions of stars painted across the sky, their light faintly illuminating the forest that surrounds the castle. A breeze brings with it a touch of the salty ocean, but the warmth of the day still lingers, making the setting nearly perfect.

The pack has already gathered, their energy filling the air with a hum of anticipation. Estee stands beside me, the newly maroon highlights in her hair catching the moonlight as she gazes out over the crowd, her lips curving in a soft smile as if her connection to this land, to this pack, has already been made official. Though that will have to wait until she sees Asher again and he can release her from the Polaris pack.

We step into the clearing, a sprawling meadow on the edge of the forest, where the trees stand like timeless sentries. Closer to the forest, the scent of earth and pine weaves around us and the grass is lush beneath our feet.

The massive oaks at the edge of the clearing tower over us, their thick branches stretching outward like a canopy of protection. I catch Estee glancing toward the shadows, and I step closer to her, our shoulders brushing briefly against one another, just before we signal the rest of the wolves that it's time to shift.

My muscles ripple with energy, the familiar sensation both powerful and freeing. My nails become claws as my bones disengage and reform. My vision sharpens, and within a few seconds, my wolf pushes to the surface, his ebony fur taking shape.

The world explodes into vibrant scents and sounds, everything amplified in this form. The wind carries

Estee's scent—bright and sweet, like pomegranates kissed by sunshine—and my wolf aches to be closer to her.

She shifts with grace, and her wolf is breathtaking. A coat of silver so pure it shimmers under the stars, with a patch of white like a shield on her chest as if even her wolf's been protecting their heart all these years. On all fours, she moves with effortless confidence, her head tilting to look at me, golden eyes bright and full of mischief.

The sight of her in her true form fills me with a surge of pride and awe. My wolf lets out a low, possessive growl, as if to declare this magnificent creature ours to anyone who might doubt it.

"Run with me," I send through our bond, the words a mix of command and plea.

Estee's wolf dips her head playfully before taking off into the forest, and mine doesn't hesitate to give chase. My wolf surges forward, paws pounding against the earth as we race after her. The forest opens its arms to us, the tall pines and sturdy oaks blurring as we tear a path through the trees.

The wind whips through my fur, carrying the exhilaration of freedom along with the sound of our pack following suit, giving themselves over to their inner beasts.

I stay close behind Estee, watching her wolf move with effortless elegance, her muscles rippling under her coat. Every few strides, she glances back at me, her tongue lolling in what I can only describe as a laugh. She's teasing me, daring me to catch her. My wolf answers with a powerful burst of speed, closing the distance between us in seconds, but still not quite enough to playfully take her down.

We break into the heart of the forest, where the moonlight filters through the canopy in soft streams. The rest of the pack stays near, their howls echoing into the endless sky, a chorus of unity and strength. Estee slows, falling into step beside me, and together we lead them deeper into the woods. For the first time in years, I feel like the king I was meant to be—not because of a crown or the throne, but because of the family running at my side.

The bond between me and Estee intensifies, its power almost tangible in the air. Her wolf nudges my side, and I nuzzle her in return, the simple gesture grounding me.

This is what I was meant for. This is who I was meant to be —with Estee by my side.

We continue, the pack following our lead as we carve a path through the forest. Their surrounding elation is infectious, and spreads with every howl and pawprint left in the dirt. For the first time since I took the crown, I can sense the rest of the pack as a whole, each soul igniting within my mind, putting off an electric energy as though they've all been waiting for this connection, this moment of togetherness.

As we begin to circle back, I'm convinced nothing can take this high away, but one voice makes my whole world go still, as if the forest is also holding its breath.

"Remember this moment, Theodore," Orix hisses through my mind, dark and venomous. *"It can be something you recall in those final seconds as I end your pathetic existence."*

I stop, frozen in place as the air grows colder, my fur

bristling while his presence slithers further into my thoughts.

Estee tries to break through to me—I can feel her panic—but it's as if Orix has the same hold over me he always has. This shouldn't be possible. How is he in my head?

His sinister laughter echoes through my mind. *I'll be seeing you soon, Theodore. And this time, there will be no running.*

A growl tears from my throat, my wolf's hackles rising as I turn in circles, searching for any sign of him. But the forest is free of his vile presence, as though Orix's voice was nothing more than a ghost in my mind.

The pack gathers around us, their howls softening as the run comes to an end. Estee's wolf scratches at me, her golden eyes narrowed with frustration but also concern. Her presence steadies my racing thoughts. Through the bond, I send her calm reassurance, though my insides churn with fury and dread.

"What happened?" Estee's panicked voice finally breaks through.

"Orix was in my head," I tell her flatly. *"He's coming."*

Her wolf snarls, teeth bared. *"We'll be ready for him."*

She's right, we have a plan, but as I start to shift back to my human form, I can't shake the lingering echo of Orix's presence still attached to me.

If he can still get inside my head, overpowering Aurora's block, what else can he do?

CHAPTER THIRTY-FIVE

ESTEE

The moment Theo tells me what happened during the pack run, a fury unlike any I've ever known ignites in my chest. My blood boils, and my wolf snaps her jaws in frustration, her senses prowling through the trees, searching for our enemy, ready to battle without hesitation.

Clueless, the pack is left to enjoy the night beneath the stars, Theo sending our mental goodbyes as we race back to the castle. I shift before we even reach the stone steps, the transition happening so fast that my muscles scream in protest, but I don't care. I need to touch him, to see him, to make sure he's truly here with me and not some illusion left behind by that dreadful god.

Theo stands before me as I approach, still dressed in his royal suit, the silver crown sitting proudly atop his dark hair. Yet my focus isn't on his regal appearance; it's on his eyes. I search their depths for shadows, for signs of Orix's lingering presence. I reach out tentatively, brushing his chest, my senses pushing through the bond, probing for any fractures.

I find none.

All I feel is Theo—his warmth, his love, his strength. It floods through our connection, steady and unyielding, as though he's reinforcing it for my benefit.

Relief crashes over me, and I collapse into his arms, gripping the fabric of his tunic. "I won't lose you to him."

He wraps his arms around me tightly, his voice a soft promise against my ear. "You won't. I don't know how he managed to reach me, but it won't happen again. I swear it."

A familiar voice interrupts us, carrying a sharp edge. "What won't happen again?"

I turn, and Elyn is standing in the doorway. Or rather, what's left of the elder wolf I once knew. Her silver hair now gleams with vibrant life, cropped neatly around her face. Her lavender eyes glow faintly, brimming with power, and her skin, once marked by time, is now smooth and youthful.

"You...you look..." I stammer, struggling to reconcile this version of her with the one I've come to know. Theo told me about her changes, but seeing them is something else entirely.

"Like someone who can finally get stuff done without feeling like my bones are about to break," Elyn replies, a wry smile curving her lips. She steps forward and hands Theo a wooden box, the Selaris insignia etched intricately into the lid. "Aurora might not return, so we need to be prepared. This will help you end Orix. Permanently."

Theo's hands hover over the latch, curiosity flickering across his face, but Elyn smacks his fingers away.

"If I wanted that out in the open, I wouldn't have put it in a box," she snaps. "This is your secret weapon. With this—"

Without thinking, I slap my hand over her mouth, rougher than I intend, and yell, "Stop!"

Elyn's lavender eyes narrow as she pulls my hand away with surprising ease. "If you weren't days away from being my queen, you'd be on your ass right now."

"I'm sorry, but Theo's mind isn't safe." I'm not actually sorry, considering this woman took joy in killing me before, but I'd rather pretend with her for the moment.

Her expression hardens, her gaze shifting to Theo. "What does she mean? Aurora's shield is still in place. I can feel its energy. No one should be able to penetrate that, except the goddess herself."

My mate's mood plummets, and I already know it's because if Orix managed to do so, he might not be as weak as we were told.

"He spoke to me," Theo admits. "We were out on the pack run and everything was perfect then his voice was in my head and his presence was nowhere to be found. His connection to me is still intact."

Elyn mutters something under her breath before stepping forward and flicking Theo on the forehead.

"Ow—what the—"

"Do you know nothing of power, young king?" she scolds. "When Aurora shielded your mind, it was just that —*your* mind. But you were in your wolf form. Orix's connection isn't to you alone. It's also to your wolf. Two separate entities, two separate vulnerabilities. As long as you don't shift, he can't reach you."

The logic is sound, yet it feels too simple. Still, I can't ignore the truth in her words. Our wolves, though bound to us, have their own souls. Something I didn't consider until she so blatantly pointed it out.

"Now, if everyone can keep their hands to themselves," Elyn says tersely, gesturing back toward the box. "I've brought you a dagger with a special ability. One that will only work once, so you don't want to open this until you're ready. I've disguised the weapon as one of the royal scepters. Break the casing and stab Orix with the blade. The stones on the hilt will take care of the rest."

"Where did you get this?" Theo asks, eyeing the box suspiciously.

Elyn smirks, a hint of mischief in her gaze. "I stole the dagger from King Airik. I found out he was planning to... well, that doesn't matter now. I just knew I needed it more than he did, and now I know why."

"How did he get away with being so despicable for so long without any of the other alphas knowing?" I ask, more to myself and not really expecting an answer, but she gives me one anyway.

"Just as Orix has been siphoning Theo's god energy, Airik was doing that to his wolves," Elyn explains. "He kept everyone in place in exchange for their sanity. The ones who questioned him too many times usually ended up losing their minds. Some of them disappeared, some died, often without anyone willing to openly wonder why."

"And you, a wolf who has the means to interfere, just

allowed all of this to happen?" The bitterness within me grows. How could someone of her strength, even before Aurora boosted her energy, stand by, knowing all that and doing nothing?

"I was waiting." Her voice is devoid of regret as her gaze falls on Theo. "I had my fun, and I protected all I could, but I knew something better was coming. Selaris didn't need a war, and we certainly didn't want to be overtaken by Polaris, which is what would've happened. We might've appeared to be a weak pack, but it took strength to keep our faith. There's a reason the people haven't revolted against you, King Theo. You were everything we were hoping for, even when you were hiding."

That makes my heart clench, and emotions burn behind my eyes. There was a dire need here when I arrived, but I had no clue these people had been surviving on their beliefs alone for this many years.

Our kingdom is much stronger than anyone's given it credit for, and I won't forget that.

A tear falls down Theo's cheek, and he reaches for Elyn's hands, holding them between his. "Thank you for that."

"You needed to know." She briefly closes her eyes then slowly pulls away from Theo. When she looks back up at us, the moment is gone. "Just don't screw this up, because if Orix wins but doesn't kill you, I will."

There's the Elyn I've come to know.

I chuckle as she slinks into the shadows, off to go do who knows what. "Are we even sure she's a wolf?"

He shrugs, shaking his head. "The alpha part of me says yes, but I honestly don't know. Aurora called her 'my child' when she was here. There could be something to uncover there, but I doubt it's worth our time as long as she remains on our side."

"Maybe Elyn is like you will be," I say with a smile. "More god than wolf. Let's just be thankful she doesn't also carry the alpha gene."

"The entire world should be thankful for that." Theo shudders and wraps an arm around me. "Let's go discuss our plans to kill a god and keep the pack safe."

"About that... I have a slight change we should consider."

His charcoal eyes brighten, and he takes my hand, his grip solid and unwavering. "Tell me more."

As dawn begins to stretch her colorful rays across Selaris, we finally make our way back to the royal suite. The night unfolded better than I could've hoped. The moment we found Queen Sloane, the plan to defeat Orix spilled out of me, to be refined by Sloane and Theo's sharp minds. Together, we built a strategy that feels as unbreakable as the bond I share with Theo.

We discussed not only the final touches for the ball but how to ensure it would be a night etched in the pack's mind—not just because Orix will show but because of the hope and magic we aim to infuse back into the hearts of the shifters.

There will be delicious delicacies, live entertainment, and dancing for however many hours we have, but most importantly, we'll be telling the pack what to expect.

Hiding the impending battle from the pack never sat well with me. I understand the argument—that if they don't know, Orix won't see them as a threat—but I disagree. They *are* a threat. This pack is fierce, resilient, and brimming with untapped strength. They've endured horrors and come out stronger. They've earned the right to know what's at stake and decide how they wish to face it.

While a team selected by Jerome and Cecil meticulously designs the evening's grandeur, the two advisors work with Orion and the guards to quietly inform the pack of the truth. They're given three choices: take shelter in the underground bunker with Queen Sloane as their guardian, join the celebration—but be prepared to escape when Orix arrives—or stay and fight alongside us.

Theo's hands find my temples as I rinse my toothbrush, and his deep voice cuts through the haze of my thoughts, making me jump. "Your mind needs an off button."

I tilt my head, having no clue what he means, and he laughs. "You just spent ten minutes barely moving that toothbrush or hearing me when I called your name."

"Oh." I reach for a towel to wipe my mouth, but he grabs it first, turning me to face him.

He pats the cotton over my mouth, grinning at me. "You did good tonight. You acted like the queen you're soon to be, you put the good of the people first, and you thought as the warrior I already know you are. We have a plan. One that includes dozens of guards, an informed pack, and our secret weapon. Didn't we already agree that anything else that might happen can't be predicted and getting rest is more important?"

I nod, but the gears in my mind keep turning as if racing toward the world's most vital finish line.

His brow arches knowingly. "Then why isn't my mate in bed yet?"

"Because as you just said, she doesn't have that off button." I grin, trying to be cute, but he doesn't seem to agree.

In one swift motion, he scoops me up and throws me over his shoulder as if I weigh nothing. "I'm going to find one." His hand lands on my backside with a resounding smack, the vibrations sparking heat low in my belly.

I tighten my grip on him as he strides into the bedroom, the raw strength in his movements igniting a fire within me. He tosses me onto the mattress, his shadow falling over me like a protective shield. For a moment, he doesn't move—just watches me, his gaze piercing and unyielding.

Which is when I see what I should've already known: the worry he's been hiding beneath his confident exterior. This isn't just about the pack or the battle tomorrow. It's about us. About what we stand to lose. And in that instant, every doubt, every second-guessing thought slips away.

My skin pebbles from his intensity, and I reach for him, needing to feel the heat that radiates from his bare chest. "We're going to be okay."

His jaw tightens, but he nods. "There's no other choice. I won't lose you."

"You never will." My fingers splay over his abs, my

touch inching to settle over his heart. "Not in this life or any that come next."

"My Starlight." The rumble that echoes from his chest has me pulling on him, and he doesn't hesitate to press the lower half of his body over mine.

He pushes the silk fabric of my robe to the sides, leaving me exposed to his powerful gaze.

Theo kisses me, his tongue sweeping through my mouth and the hum of his alpha power rippling through the room in waves. His strength surrounds me, a cocoon of safety and love that drowns out every fear.

No matter what happens tomorrow, win or lose, Orix can never take this away from us. Not this moment, not our bond, and not the future we've fought so hard to claim.

I'll fight to the death for this man and this pack, whether it's the end of Orix or me. This stops for all of us within the next twenty-four hours.

But for this moment, as Theo touches me, loving me with every ounce of his being, I know this is only the beginning for us. Tonight will come soon enough, and when it does, we'll be ready.

CHAPTER THIRTY-SIX

ESTEE

The murmurs and music of the ball spill through the heavy oak doors of the great hall, muffled but pulsing with energy. My hand tightens on Theo's arm as the doors swing open, revealing a scene so breathtaking it makes me momentarily forget what tonight represents.

The steward steps forward, his voice clear and commanding as he announces, "His Majesty, King Theo Northcroft, and Her Highness, Princess Estee Blackwood."

Every eye turns toward us, and the air shifts as the whispers die, replaced by hushed awe. My heartbeat quickens, the attention heavy on my shoulders, but Theo's reassuring presence grounds me. He presses my lower back gently, a silent reminder that I'm not alone.

I step forward, my gown trailing behind me in a cascade of maroon silk and intricate embroidery. A plunging neckline dips just enough to be daring but remain elegant, while the fitted bodice flares into a full skirt that sweeps the polished marble floors. Tiny crystals are stitched throughout the fabric, catching the light with every step and creating the illusion that I'm wrapped in the stars.

Theo walks beside me, regal and composed, in his black tuxedo. A maroon sash lays across his chest, bearing the crest of Selaris, and his gold crown glints under the glow of the chandeliers. He's magnetic, his strong jawline and commanding presence drawing every gaze. My wolf hums in appreciation, and I can't help but steal a glance at him.

He catches me looking and smirks, leaning down just enough to whisper, "You're stealing the show, my Starlight."

"You're not so bad yourself," I murmur back, my cheeks warming under the intensity of his gaze.

The great hall is a masterpiece of architecture, its vaulted ceilings stretching high above us and adorned with intricate carvings of wolves, the forest, and an enchanting night sky. Massive arched windows line the walls, their stained-glass panels reflecting the flickering light of hundreds of candles. Garlands of greenery and dark red ribbons drape the balconies, while crystal lights hang like constellations, their glow casting a warm, ethereal presence over the crowd.

The floors gleam, polished to a mirror-like finish, and the air is rich with the scent of fresh flowers and aged wood. On one side of the room, musicians play a lively melody as couples dance in sweeping circles. On the other side, performers entertain with feats of acrobatics and fire, their movements captivating the crowd.

The pack is dressed in their finest, the women in flowing gowns and the men in sharp suits, their excitement tempered by an undercurrent of tension. Even with the joy and unity on display, there's a shared awareness of what tonight could bring. The knowledge of Orix's likely arrival lingers in the air, unspoken but felt by all.

As we make our way through the room, the pack parts for us, offering smiles and bows. Theo nods graciously, his expression calm and collected, but power radiates from him. His presence is captivating, and I know the pack feels it too.

Drea and Orion approach us, their expressions a mix of pride and caution. Drea's dark green gown hugs her frame, her brunette hair pinned up with tiny pearls woven throughout. Orion stands beside her, his broad shoulders and stoic expression making him look every bit the warrior he is.

"Quite the entrance," Drea teases, her eyes sparkling as she looks between me and Theo. "I think you've set a new standard for royal appearances."

"Just trying to make an impression," I reply with a grin, though I know she can sense the underlying nerves I'm trying to suppress.

Orion nods respectfully to Theo. "The pack is ready, Your Majesty. They're alert but calm. Everyone's taking their cues from you."

Theo claps Orion on the shoulder. "Good. Let's keep it that way. Thank you for your diligence tonight."

"And those not present?" I ask, hating that we're separated but also knowing it's for the best.

Orion glances left and right then lowers his voice.

"Queen Sloane has secured the doors and stands guard with two of our best."

I asked earlier if that was enough and the look of indignation Sloane gave me seemed to be answer enough. While I trust her intentions, I hope she's right. At least the pack feels better having an alpha present.

Before we can say more, Jerome appears at Theo's side, his expression carefully neutral but his eyes sharp. "Your Majesty, Princess Estee, everything is proceeding as planned. Everyone's in position, and Cecil's overseeing the final security checks."

Theo nods. "And how is the pack feeling?"

"United," Jerome says, his voice low but firm. "The tension is there, but they trust you. They're ready for whatever comes."

As Jerome steps back, Theo and I move further into the room. We need our people to know we're here for them and that spending this time with them isn't just for show or a trap. We greet everyone we pass, exchanging pleasantries, and the more we do this, the calmer the room becomes.

The music shifts to a slower melody, and Theo pulls me into his arms, guiding me effortlessly onto the dance floor. The pack clears a space for us, watching as we move in perfect harmony.

"You're quiet," Theo murmurs, his hand warm against the small of my back.

"Just thinking," I admit, scanning the room. "Do you think *she'll* show?"

"Aurora?" He sighs. "With that goddess, who knows? But if she doesn't, we'll manage. We have each other, the pack, and," he pats his suitcoat, gesturing to his inner pocket, "the scepter."

I nod, but the uncertainty remains. As we pass near the edge of the room, I spot Elyn, her rejuvenated form standing out among the crowd. She sips champagne, her lavender eyes sharp and observant.

Briefly, I consider asking her about Aurora, but I can already hear the snarky wolf's response. Something along the lines of *"She's a goddess. She doesn't answer to you."*

"Do you think the kids in the bunker are scared?" I ask as the song we're dancing to ends and rolls into another.

Theo presses his lips to my temple, and I feel his smile over my heated skin. "I took you there earlier so that you would quit worrying. They have more than enough distractions to entertain them for the night. I promise, they'll be fine."

Keera said the same thing when I visited them. I told her as much of the truth necessary to keep her from being taken by surprise. She's been a parent to the younger ones, and I hate that she is still, but after this is over, my focus will return to finding them proper homes. At least everyone's been happy in the castle so far.

Mostly, I'm just ready to know what the fallout might be, to be done fearing the unknown. The life I never thought I'd have is right there at my fingertips, and facing Orix, ending his threat over us is the only thing that stands in the way of happiness for so many.

Waiting for this fight feels like an eternity passing at a snail's pace.

Still, I manage to keep calm, being the mate to the king and strong for the people. Theo and I rotate between dancing, speaking with the members of the pack, and communicating with Jerome, who oversees the pack on Theo's behalf.

While everyone smiles and seems to enjoy themselves, I'm not the only one who's eager. The overall tension within the room never quite dissipates as the night continues. The more time passes, the more I begin to fear we've built this evening up only for Orix not to show.

It's nearly midnight, time for our closing speech to the people. Hand in hand, Theo and I make our way to the dais at the front of the hall. The crowd quiets as we step forward, their eyes full of hope and expectation and maybe even relief that, without incident, the evening is almost over.

Theo's voice is strong and steady as he begins. "Tonight, we celebrate not just our victories but our unity. While Selaris has faced its share of challenges, we've survived and even begun to thrive, despite those who wish otherwise. Most importantly, we've learned that together, we are stronger than any force that seeks to divide us."

He looks at me, his gaze softening. "I found my strength the day Estee came into my life. With her as my mate, we're forging a new future for Selaris, one built on trust and hope."

I step forward, my voice clear. "This ball is a reminder of all we've overcome and all we stand to gain. This pack is not just our kingdom—it's our family. And together, we'll face whatever comes with courage and determination. As you know, a god recently held me captive, but even his strength was no match for that of our Alpha

King. That alone is worth celebrating tonight, wouldn't you agree?"

The crowd erupts in applause, the sound echoing off the high ceilings. The louder their cheers grow, the more the tension leaves my body. As much as I wished for this to be over, maybe a night without drama is exactly what we all needed.

As the pack begins to quiet, the hope radiating through the room settles over me. Theo intertwines his fingers with mine and lifts our joined hands in the air. The movement reignites the cheers, and I find myself grinning from ear-to-ear at my mate.

"I love you," I whisper beneath the applause.

But as he opens his mouth to respond, the air shifts. A sudden chill sweeps through the room, extinguishing the warmth of the chandeliers. The pack's euphoria shatters into silence as a deep, sinister voice echoes through the hall.

"Well, isn't this a charming display?"

Orix's presence is suffocating, pressing down on the room as he materializes at the far end of the hall. His dark eyes glint with malice, and a twisted smile spreads across his face.

"Did you really think you could outmaneuver me?" he sneers, his voice dripping with contempt. "That you could celebrate a win you have no right to claim? How about we show your people just how pathetic you really are, Theodore?"

A tear forms in the now-dark ceiling, a portal of some sort, black as the night sky on the other side and flooded with evil intent. Shadows come through, swarming the ballroom and plunging the place into chaos. Our pack scrambles, some of them running for the exits, others looking to us for instruction as Orix's power fills the space.

We knew there'd be a fight, but these shadow creatures... We didn't prepare for this, and I haven't the first clue how to fight them.

"What do we do?" I murmur, already hearing the screams of our frightened shifters.

Theo steps in front of me, his body tense and eyes moving around the room as if he's doing too many things at once. I imagine he's giving a half dozen commands to those we've designated as leaders tonight.

His gaze settles on mine a couple of seconds later. "Exactly what we planned. We kill Orix. Elyn will find a way to close that portal, but until then, don't touch the shadows. Their darkness will cling to you, sucking the energy from your body and weakening your soul."

Great. We're faced with the fight of our lives, and we can't actually strike the enemy. Still, my wolf surges to the surface, ready and waiting to take over the moment I release her.

This is it. The moment we've been preparing for.

Orix's sinister laughter echoes through the ballroom, and the fight for Selaris has finally begun.

CHAPTER THIRTY-SEVEN

THEO

Chaos rains down all around us. The pack hall, once a sanctuary of celebration and unity, is now overrun with beasts made of shadows. Dozens of them pour from the portal Orix ripped open in the ceiling, their inky forms swooping low, searching for prey as my people run, unprepared for this form of attack.

Orix stands at the center of it all, a smirk of satisfaction curling his lips as his dark gaze locks onto mine, cold and calculating. "This is what you've brought upon them, Theodore. I must admit I'm impressed. I thought you'd face me alone, but like the king before you, you're sacrificing the people for your own wellbeing."

I shake my head, my wolf snarling deep within me, his fury echoing through my chest. "No."

This was never the plan. We were supposed to be stronger together, prepared for whatever Orix threw at us, but none of us could've predicted this—an army of shadows, untouchable and relentless.

"Yes," Orix presses, his accompanying laugh haunting.

"You've led them to the edge of hell. I'm going to take them from you, one by one, just like I did your last family."

As if to prove his point, one of the shadows finds its mark, wrapping around a young shifter near the front of the room. His scream cuts through the chaos as his knees buckle, his skin paling as though the life's being siphoned from his veins.

He claws at the shadows, but his movements cease within seconds.

A surge of helpless fury floods me. I lunge forward, desperate to reach him, but Jerome's voice sounds through my mind.

"We'll help the pack as best we can, Sire. You're the only one who can end Orix."

He's right. My people need me to end this nightmare at its source, but my chest constricts with every anguished cry that fills the hall. I won't lose everyone like before. I refuse.

Cecil's booming voice sounds above the cacophony. "Use whatever's at your disposal to protect yourselves. Just don't let them touch you."

Estee stands beside me, rigid with tension as she points toward a few of the guards. "Look."

Three of our wolves have ripped tapestries from the walls and are using the rods holding them up as weapons to swipe at the shadows. With every swing, the inky forms disperse, breaking apart into black mist. Though the figures reassemble within seconds, those fleeting moments of reprieve are enough to give the pack hope.

Cecil and Orion bark orders, rallying the shifters,

while Jerome ushers the others toward the exits. It's chaotic, but they're holding their ground.

Estee was right. They can handle this, and I need to focus on Orix as I've already been told.

Hand-in-hand, we walk toward our biggest threat. He stands near the back wall of the room, taller than I've ever seen him. The devious god's joyful expression never falters, but there's a glint of uncertainty in his eyes. One I fully intend to draw on until he's on his knees, drained of my energy.

I bare my teeth, my wolf snarling in unison. Though, I don't dare shift, having no clue what Orix might do to my wolf with that connection still intact. "You'll regret this," I growl, my voice carrying the power of the alpha I've always been, even when I allowed myself to forget.

"Hmm," Orix muses, his tone dripping with mockery. "Maybe, but even if you manage to win today, what will the two of you lose?" His eyes dart to our left.

Estee's gaze follows and she snarls. "Drea."

The shifter is alone, swinging a candelabrum at the three shadows closing in on her, herding her into a corner of the room, likely without her even realizing it.

"Go," I tell Estee, my voice firm. "Help her."

As much as I'd rather have my mate at my side, Orix is my problem, and Drea's only here because of me and Estee. I won't allow either of us to live with that guilt if something happens to her and we did nothing to help prevent it.

Estee glares at Orix but speaks to me. "I'll be back."

I give her hand a squeeze before she turns sharply, running toward the inky demons.

"And then there were two," Orix says giddily as if this scenario is exactly what he hoped for.

Even if it is, I'm done playing his games. I don't need idle chatter while these shadows destroy my pack. I want this done, and I want it done now. Without another word, I charge.

"Finally." Orix meets me head-on, his dark energy crackling around him like a shield. I feel the impact as our bodies collide, the force reverberating through my bones. My claws lengthen, slashing through the air as I drive him back, my focus singular: ending him.

My knuckles cut into his nose and onyx blood drips down his face, but then he strikes my ribs, cracking at least one of them and making it hard for me to breathe.

I draw on my wolf, pushing him further to the surface, but as I feel the shift trying to happen, I stop myself.

Orix hovers over me, glee in his soulless eyes. "Come out and play, Wolf."

He needs me to change. Whatever connection he still has to me is important. I don't know why, but he's shown his hand too early, and I won't give in.

My inner beast retreats, just enough that I no longer have claws, but I can feel his power beneath my skin. I'm not alone, and his strength keeps me moving despite my worry for Estee and the pack.

A quick glance shows me that Estee's now at Drea's side and they're slashing their way back to the center of the room. I want to keep watching, but Orix sends a tendril of dark energy at me, lashing the whip of power across my chest.

My clothes are ripped open, and a red line mars my

skin, but the hit doesn't cut me. "I'm done playing your games, Orix."

His laughter surrounds me. "Oh, Theodore. And here I was hoping that we were only just getting started."

I lunge at him again, unleashing blow after blow. For every hit I land, Orix counters with shadowy wisps that snake around me, seeking to trap my limbs. I twist and dodge, but the bindings are relentless.

I let them close in on me, feigning weakness as I grab Orix around the waist and slam him to the ground. The force of our impact cracks the floor beneath us, and the shadows shatter like glass, freeing me from their grip.

Taking advantage, I position myself over Orix, striking him with my fists. I expect him to fight back, but he laughs harder. "I used to hate your stupidity, but I see now that I should've been grateful for it."

Confusion fills me, and it's not until I pause that I realize the wisps of his power didn't dissipate completely. Where he already ripped open my tuxedo, onyx lines of poison spread over my chest, and my heart slows, making my breathing worsen.

I don't know what's happening to me, but I do know I'm not giving up that easily. With Orix still staring at my growing wound, I use his distraction to reach for the dagger disguised as a royal scepter.

"The crown jewels won't help you now," he taunts, but the moment I break the metal, revealing the weapon, his eyes go wide.

Orix scrambles, trying to shove me aside, but I won't be stopped, not when I'm this close to freedom. I reach for his shirt, risking everything when I allow my wolf to surge forward, borrowing his strength to keep Orix close as I drive the dagger into his chest.

"I'm taking back what's mine."

Ancient power warms my palm as I hold the hilt, doing my best to keep the blade in place while he bucks beneath my weight.

"No," Orix groans, but his refusal means nothing.

The blue stones glow around the dagger, and the dark magic bleeding through my skin, attempting to claim my heart, starts to fade.

This is it. Our nightmare's going to end.

Power thrums with purpose around us—*my* power—as Orix weakens, barely able to fight back as his energy fades. He's done. There's nothing more he can do to hurt me or the people I care about.

The relief is nearly as joyous as bonding with Estee, but it doesn't last long.

He shakes his head, his dark eyes filled with defiance. "Even if you kill me, have you already forgotten my warning, Theodore? You're still going to lose. I've made sure of that."

I have no clue what he's talking about, and I don't want to know. He's trying to take advantage of me like he has all these years, and I won't allow it. Never again.

"Listen to their cries," he taunts, chuckling despite the blood flowing freely from him and the translucency of his skin. "Do they remind you of the last family I took from you?"

There's a roar pulsing in my ears, a thunderous pounding of unfiltered power as I reclaim the god energy he's stolen from me. The rush is intoxicating—a storm of strength and purpose coursing through my veins, filling the void Orix created. His essence bleeds into the air like the last notes of a dying song, and my rightful energy settles into every fractured piece of me.

"You're more like me than I wanted to admit," Orix garbles, his once-commanding voice raspy and weak. "Congratulations, Theodore. Just remember, this kind of power always comes with a price."

His words are hollow, laced with malice and mockery, but I don't falter. The pulsing desire to never hear his vile voice again is all I need to ignore his words, focusing only on his once-untouchable form as it trembles and shudders.

The heat from the dagger begins to brand my palm, the transfer of power reaching its peak. I'm tempted to let go, but I don't. Maybe it's my greed or just the desire to be done with this nightmare, but I hold on tighter, fighting for the moment this god finally takes his last breath.

My fingers start to blister and no matter how hard I try to stay focused, the burns moving up my arm shatter my concentration. The first thing I hear is Orix's haunting laughter and then…

The screams. And not just any screams.

Estee.

Hers cuts through my haze like a blade, and I drop the dagger without a second thought, ready to find my mate. I whip my head to the side, my gaze sweeping around the chaos. The shadow beasts are everywhere, their inky shapes latching onto my people, possessing their bodies, and turning them into weapons against one another. Jerome and Cecil are among the few still standing, rallying those who remain fighting, but even they look moments from collapse.

But I don't see her. I don't see the one person who matters most.

"Where are you?" I yell through our bond.

"Foun...tain."

Her voice is labored, but she's alive. I spot her then, her silver wolf shaking with determination amidst the chaos. My heart clenches at the sight. She's cornered, the darkness closing in, and she's trembling with exhaustion yet refusing to yield. The shadows slither closer, circling her like predators savoring their prey.

"Shift back and fight!" I command, knowing her wolf's bite will do nothing against these incorporeal beings.

"She's faster than I am right now," Estee pants. *"I need her."*

"No, you need me," I murmur, a wave of helplessness surging through me.

I can't fail. Not again. Not like before.

I glance down at Orix, still pinned beneath me, his blackened blood pooling around the dagger. He's alive, though barely, his hand weakly reaching toward me. My teeth clench, rage and despair warring within me as Estee's voice screams through the bond.

"Finish him, Theo!" Her plea is desperate, commanding even, but I can hear the fear in it, the unspoken knowledge that we're running out of time.

"I can't," I rasp, my voice breaking under the weight of my memories. My mind flashes back to my old pack, to the blood and the bodies, the screams that have haunted my nights. I won't let it happen again. I won't be the only survivor. Not this time.

"This isn't like before," Estee reminds me. *"You can do this, Theo."*

Her words are the anchor I need to bring me back to the present. I made the choice to forgive myself for the past and to move forward. I can't go back now. I vowed to be better, and this is the time for me to prove that I can be.

The sooner I end this, the safer they'll all be.

Except I've already paused for too long and lost my advantage. Orix's hand shoots up, clamping around my throat with supernatural strength. His grip tightens, and I feel the god energy I've reclaimed slipping back into him.

"You're pathetic," he snarls as he pushes me off him while reversing our positions, his black eyes glinting with triumph. "Unworthy of the power you've been given."

The edges of my vision blur, spots of darkness creeping in as his energy drains me. I can feel my strength waning, my body succumbing to the intensity of his power. But then, above it all, Estee's voice slices through, raw and filled with fire.

"You made me promises, Theo Northcroft. Don't you dare give up."

Her strength and belief in me ignite something primal and unyielding from deep within me, a reminder that I'm more than just a wolf shifter.

Orix can take my energy, but that doesn't change who I am. An Alpha King, a shifter who is more god than wolf. I've bowed to this monster for too long and I'm done.

His nails cut into my throat, keeping me pinned as my lungs burn for air. I close my eyes, blocking out the pain, and search inside me for the power I need, something Orix will never be able to take from me.

The love I have for my people.

My link to the pack, and even the tether to Estee, glows at my core. I hold tight to that connection and the longer I do, the more I realize I never needed that dagger to take my essence back from Orix.

There's a simmering shift in the air around me and when I open my eyes again, I know everything is about to change.

Orix tenses above me and opens his mouth to speak, but his time here is done.

The dagger is still lodged in his chest, but I quickly remove it. Ignoring the blisters still on my palm, I keep a tight grip around the hilt and shove him off me as I stand.

He scrambles back but gets to his feet within seconds. "You can't kill me." His hiss is venomous, his voice dripping with hatred.

"Maybe not, but I will stop you." I charge forward as a new presence fills the room.

Aurora.

I'm not sure if she's here to kill Orix herself, but I don't stop. This has always been my fight and I'm going to finish this.

He tries to turn away from me, but I kick the back of his leg, forcing him to his knees. Gripping the back of his head, I step around him and tilt his head up. "Goodbye, Orix."

"This isn't over," he mutters, but his words mean nothing to me anymore. He means nothing.

I drag the blade across his throat, the cut deep enough

to nearly take his head off, then release him. His body drops to the floor with a thud and his eyes stay open, unmoving, while black blood paints the floor beneath him.

There's a brief moment where I'm tempted to celebrate, but Estee is still at the forefront of my thoughts. I start to go to her, but before I can take a step, I find her at Aurora's side, back in her human form and walking toward me.

One of the shadows moves to attack them but seems to be repelled by Aurora's aura. Her lip curls as she snaps her fingers. I watch as the creature is forced upward, back into the portal it came from. Two more follow suit and I realize that's the last of them just as the opening begins to stitch itself back together.

With the threat seeming to be taken care of, I run to Estee and wrap my arms around her waist as I lift her off the ground. "Thank you."

The goddess next to us scoffs. "You should be thanking me."

Aurora might have helped with the shadows, but it was Estee's belief in me that won this fight. Something I'll spend the rest of my life repaying her for.

Shouts of victory ring out from the pack members still present, most of them barely standing, but each filled with pride.

We did it.

Aurora steps forward until she's standing over Orix and sneers. "This one's being burned. I won't let anyone get in my way again."

Her way? I glance at Estee, and she seems just as

confused, but before we can question the goddess, she turns back, her commanding expression locked on me.

"You've surprised me, King Theo," she seems to reluctantly admit. "I didn't believe you were worth my time, but I see I was mistaken. Just don't make me regret coming to clean up after you. If you abuse that which you've been given, I will be back." She places her heel on Orix's limp hand, and his body takes on a brief purple glow before disappearing. "I'll dispose of Orix. A favor for you. One I'll be back to collect on."

Her words linger as she vanishes in a burst of light, leaving us alone in the aftermath of the battle. I should worry what the goddess means to collect from us, but as I look over at Estee, I only care that she and my pack are safe.

CHAPTER THIRTY-EIGHT

ESTEE

Remnants of the battle linger like a storm—both turbulent and strangely soothing—over Selaris. I stand on the balcony of the royal suite, the early morning air cool against my skin, as the kingdom below awakens to a new era. From here, I see the heart of the kingdom: shifters working tirelessly, bringing supplies into the castle, their movements swift and purposeful as they begin to repair the damage caused by the shadows. Yet, even amidst their labor, distant laughter echoes—a group of children running through the square, their joy like sunlight breaking through the clouds.

Theo joins me, the warmth of his presence grounding me in the way only he can. He wraps his arm around my waist, his warmth seeping into me as I lean into him. "They're resilient," he says softly. "Stronger than I ever gave them credit for."

"And so are you," I reply, tilting my head to meet his eyes. The haunted shadows that lingered in his gaze for so long are fading, replaced by something brighter, more certain. Hope.

Still, the road ahead won't be without its challenges. Aurora's intervention may have saved us from complete devastation, but the battle left scars—some visible, others buried deep. We lost several wolves to Orix's shadow creatures: the young man who was attacked first, along with some of our elder members not strong enough to fight the darkness.

Their deaths won't be in vain, though. We'll honor each of them in the coming days and, with this new start, do better for the pack as a whole. The people have continued to show their support, but after so much destruction, I can sense their unease, their need to see that the rug isn't about to be pulled out from under them once more. It's our job as king and queen to give that to them and I know we will, every day moving forward.

"I do have some good news," Theo admits, and his heart pounds faster beneath my touch.

Our bond pulses wildly within my chest, his excitement becoming my own, as I reach to hold him tighter.

Smiling brightly up at him, I give him a brief yet lingering kiss, keeping my tone light. "And that would be…"

"I spoke with your sister," he says, his energy going wild with joy and relief. "She'll be here in two days with Asher, but she also delivered a message from your mother."

My mom? I haven't spoken with her in much too long. Gods, I hope she's not furious with me.

"Isla didn't want to tell you before with all we had

going on, but apparently Florence can receive messages while she's dreaming from those who've gone to rest," Theo says, his eyes glazing over and making mine do the same. "My mother. She's…" His voice cracks as he grins. "She's safe and happy and at peace."

"Oh, Theo." I throw my arms around him, but the tighter I hold on, the more erratic my emotions become. I go from happy to overwhelmed within an instant and guilt begins to choke me.

I try to pull away from him, not wanting this moment to be about me when I know how much this news means to my mate, but he holds onto me, his touch filled with only love.

"I've got you, Starlight," he promises with a certainty that I find myself clinging to.

"I don't know what's wrong with me," I mutter against his chest. "You've just shared good news, but…"

He kisses the top of my head. "Even something positive can push the strongest of us over the edge. You've spent centuries carrying your emotions on your own and you've done so with strength and grace. But you don't have to do so alone anymore."

His words crack something inside me, a fissure that's been forming since the moment I arrived in Selaris. I've held on to every burden, every scar, every moment of pain, convinced I had to bear it all on my own. But all this good news combined with Theo's love and his unyielding belief in me…it dismantles my defenses in ways I never thought possible.

His godly alpha energy pulses through me, shattering

the last of my walls. The dam breaks, and I collapse against his chest, sobbing with a force that shakes me to my core. I cry for the lives lost, for the battles fought, for the little girl who spent her life searching for a place to belong. I cry for the woman I've become and the one I'm yet to be.

Through it all, Theo holds me, his arms a fortress, his presence unwavering. He doesn't try to silence my grief or rush my tears. He simply lets me be, his love a steady current that anchors me even as I feel like I'm falling apart.

When the rush of emotion finally subsides, a quiet peace settles over me—a soul-changing calm that I've never known before. I take a shaky breath, lifting my gaze. Theo's grey eyes are luminous, filled with pride and something even deeper.

"You're going to be a glorious queen," Theo whispers in my ear as I begin to settle. "You have so much love within you. I'm not even sure you realize how it beats around you, a tangible energy that draws people to you. The fact that I get to call you mine makes me the luckiest man in all the worlds."

I look back up at him, and as his stare sparks with new light, I know exactly what I want to do next.

"We need to plan my coronation," I say. "A proper celebration for the kingdom that has nothing to do with baiting a god. With Asher and Isla here, I can be released from Polaris and officially become part of our kingdom."

He flushes and grins cheekily. "I might've already told Asher that was something he needed to do while he was here. They mentioned finding the source of the threats and—"

"Who was it?" I try not to lose myself to the rage, but it's hard when I'm reminded of my sister being endangered.

"A young woman who thought she was in love with Asher for the last few weeks," Theo explains. "She worked in the castle, giving her easy access to Isla, but after talking with Asher, we both believe that she was influenced by Orix to be a distraction. The timing of her confession, along with her confusion over her actions, came too close after killing him to be coincidence." His gaze darkens briefly. "Elyn told me he was cunning, but I didn't realize his reach extended that far."

If that bastard of a god wasn't already dead, I'd be on the hunt once more, but I have to trust that Aurora's already disposed of his body and soul with harsh and deserved justice.

"Hopefully, this means there'll be peace in our lives for the foreseeable future," I say with a sigh.

The tension doesn't leave Theo. "Maybe. Aurora said we owe her a favor. I don't like not knowing what that means."

"She said the same thing to Asher," I remind him. "Whatever she wants, it doesn't matter. We'll get through it together so there's no need to stress about what hasn't even happened yet."

He places a light kiss on the top of my head, and I can feel his smile before I see it. "You're absolutely right, Queen Estee."

A few weeks ago, hearing that might've made me spiral, but now, there's only peace within me.

"So." I smirk. "We have another celebration to plan?"

He cups my cheeks, his thumbs brushing my skin with a reverence that makes my heart ache. His lips press to mine in a thorough kiss, one that pulls me completely into the moment with only him on my mind.

"It's already being done," he murmurs against my lips before taking my hand and lacing our fingers together. "But in the meantime, I have another surprise for you."

A spark of curiosity ignites inside me, and I follow eagerly as he leads me out of the room. "Where are we going?"

"You'll see," Theo replies, his grin wide and mischievous, like a boy with a secret too big to keep. His enjoyment of this moment sweeps through our bond, becoming my own.

Except that doesn't last long as confusion begins to fill me. He's taking us toward the guest quarters, but he already said Isla wouldn't be here for two more days...

And then we stop in front of the room where the children have been staying.

"When we walk in here," Theo begins softly, his voice carrying a warmth that wraps around me, "you're going to see two of our pack members with the kids. You've been trying to find placements for each of them, but there's a home for all of them. Together."

My heart stutters. "They don't have to be separated?" The words are barely a whisper, laden with disbelief and hope. As much as I dreamed of keeping them together, I'd forced myself to accept the reality that asking one family to take on six children was an impossible task.

Theo's hand tightens around mine, his steady gaze grounding me. "A couple who couldn't have children of their own and lived outside the kingdom heard about what's been happening here. When they came to see the changes for themselves, they learned of the orphaned pups. The moment they met the kids, they knew what they wanted to do. They've even volunteered to move closer to the castle, so things stay familiar for the younger ones."

My throat tightens with emotion as I process this news. "They really want them—all of them?"

Theo nods, his expression softening. "Every single one. They didn't hesitate."

The urge to cry again surges with a ferocity that takes me by surprise, but I manage to keep some of my composure as I push the door open. The sight that greets me will forever be etched into my heart.

The room is filled with the sound of laughter and quiet chatter, a scene of pure, unfiltered joy. The man, his broad frame strong, has the two youngest climbing over him as though he's their personal jungle gym. The woman, with a serene smile, is braiding Neri's hair while Keera sits in front of them, reading a book. The others are sprawled on the floor nearby, coloring and giggling in a way that feels so natural, so right.

For the first time, they look like children—carefree and happy.

I blink back tears, unable to speak as the reality of this moment settles over me. I glance up at Theo, who's watching me with a tenderness that makes my chest ache. "Thank you."

He wraps an arm around my waist, grinning. "You did this," he says firmly. "None of this would've been possible if you hadn't searched them out and brought them back here. They're safe because of you."

Maybe he's right, maybe not. Either way, the moment Keera looks up and sees me, her face glowing with a youthfulness I couldn't find when I first met her, I know this is a moment I'll cherish forever. That guarded, wary girl has been replaced by someone who feels safe enough to let her walls down. It's a transformation that fills me with so much gratitude.

Keera jumps up and runs to me, wrapping her arms around my waist in a hug so tight it nearly knocks the breath out of me. "Thank you, Estee," she says softly, her voice muffled against my dress.

I stroke her hair, my own tears finally spilling over. "You don't have to thank me. This is what family does."

"I'm going to have a real home." Keera's precious words leave a mark on me that will last a lifetime.

Addie calls for her to come look at the drawing she's just finished, pulling Keera away from me. My hand covers my heart as I gaze around the room. There's not much that could be better than this.

Theo clears his throat, his voice breaking the moment with gentle ease. "Why don't you visit with them for a while? I'll send Drea for you when it's time for the coronation dress fitting."

I tilt my head up to kiss his cheek, a small gesture of thanks for everything he's done. "That sounds perfect."

He smiles, his expression soft and full of love. "I'll see you soon."

As he leaves, I turn back to the children, the warmth of his love remaining with me. For the first time in as long as I can remember, everything feels right. Everything feels like home.

CHAPTER THIRTY-NINE

ESTEE

Three days have passed, yet it feels as though time itself has folded in on me, rushing to this singular moment. My coronation. My heart beats a steady rhythm of nerves and excitement, but above all else, there's a sense of purpose—a need for this ceremony to mark not just my new beginning but a fresh start for Selaris as well.

Isla fusses with the curls around my shoulders while Drea meticulously presses the last wrinkle out of my gown. Both have been like mother hens with me all morning, but even with all their poking and prodding, I wouldn't have it any other way.

When Drea stands back up, I reach for her and then my sister, pulling them into a hug. Their warmth is an anchor, their presence a reminder that I'm never alone. "Thank you for being here with me," I whisper, an overwhelming appreciation for them thickening my voice.

"I wouldn't be anywhere else," Isla says firmly, her arms tightening around me.

"Agreed." Drea smirks, stepping back with a wink. "You're stuck with me now, you know."

Isla lets out an exaggerated sigh, crossing her arms in mock exasperation. "I want to hate you for getting to stay here with Estee, but honestly, I'm just glad my sister won't be alone."

I shake my head, chuckling. "You know I'm staying because my *mate* is here. I wouldn't be alone either way."

Isla scoffs, though there's a glimmer in her eyes. "There's nothing more important than having that one woman in your life who not only accepts you for who you are but embraces every part of you."

The truth of her words hit hard, and I realize something I hadn't before. I'm leaving her. I've always been that person for Isla, her confidante and constant, and now I have Drea. But who will my sister have?

"Oh, Isla," I whisper, pulling her into another hug. "I'm so sorry."

Her soft laughter fills the room. "Why in the world would you be sorry?"

"Because I'm leaving you without *your* person," I reply, guilt curling in my chest.

Isla steps back, placing her hands firmly on my shoulders. "I love you more than all the stars in the universe, Estee, and no one will ever replace you as my soul sister." She hesitates, her cheeks flushing slightly as she adds, "But I do have someone in Polaris."

I blink in surprise. "Who is this 'someone?'" I ask, feigning insult even as a grin spreads across my face.

"Her name is Maegan," Isla says, and her face lights up in a way that makes me want to both cry and laugh. "She applied to be one of the royal guards. The way she spoke to Asher when we met her… You'd have been in love with her right then and there."

I smirk, though jealousy nips at me, irrational as it is. "I look forward to meeting her," I say, though my tone must betray me because Isla bursts into laughter, her joy infectious.

"Liar," she teases, wiping a tear from her eye. "But I promise, when you do, you'll love her just as much as I love Drea."

Before I can reply, a knock at the door startles us, and my stomach flips with anticipation. The three of us exchange a glance before I nod. "It's time."

"You're going to be amazing," Isla says, her voice firm and filled with sisterly pride.

"What if I trip on my dress the second I walk into the great hall?" I ask, half-joking, though the fear is real. It's a scenario that haunted my dreams last night.

Drea loops her arm through mine, her grin confident and reassuring. "You're going to be fine. I promise."

With a deep breath, I straighten my spine and push away the last of my nerves. She's right. "Let's do this."

"As you wish, Queen Estee," Isla quips, her grin mischievous as she ushers me toward the door.

Jerome is waiting in the hallway. He bows deeply as we step out. "If I may say, Your Majesty, you are breathtaking."

"Thank you, Jerome." My palms lightly glide over the multiple layers of fabric.

The dress is…extravagant, but the moment I slipped into it, I knew this wasn't just a gown—it's a declaration.

The pristine white fabric, flowing and heavy, makes me feel like I'm draped in energy that comes directly from the gods themselves. The golden embroidery along the top of the bodice also circles around my waist, then splits the top layer of the skirt, continuing the intricate design beneath. Every stitch screams royalty, as if the dress alone could command a room.

And then there's the cape. A deep red, bold and dramatic, cascading from my shoulders as though it's trying to remind me of the responsibility I'm accepting today. This isn't just about me—it's about a kingdom, a future, a throne.

Jerome gestures for us to go ahead, and as we make our way to the great hall, where Theo and the rest of the pack await, I can't stop the smile that spreads across my face. This is real. This is happening. I've found my mate. I'm about to become queen. And I have my family here with me. For the first time in much too long, everything is exactly as it should be.

When we reach the grand double doors, Cecil is there, his expression a mixture of pride and warmth. He knocks once, and the doors creak open slightly to allow my parents to slip out. Their eyes shimmer with unshed tears, and the sight of them nearly undoes me.

"Our precious girl," my mother whispers, pulling me into her arms. Her embrace is welcome and familiar, and for a moment, I'm not a soon-to-be queen, I'm just her daughter.

"Thank you for being here," I say, my voice steady but soft.

Their arrival with Isla and Asher was the best surprise

of all. When they stepped off that ship, I'd never run faster to get to them.

"We wouldn't be anywhere else today," Dad adds. "Plus, I needed to see for myself that Theo was good enough for my little girl."

That makes everyone chuckle, and I swipe at my eyes before I can ruin the work Isla and Drea did on me.

"All right," Isla says with a clap of her hands. "Shall we?"

I inhale deeply. "Absolutely."

The rest of them enter the room, and I remain behind by myself, waiting for the sound of the trumpets. It comes only seconds later, giving me no time to spiral. Though, I don't think I would have.

The doors part, and everyone stands, staring at me as I walk toward Theo where he waits at the end of the maroon runner.

Sunlight streams through the towering stained-glass windows, casting vibrant hues of blue, green, and deep purple across the polished marble floor. The air hums with energy, a mix of anticipation and hope from the hundreds of shifters gathered to witness this moment.

My heart pounds in my chest as I put one foot in front of the other, but not with nerves. Only eagerness.

Theo's gaze locks on me, and I easily lose myself in his stare. His essence brushes against mine, a quiet reassurance that keeps me steady. He looks every inch the king, dressed in a tailored charcoal suit, his crown gleaming atop his dark hair. The pride and love in his eyes nearly threaten to undo my composure.

The dais he waits for me on is flanked by two statues

of wolves, carved from gleaming obsidian stone, as though they're watching over the ceremony with stoic poise. At the center is a stone pillar with a velvet cushion holding my new crown.

The gold points catch the light, casting off a soft, ethereal glow that highlights the garnet stones set within them. It feels ancient and sacred, a symbol of a legacy I'm now part of.

As I ascend the steps, the hall remains silent except for the faint rustle of my gown. Theo reaches for me, his hand warm and steady around mine. His lips curve into a small smile once I'm standing in front of him, and he murmurs, "You are the most stunning being to ever grace these lands, my queen."

My cheeks heat. "Thank you."

Asher joins us, taking the lead in the ceremony as the next-most powerful Alpha King present. Though Sloane is here somewhere, I'm glad it's my brother-in-law up here with us.

"Estee," he begins, his voice clear and strong, carrying easily through the hall. "You have proven yourself in ways that go beyond what's required of a queen. You've fought for this pack, not only with strength but with wisdom and compassion. You've brought hope to Selaris in its darkest hour, and it is my honor to bestow upon you the title of queen."

Asher gestures for me to kneel, and I lower myself onto the velvet cushion provided, folding my hands in front of me, bowing my head as he continues.

"Do you vow to protect Selaris and its people, to lead

with courage and fairness, and to uphold the honor of this kingdom above all else?"

"I do," I say, my voice steady despite the lump in my throat.

"Do you vow to stand as a symbol of strength, unity, and hope for your pack, to guide them through light and darkness alike?"

"I do," I repeat, feeling the certainty of each word settle into my soul.

I sense Theo reach for the crown, and this is it. There's no going back. Not that I'd want to, but the power of finality seeps through me, my energy and the bond I share with Theo pulsing wildly throughout my body.

As if the entire room holds their breath, the only thing I hear is the rapid beat of my heart and Asher's next words. "Then by the will of the gods and the trust of your people, I declare you Queen Estee of Selaris. King Theo, crown your queen."

Theo's behind me and he lowers the crown onto my head, its weight surprisingly comforting, as if it's always belonged there. He steps around to face me, kisses both my cheeks, then offers me a hand. "Absolutely perfect," he murmurs with a dazzling grin.

As I rise, the room erupts into cheers, the sound a deafening roar that shakes the very walls of the hall. My vision blurs with unshed tears as I turn to face my people, who are clapping and cheering with an energy I can feel in my bones.

Theo stands beside me, my hand still firmly in his. "Your Majesty," he says softly, his voice filled with pride.

"My king," I reply, the words feeling right as I look into his eyes.

We step forward together, facing the pack as one. I see familiar faces among them—Drea and Orion standing near the front, their smiles wide; Jerome and Cecil looking proud and relieved; even Elyn, who nods at me with what almost looks like approval. My parents and Isla remain close as well, their support meaning the world to me.

But it's the rest of the pack, the ones who don't know me, yet would fight alongside me just the same. Their essence begins to unfurl within me, my bond as their queen coming to life. I sense their resilience, hope, and acceptance, reminding me that I'm exactly where I was always meant to be.

Theo raises his free hand, signaling for quiet. The cheers gradually die down, and the room falls into a reverent hush. "Selaris," he begins, his voice resonant and steady, "today marks the beginning of a new era. A stronger present and future. We've faced trials that could've broken us, but instead, they've united us. And with Queen Estee by my side, I have no doubt that our lands will thrive."

The crowd erupts again, their cheers filling the room with a palpable sense of duty and hope. I squeeze Theo's hand, my heart full, and as I look out over our pack, I know we can face anything that comes our way.

Even the gods.

EPILOGUE
SLOANE

A month has passed since my return to Alcaris, the land I've ruled for over two centuries. Once, its rolling hills were lush and vibrant, its forests teeming with life. Now, cracks crawl across the earth like veins on a withered leaf, and the forests are becoming little more than skeletal reminders of what they used to be. Alcaris is dying, and I've exhausted every option to save it.

The only choice I'm left with is the one that terrifies me most—merging my kingdom with Venaris, under the rule of King Aeson.

The treaty sits on my desk, its edges worn from count-less nights of deliberation. I'd been ready to sign it once, desperate to give my people hope of a brighter future. But then, I visited Selaris. I saw the undeniable love between Theo and Estee as well as Asher and Isla. The strength of their bonds is profound. It made me crave something I've long convinced myself I didn't need.

Now that I'm back in Alcaris, the ache for something

more plagues me. But to sign this treaty—to bind my future and my people's survival to Aeson—feels like sacrificing the last shred of hope for myself.

Aeson isn't my mate. He's not even my friend. An ally, yes. But can I trust him? That's something my wolf refuses to extend to him.

It doesn't matter that he promises we would become the king and queen of the new kingdom, where not only my people would be taken care of, but so would I. He seems to think I should take this as further incentive, but tying myself to him sounds like a life sentence.

It's not that he's a bad person. His pack seems happy, he keeps an advisory council, abides by all rules, and almost always has a smile on his face, but none of that changes the facts.

He's *not* my true mate and the terms of his proposed agreement are clear.

My people will have a new and better place to call home and Aeson will have me as his queen, by his side, in all ways. Something he seems even more eager to obtain now that both Asher and Theo have theirs.

I want to believe that he means well, especially knowing that whenever I visit the Venaris castle, I have the oddest sense of home and belonging. Even when I'm in Aeson's presence, there's a connection there, but it's not one built from love or even lust.

Not that I've dreamed of fairytales all my life. I've spent years fighting alongside my people, unafraid of getting my hands dirty and proving my worth as an unmated queen. Still, I thought I would find my mate by now, that I'd no longer be alone in my struggles.

The fact that I haven't has made me work ten times harder in this world. Not only for my people, but for the respect of my peers.

There isn't a war or conflict that I've avoided over the years, knowing that the chance to show my strength was never something I could pass up. Yet, the fiercest battle I've been fighting, the one I need to win most, is the only one I can't seem to figure out.

Why are my lands dying?

"Your Majesty," Clara, my closest advisor, says as she enters my office. "You wanted to see me."

I nod, gesturing for her to enter. "Close the door behind you."

She does so quickly and turns to face me. Her blonde hair is pinned back, tightly wrapped at the base of her neck, and her piercing green eyes somehow see through my pretenses. I shouldn't be surprised. There's a reason I've called her here. Not only is she my closest confidante, her sharp wit and unwavering loyalty have made her indispensable to me.

I place my hand over Aeson's proposal. "Tell me what to do about this."

Her lips twitch, a barely suppressed sigh escaping. "My queen, you know I can't *tell* you anything."

"With every matter apart from this one, you seem to have no problem doing so," I counter her snark. "Now, quit being difficult."

She grins. "I've already given you several scenarios on how this treaty could work out, both in and out of our favor. Would you like me to repeat them?"

I grimace. "You know what I'm asking, and it's not as your queen."

I can't remember when we crossed the line from queen-and-advisor to friends, but I need the latter from Clara right now. Unfortunately for me, she enjoys dragging this out of me, especially over this particular subject.

She takes a seat across from me and reaches above her head. "I'll take off my advisor hat, but only for you." She pretends to toss the imaginary object across the room before offering me a compassionate smile. "As your *friend*, I think you should throw that agreement in the fire. We'll figure this out ourselves. We still have time."

"Do we? Half the pack has already begun requesting transfers to other kingdoms," I remind her.

"Think of it this way," she muses. "You're weeding out the weak. Those who're already jumping ship were never completely loyal to you anyway."

I scoff. "Or maybe they're just being smart, jumping before they risk sinking with the rest of us."

Clara levels her gaze on me, clasping her hands together. "You don't love Aeson, and for him to only offer to help our people if you willingly become his mate doesn't make me think kindly of him. If he had pure intentions, he'd offer to do something about our problems, instead of trying to sweep them under the rug."

This is another discussion we've had more than once, and I agree with her. Yes, Aeson has allowed my people to come and go from his lands, getting the necessities we need to survive from Venaris as often as we choose, but outside of opening his doors to us, he's offered no potential solutions that will save Alcaris. He wants me at his side, and the fact that I can't figure out why drives me insane.

"And knowing that his mate died and chose not to be reborn…" Clara shakes her head. "Something isn't right there, Sloane, and you know it."

Gods, do I, but the choices I'm left with aren't ideal. If I deny Aeson and can't save what's left of my land, I'll not only lose my home, but so will everyone who's trusted me and stayed. I'll lose my crown and the power to advocate for them and then what?

She groans and covers her face with both hands, bringing her elbows to her knees. "Why am I so smart?"

I laugh at her seemingly self-imposed misery. "Because you've been learning from the best for the last hundred years."

Her glare cuts me as she looks up. "I have a thought. I don't like it, but the advisor in me can't *not* tell you now that I've thought of it."

I lean forward, my brow arched. "Do tell."

"What if we did a sort of trial run?" Clara suggests. "The two of us go to Venaris for a moon cycle. We stay in the castle with Aeson and see what life might actually be like should we choose to leave Alcaris behind."

The suggestion settles over me, heavy but not unwelcome. It's risky, yes, but it's also practical. A chance to see beyond the facade Aeson presents, to understand what I'd be committing my life to.

I nod slowly. "Let's do it. Make the arrangements"

Clara blinks, clearly taken aback by my quick agreement. "Just like that? No questioning the craziness of this idea? We're just doing this?"

I hold her gaze and sigh, the fate of hundreds of lives rests on my shoulders. "I don't have a choice. I need to know that I've done everything I can to keep our pack safe, and we're running out of time."

She pushes up from the chair and nods, her enthusiasm waning. "I'll go pack a bag, then speak with the other advisors. They'll need to know what to manage while we're gone. Anything else, my queen?"

I shake my head at her feigned formalities and she winks, but even the smile on her face doesn't hide the regret I sense from her as she exits my office.

And I don't fault her for it. As much as this might be a bad idea, we need to do it. Otherwise, I might be left hating myself, no matter what I decide, and by then it will be too late to go back.

The door closes behind her, and I pick up the treaty once more, running my fingers over the embossed seal of Venaris. My wolf stirs uneasily, her instincts warning me that this path won't be as simple as I hope, but at least she's not in complete disagreement with me.

I made a commitment to Alcaris when I took the crown. I vowed to put the people above my own needs, and it's time I did just that.

There's no more worrying about how this might cost me my heart. A decision needs to be made, and I'm the only one who can do it.

Consequences be damned.

Thank you so much for reading A Crown of Fates! I hope

you enjoyed Estee and Theo's story as much as I did writing it. If you did, please consider leaving a review on Amazon and/or Goodreads to let me know!

A Reign of Malice will be Queen Sloane's story and I'm so excited for the twists that happen in this one! Get ready for even more mysteries and maybe even a trip to the god realm...
The final book will release Summer 2025!

In the meantime, flip the page for ways to stay in touch and talk all things Wolves of Lunara!

ALSO BY HEATHER RENEE

Paranormal Romance Books:

The Mystics and Mayhem World—These series are connected by characters crossovers, but not the plots. You can read them in any order. Though, this is their timeline order.

Broken Court

A complete New Adult Urban Fantasy series featuring an unconventional and anti-heroine leading lady, a broody love interest, and a fae kingdom with a vile king.

Luna Marked

A complete New Adult wolf shifter series (dual POV) featuring a strong-willed leading lady and a patient, yet fierce alpha male.

Scorned by Blood

A complete New Adult Vampire series featuring a supernatural hunter and the sexy vampire bound to protect her no matter the cost.

Fated to the Wolf

A complete New Adult Witch and Wolf series (dual POV) featuring an abandoned witch, a rogue wolf, and their broken bond.

The Hidden Realm

A complete New Adult wolf and dragon shifter series (dual POV) featuring a feisty wolf shifter just looking for her freedom and a broody dragon trying to save his world.

Mystics and Mayhem Novels

This includes *Christmas Mates, Fractured Mates,* and *Shattered Mates.* Each book is a standalone and between the three stories, you'll find a holiday gathering with all the shenanigans, vengeance to be had, and risks to be taken.

Individual Series

Raven Point Pack Series

A complete Upper Young Adult Paranormal Romance series featuring wolves, witches, vengeance, and fated mates.

Shadow Veil Academy

A complete Upper Young Adult Urban Fantasy Academy series featuring shifters, elves, witches, and more.

Elite Supernatural Trackers

A complete New Adult Urban Fantasy series featuring witches, demons, a smart-mouthed female lead, alpha males, and a snarky fairy sidekick.

Royal Fae Guardians

A complete Young Adult Urban Fantasy series featuring fae, magic users, a sweet romance, along with snark and humor.

Standalone Fantasy Books

Ignite Me - A spicy wolf shifter story featuring a lost heir, the mate who doesn't want her, and the enemies who wish them dead.

Cage Me - A spicy wolf shifter story featuring a shadow cursed wolf and a mate who's on the run.

Marked Paradox - A Young Adult fae story about a realm divided and one fae to bring them back together.

Contemporary Romance Books with Harper Reed:

The Wicked Duet

A mafia romance with enemies-to-lovers, forced proximity, and more than a bit of unaliving before there's a happily-ever-after.

Ruthless Truths

Tangled Deceit

The Unexpected Series

A Spicy RomCom trilogy featuring three best friends and their happily-ever-afters!

A Mutually Beneficial Proposal

A Mutually Beneficial Mistake

A Mutually Beneficial Secret

Standalone

A Royal Oops

A Spicy RomCom with royal antics, an epic second chance romance, and a kingdom that needs their new queen.

ABOUT THE AUTHOR

Heather Renee is a USA Today Bestselling author who lives in Oregon. She writes Paranormal Romance and Fantasy novels with a mixture of romance, humor, and sass. Her love of reading eventually led to her passion of writing and giving the gift of escapism.

When Heather's not writing, she's spending time with her loving husband and beautiful daughter, going on their own adventures. She loves to hear from her fans, so visit her website: www.HeatherReneeAuthor.com and check out the Contact Me page for ways to connect.